Requisite

Vices

Miranda S. Veil

For my muse. Without you, there would be no story to tell.

For K.A, who helped encourage me, and who listened to my hours' worth of ramblings over many moons. Thanks for letting me bounce ideas off of you, for helping to inspire new ones, and for always being there for me.

And to all others who, at some point during this process, convinced me to keep going. I would have never done it without your constant reassurances.

Prologue

"*The sound of her voice* sets my teeth on edge."

Sighing, I slide my phone face down near the edge of the table.

It's a particularly brutal Thursday afternoon, with the sun beating down on us from directly overhead. Waves of heat emanate from every inch of our surroundings, and the humidity is unbearable; it floods every pore and drowns my lungs, making it near impossible to breathe. Riley, however, insisted on sitting outdoors, most likely to show off her new shoes to whoever happens to walk by. What a princess.

It's become a bit of a ritual for us to come out once a week and spend time together. It offers a much needed respite to reconnect, and gives us an excuse to get the frustrations of our week out in the open. It can feel, at times, like everything flies across the screen of our lives. The minutes, the hours, the days, and before we know it, we're lost in a whirlwind of what has become the day-to-day.

And so we've settled here for our weekly date. Though the place is very obviously Italian, every restaurant down here has thrown a bit of Cajun flair into every dish. I've always had a taste for a bit of heat in my food, so I'm definitely not complaining.

It's that golden hour just after the lunch rush, but before the dinner crowd, when everything is quiet and serene, and thankfully, we're left in peace as we sit beneath towering palm trees, enjoying a liquid lunch, and nibbling on delectable stuffed mushrooms.

"What does she want this time?" Riley asks, just before tilting her head back and draining the remainder of her glass. She lifts her finger, motioning to the waiter for another round of drinks.

"She was frantic, which only makes her voice that much harder to listen to. She may have hit glass-shattering notes this time around." I roll my eyes at the memory of Angela's voice. "Her choice for the interview with an author from New Orleans backed out on her at the last moment. She already has a hotel room booked for the weekend, and doesn't want to miss this chance, so she called to see if I had plans."

The waiter stops by our table, dropping off our drinks. I stir my whiskey sour by the cherry stem, watching the shockingly red fruit swirl around the glass.

"This is a big thing for her, and for the magazine. She must really be scraping the bottom of the barrel if she wants me to conduct the interview. I haven't done an interview since freshman year, but it can't be that bad, right?"

"Right! Besides, it may really help launch your career, you know? It could shine a bit more light on your work. Maybe you'll become some superstar interviewer, like those people on TV. You'll have your own show and everything!"

"Riley, your imagination is bigger than your boobs, which is certainly saying something."

"You love my boobs! Don't pretend otherwise." She winks, laughing playfully from across the table.

"Okay. I may be a little envious, but I've definitely got a better ass."

We share a laugh and, drawing my glass to my lips, I take a sip, letting the drink wash over my tongue and dance down my throat. It's been a few days since I've had my taste of alcohol. Never again will I wait this long.

Days like this have become the highlight of my week. It makes me feel connected to someone again after walling myself away from the world. I've never trusted anyone more than I trust her. She makes me feel like your normal, everyday twenty-something.

"So, what's this guy's name? Is he cute? Maybe you can get a *personal* interview." She winks.

"I think not. He's probably some old, stuffy writer who thinks tweed jackets are still in. I'm not overly familiar with him. He's new, I think. Well, new to mass popularity, at least. His name is Alexander Delacroix."

"I bet he's full of himself, but I guess you'll have to find out first hand, huh? You *are* going, aren't you? Regardless of how much of an ass he may turn out to be, you really can't pass this up."

"Yeah. I'm going." Tilting my head back, my eye catches the palm trees rustling in a phantom breeze. "I'm fairly certain Angela only asked because she knows I don't do anything on weekends. I should've made up something, just to make myself seem more interesting."

"And she would've called you on it."

"Yeah," I sigh "she probably would have." Palming the glass, I tilt my head and drain the drink in one shot. "How does anyone survive in this heat? It's too hot to be out here."

The sweat, which had been accumulating on my skin the entire time, has now become a steaming river running between my breasts and down my back. I'm sure the alcohol isn't helping…

"Ready to go home?"

The heat seems to have gotten to Riley as well, and shows itself on her flushed cheeks as the sweat beads threatening to fall from her forehead.

"Definitely."

Chapter 1

Opening my eyes, I stare at the clock in a stupor as it sits on the bedside table. It looks so innocent; it's cold, blue numbers flashing in time with the obnoxious racket ringing from its speakers. Slipping the covers off my skin with a groan, the warmth and security of my precious bed falls away, giving rise to a host of goose bumps in response to the stark cold of the barren room.

Chancing a glance at the clock, it continues to scream, mockingly, from the nightstand. If only my glare could cause it to shatter, and lie peacefully upon the floor among the scattered remnants of clothes from the night before. Rolling my eyes, I knock the alarm to the ground with a sweep of my hand. No one wants to wake up this early, and I'm no exception. I'm honestly surprised the damn clock still has the strength to make any noise at all, after the abuse it's received recently.

The room is instantly cast into a deafening silence, ominously pressing against me from all sides as it couples with the near darkness of the early morning hour. Staring out across the bed, I can barely make out the indentation of my partner from last night. All other evidence of his stay has been meticulously removed, at my request. I'm glad to see he remembered to follow my instructions, after all, they're there for a reason.

Stumbling my way into the bathroom, I catch a glimpse of myself in the mirror. My hair is a tangled mass of chestnut curls, my eyeliner, more reminiscent of war paint than a beauty aid, and the fading red stain against my lips portrays a telltale story of the night before.

The memories blur, dripping into one another as my mind grasps to piece together the night. I shake my head to banish the thoughts.

No, it didn't happen. Nothing happened last night.

Running the cold water from the tap, fractured thoughts stubbornly pull at the surface, struggling to bind together into a clear image. Bending my head over the sink, I scour my skin with my palms until all signs and symptoms of my sins give way to pure thoughts and raw, reddened flesh.

Once I've cleaned up, I glare at my reflection. My skin quickly fades to porcelain, and the image that stares back at me morphs into picture of perfect innocence. I'm a common face among the crowd, a whispered voice indistinguishable among a roaring sea of people. I'm nothing special, and I endeavor to keep it that way.

I've decided on a simple outfit for today — a pair of ash gray slacks and a cream colored blouse — then pull my cell from where I had tucked it, unceremoniously, into the strap of my bra. Swiping through the messages, there are texts for coffee and cocktails, breakfast to dinner, and every meal from now until the end of the month from half a dozen lovers. They didn't honestly think there would be anything more, did they? I made my intentions perfectly clear, after all.

With an exasperated sigh, I delete every message other than those work related, and close my eyes tight to concentrate on the day ahead. None of them happened. They don't exist.

Breathing deep, I force down the shredded thoughts of last night, the night before that, and the one before that. Last night was lonely. Riley went out, and I spent my night curled up on the couch in front of the fireplace reading a book. That's it. I sipped on a glass of wine and fell asleep alone. I fell asleep alone…

I take a final deep, calming breath and slip into my heels.

Chapter 2

Life in Louisiana is such a drastic change from the life I was used to in New York. Everything was so fast paced up there, and you never ever looked anyone in the eye. Since I lack the don't-fuck-with-me attitude so famous when thinking of New Yorkers, I survived by keeping my head low and my voice even lower amidst the undulating mass of bodies that surged from every corner of the city. I often thought of its inhabitants as hordes of wild animals. They would weave and dance and collide into one another, which resulted in cursed words and verbal shouting matches that often weren't worth the time it took to gawk.

There was something magical about it though. Something that still tugs at my heart and makes me think back with longing. Perhaps it was the way the steam curled its fingers up from the depths of a manhole on a cold day or the soft seduction of music and smells that came wafting out of every restaurant. Maybe it was the abandoned streets in the early morning hours of the winter, covered in fresh virgin snow that hid the grime of the streets beneath its skirt.

It was a place for everyone, and yet, I still didn't feel comfortable there. I was awkward. I didn't fit in, I'm not sure I will fit in anywhere. Even here, I find myself gazing out the window and wondering where I'll wind up next. What's the next adventure, where's the next stop? Where can I go, what can I do? Where will I move to next in order to start over? I'm hoping this time will be different.

My long-time friend, current roommate, and the closest thing I have to a sister, Riley, convinced me to move to this state. Compared to New York, this place feels bleak, and entirely uninteresting.

The city she decided on is, honestly, a bit boring. She moved for the silliest of reasons too — a man — and though I spoke against it, she was pretty adamant. The opportunity to tag along came up, and I had a hard time passing up the chance to add yet another state to the list of places I've tried to turn into a home. Besides, I couldn't let her come here by herself, could I? She'd get in to all sorts of trouble without me!

The man I'm meeting this morning, Alexander Roderick Delacroix, has already sent me the address of where we are to meet. He's changed the venue three times since Angela sent me the original address yesterday. It's in times like these that I'm actually thankful Angela gave out my number so he could reach me. I'd be livid if I showed up at the wrong location and waited for hours only to realize I'm not where he wants me to be.

Alexander Delacroix is a writer based out of New Orleans, and I was encouraged to gather as much information as I could on the ins and outs of his work by Angela Leveaux, Editor-in-chief of LAddict magazine. According to her, he's a hard guy to get in contact with, and she has stressed over and over, the importance of this meeting. She called in a fit yesterday, begging me to take over this interview, since the guy she had originally picked for the job ducked out on her. Seeing as how I had nothing better to do, I figured the extra cash couldn't hurt. I imagine I'll get at least a pat on the back and a coffee out of this, if I manage to spin a decent piece on the ever-elusive Alexander Delacroix for her precious magazine.

Through the few years I've lived here, I've never bothered to venture into the city of New Orleans. I have always heard of the crime, and how gross Mardi Gras really can be, but I still hoped to experience it for myself one day. I'm sure I'd never forgive myself if I moved away without enjoying the celebration.

My palms slip across the wheel as I near the city, sweaty from my poor attempt to repress my nervous thoughts. Mr. Delacroix is a fairly prestigious author, from what I've managed to scrape up; the winner of multiple awards, with some of his best work topping the best seller lists. It's normal to be nervous, right? I wish my stomach would stop flipping head over heels like an acrobat tripping on acid. I feel sick, like that mix of excitement and dread you feel the night before the first day of a new job.

Majestic silver giants rush up to greet me as I approach the city, cruising by the Mercedes-Benz Superdome in what I believe to be the Central Business District. The city is beautiful, and not at all how I expected it to look. I didn't expect skyscrapers or gleaming streets. I imagined dilapidated buildings, crumbling architecture and half-flooded streets with buildings so tightly packed together, one would become claustrophobic just walking by them. I expected worn homes and unfriendly alleyways surrounded by a desolate landscape; the ruins of a once great city, but what I encountered today was something entirely different.

Glancing over at the GPS, it chimes in with its all-too-chipper voice, directing me down a street on the left. Ushering me past the skyscrapers of the business district, it guides me toward smaller, more compact buildings that had been hidden from view. These buildings are much more charming, with architecture the likes of which I've only ever seen in history books. Being here amidst the historic homes and horse drawn coaches plodding down the side streets, transports me to another time; a simpler time, that harbors street musicians streaming jazz into the streets, and closely packed homes decorated with French doors and wrought iron balconies.

A space clears to the left dominated by walkways, perfectly trimmed hedges and impossibly green grass. Between two tree lines stands a breathtaking, regal, white building topped with three grey spires that stretch toward the heavens. This is the St. Louis Cathedral I've read about, and it's every bit as prepossessing as I had imagined. As much as I'd really love the chance to take a closer look, my time is a bit pressed this morning.

The thought of being in the city makes me nervous. Physically being here, is much more nerve wracking than I thought it would be. It's beautiful, really, but there are so many people. I hated New

York for that reason. The crowds always made me anxious.

I can still hear Angela's shrill voice in my ear and feel those cold, black eyes staring me down as she slaps the paper in front of me detailing this assignment. I know. It's a once in a life-time thing; she made that abundantly clear, and I'm honored, really. I'm surprised she would trust me with such a heavy hitter, but, she could've given me more forewarning. I didn't prepare well enough for this! I only managed to think of a handful of questions to ask, shrugging off the rest of it by thinking I'd just wing it. Wing it!? What the hell made me think I could wing this interview? This is going to be a disaster.

As I wander down the road, my eyes frantically search for some obscure coffee shop in a city I've never stepped foot in before today. The oppressing heat and humidity does my poor curls no favors, and I can feel the sweat beginning to bead on my skin. The sun has come up just over an hour ago and the weather has already become unbearable.

Shit, where the hell is it?

Nervously glancing at my wrist watch, I stare in horror as the hands meticulously slip to rest at 8 o'clock. This is not the type of meeting I want to show up late to. Angela will have my hide if I ruin this for her.

My heels echo on the pavement and the sun assaults me with its glare as I wander past the crowded square. The sight of the people surging against the sidewalks makes my skin crawl. I can't wait till this is done, then I can get away from the city center, and I'll be okay...

Creeping up on my right, is a large green and white striped awning with white letters printed along the side.

This must be it!

Pulling my notepad from my purse, I head across the street with renewed haste, and leaning precariously against a pole holding the awning, is Alex Delacroix. It's not hard to recognize him after I spent the greater part of yesterday night skimming every website with information on him, and their accompanying pictures, in order to get more of a feel for my subject.

He's taller than I am by about six or seven inches, with loose auburn curls, and what looks to be the beginnings of a beard borne from a few days of missed shaves. His hair rebels against the frizz that so often accompanies this disgusting humidity, and cascades down to his shoulders with silken perfection. I really should find out what he uses in his hair…

Dressed casually, in a pair of dark jeans and a thin gray shirt with the top button undone, his eyes are accented by a pair of slim, silver glasses. I take a deep breath to calm nerves, smooth my outfit and pray that any sweat from this incessant heat hasn't shown through my clothes. He's incredibly attractive, far more than I thought he'd be, with a fire glinting in his eyes as he glances up to watch me as I draw closer.

"Mister Delacroix?" I ask, awkwardly holding out my hand.

"Ah, Miss Roman, is it?" He takes my hand in his, raising it, and brushing his lips delicately against my skin.

I blush in response, and he treats me to a knowing smile. His eyes meet mine then slip quickly over my body, scrutinizing every inch of me, and I'm suddenly self-conscious.

Is there something on my shirt? Am I sweating? I should've worn something darker to hide it!

It's a matter of seconds, but as his eyes run over and through me; a shiver runs up my spine. His eyes meet mine and crinkle at the edges as he pulls a soft smile to his lips, but I feel exposed, as if his eyes sliced me from head to toe, and peeled back my skin to take a peek at my soul.

"Shall we?" he asks as he opens one of the doors into the café.

I return his smile uneasily, step through the door, and am instantly assaulted by the noise of dozens of different conversations going on at once, as well as the ever-present clattering of kitchen dishes. The smell is overpowering; a delightful mix of coffee, sugar, and fried dough. The sugar is absolutely everywhere. It's on the floors, on the tables, on everyone's fingers and clothes and yet no one seems to pay it much mind. It takes more than a bit of willpower not to ask for a broom and go on a massive sweeping spree.

He leans in close and whispers something into my ear, but I can barely hear his voice amidst the noise. Linking my arm in his, he leads me to the front counter, where he leans over to speak with the barista. She nods and passes off the orders to her coworker, who readies two Café Au Laits, and a plate of some breakfast pastry doused in the same sugar that makes up the entirety of the shop. Leading me to a table outside in the heat, he places the plate and both coffees on its surface, then gestures to the chair across from him.

"Please, have a seat. Have you ever had one before?"

"Have I had what?"

"A beignet," he chuckles and waves a hand to the plate with pastries that are still piping hot from the fryer. "It's a rite of passage. If you live here, you have to try a beignet."

He tears off a piece of fluffy, still steaming hot, dough saturated with powdered sugar, and hands it to me. I take it, not wanting to offend, and pop it into my mouth. It dissolves completely on my tongue, like melted silk. The texture of it is incredible, but other than that, it doesn't seem any different in taste than something I could pick up by hitting up the local donut shop first thing in the morning.

"Well?"

"Well what? It's a fresh donut without the hole, and smothered in powdered sugar."

He laughs lightly, picks up his coffee and takes a small sip.

"And how long have you lived in Louisiana, Miss Roman? I thought you would have indulged in some of the local cuisine by now."

The local cuisine, huh?

I bite the inside of my cheek to keep from blurting out something that would leave me sounding like a horny teenager.

Sipping my coffee, my eyes slip from his eyes to his lips, then down his neck before I catch myself and quickly avert my eyes to a passing horse and carriage.

"I've only been here a few years. Two or three now, I don't keep track anymore. I've tried a few things, but just haven't had the time, I suppose, for this particular…delicacy. It wasn't something that seemed important."

"Oh, but to really find yourself at home in new surroundings, you must take part of the local culture and their cuisine. How else will you find comfort in your new residence?"

He shakes his head, as if banishing some wayward thought, or perhaps he's disappointed in my previous answer. Great. This is already getting off to a bad start.

"So, Miss Roman, I'm under the impression that you've been trying to get ahold of me for quite some time. Or rather, your relentless employer has. It seems she's very keen on having someone speak with me."

"She has. I'm sorry. She can be a bit stubborn when she gets her mind set on something. Thank you again for agreeing to meet with me. I really have enjoyed much of your work, and was hoping to talk to you about it, if that's okay?"

Enjoyed his work? God, I hope he doesn't call me on that load of bullshit. I didn't know he existed till yesterday, but then again, I haven't exactly been keeping up on much of anything other than work.

"Of course." He smiles, then his eyes waver, focusing on a bird that's landed on the edge of the wrought iron fence that surrounds the outdoor patio. Tilting his head, he refocuses on me, curiosity sparking to life behind his eyes.

"You have a few interesting pieces yourself, Miss Roman. It was you who wrote that exquisite piece on the state of our educational system, was it not?"

I nod, trying to hide the look of shock from my face. I'm surprised he is familiar with me at all.

I'm not exactly well known, and often I find my own work to be lackluster at best. Nothing I've written would hold a candle to a paragraph penned by the esteemed Alexander R. Delacroix, I'm sure. The piece he's referring to is nothing more than fevered ramblings of an inebriated journalist.

Damn, a successful subject change. Was he trying to switch the focus to me, instead? Is he actually interested in answering my questions, or has he only agreed to meet with me in order to amuse himself.

I look up from my coffee to find his eyes locked on me. They're a soft, light brown, splattered with specks of green and gold, and they're holding mine firm.

"Well?"

I blink, knitting my eyebrows together, then realize I had been holding my coffee and staring into it, completely lost in my own thoughts.

"Drink, before it cools."

I doubt anything would cool in this heat, but his words overflow with the subtle power of confidence, and a sense of authority.

My cheeks burn with the excitement of forbidden thoughts, which have slipped into each crevice of my brain. Drawing the mug to my lips, I take a sip, his eyes never wavering from mine. A budding hunger peeking out from behind his eyes, causes me to shift uncomfortably in my seat. My thighs press together and my muscles clench, sending a pulse of pleasure through my quickly aching body.

Clearing my throat, I pick up my pen and poise it over the pad.

"Well, is there any advice you could tell our readers about your sudden success? Any tips or information on your personal writing process, or how you went about getting published? There are so many options, these days, for aspiring writers, and I'm sure we would love to hear about your personal experience."

"Well, Miss Roman, if I could give you any advice, it would be to write every day. Think of it as a muscle you must exercise daily. If you want it to improve, you have to work at it constantly, even if they're little spurts, say, ten minutes here and there. You'll be surprised how much the way you perceive things changes and molds your work from an ugly lump of clay into a beautiful vase. I must stress, however, that everyone's writing process is completely different. You need to find what works for you. As for publishing, well, that's a bit harder to explain. It certainly doesn't happen overnight." He pauses for a brief moment, clearly amused with himself, and asks, "How's that?"

Cocking my eyebrow, I glance at him from my notepad, where I had been furiously scribbling notes.

"I'm sorry?"

"That's what I'm supposed to say when being interviewed, right?"

"I uh, I suppose?"

He chortles, and brings his coffee to his lips. The steam rolling off the top of the mug fogs up the bottom half of his glasses for just a moment while he takes a sip, and I notice the sweat beading up on his forehead and sliding down his temples. The heat is having an effect on him too, but he seems far more comfortable in it than I am.

Maybe he enjoys being a sweaty mess.

"In all honesty, writing can be awkward and difficult. This field is solitary and unstable for the first several years, much like most people's early 20's. It takes time to find your stride, and in the process, it may often result in many long, lonely nights." he laughs. "You find yourself seeking out your place in a world filled with many others who are trying to do the same thing. Finding a way to distinguish yourself from the crowd isn't always easy, and leads many to throw their hands up in exhaustion, as they come across rejection after rejection. It is a solitary, humbling experience, and I don't think anyone should pursue it unless they're truly passionate about it. Writing isn't something you want to do; it's something you need to do. What about you, Miss Roman? Why do you write?"

"Why do I write? Right now, because it pays my bills. I know that's not a good reason, and I've had ideas for things that could become something more, but usually those ideas are nothing more than a quick release. I have trouble sticking with it once the mood has passed, and they wind up in a pile cast off to the side."

"Well, have you thought about a blog? It's a good way to force yourself into writing daily."

Clearing my throat nervously, I take another sip of my coffee as I think back on a brief spurt of blogging experience. It was definitely more X-rated than your typical blog on cooking or on the one hundred different types of hats to knit. The blog mirrored some exploratory work as a phone sex operator I picked up, in order to gather experience for an article I was writing, and of course, for the extra cash. It lasted a week before I felt myself questioning my own morals. The day I began to dread getting on the phone is the day I called it quits.

"No, I haven't had any blogging experience. Not really. My only real writing experience has been in the articles for Angela, and those few things I have submitted were randomly thrown together over the course of a few nights. I suppose I tend to write a bit more on impulse, and that's something I'd like to get away from. I want to organize it all, I just have a rough time sketching my thoughts out in some kind of order. And yes, I tried an outline under a college professor's instruction. It was so bad; he was struggling not to laugh. I guess outlines aren't my thing."

My eyes slip from his as he turns his attention back to his coffee, lost in thought, then trail down the side of his neck, over the slight bulge of his Adam's apple and linger on the hint of chest hair visible only due to the carelessly unrestrained top button of his shirt.

"Are you okay, Miss Roman? You look flushed. Is the heat too much for you?"

The pink on my cheeks must have grown to a bright scarlet as I fumble with my pen. His voice is soft, aching with concern, and it seeps through my skin, threatening to set a spark to my already boiling blood.

"Yes, yes. I'm sorry. I suppose I'm still not accustomed to the temperature down here. I wasn't made for this extreme heat."

"Oh? I would have thought you could handle the heat, Miss Roman." He smirks, with a twinkle in his eye that stirs my blood. Fantastical images of twisted limbs and impassioned moans push to the forefront of my mind "Would you like to finish our discussion indoors?"

Indoors, perhaps, but the coffee shop isn't the first thing that comes to mind. I was thinking something a bit more…private.

Biting hard on the inside of my cheek to focus my thoughts, I think back on the sound restrained just beyond the doors to the café, and know it would be pointless. I wouldn't hear a thing in there.

His phone chimes from the depths of his back pocket, and saves my scattered brain from trying to piece together more innocent thoughts. He pulls it out, apologizing for the interruption, and swipes his finger across the screen. His brow furrows as he reads over the message.

"I'm really very sorry, Miss Roman, but my free time has been cut short yet again. Perhaps we can continue this another time? Do you plan to stay in the area?"

"Yes, for the next few days. I have a few things around the city that I need to take care of, but plan to head home on Sunday."

"Wonderful! Then we'll set something up. I'll text you the details."

His lips curl into a soft smile as he rises from his seat and offers his hand. Slipping my hand into his, I give it an awkward shake.

I really hope that's why he was offering it...

His eyes peer down at me from behind his silver rimmed glasses, and his smile takes on a seductive twist to my hormone riddled brain. My imagination is running away with me again, causing enticing delusions to implant themselves into everything I perceive.

I'm glad he's was called away, before my imagination had time to fully wrap him into another one of its fantasies.

As he turns his back, I look down at my fairly empty notepad and write this off as a failure. I'm sure I know what his schedule is like; events, future projects project or helping with various activities around the city. Honestly, I'd probably have better luck seeing him on television than I would in person.

I finish off the rest of my coffee, and leave the noise of the café, and the memories of my failure, behind me. As I turn the corner towards my car, I find him leaning against it, swiping through his phone. He looks up as I approach and grins, his fingers raking insouciantly through his hair.

"Ah, Miss Roman. My apologies, is this your car?"

"Yes, in fact…"

He can't seriously think I'd write this off as a coincidence, could he?

"Well, quite the stroke of luck, then! As I was heading home, I realized that I'm terrible at contacting people."

He smiles, and I could feel that oh-so-familiar ache grow inside of me as my eyes try to focus on his, and not on the visible sprinkling of chest hair, how delicious he looks in those jeans, or how sexy his smile is.

"Why don't you try me tomorrow night?"

He eases his hand into his front pocket to fish out his business card. I thank him, and watch as he heads off again.

The usual questions such as 'How did he know what car I drove?' pale in comparison to the mental images assaulting my thoughts as I watch him walk off, and as I climb into my car, I begin fantasizing about how he'd look shirtless.

Shaking the images from my head, I check my phone to see several missed calls and a handful of messages from Ann begging me to stop by as soon as I can. I had mentioned I'd be in the city to her, and she was overly eager to have me check over her work. Sadly, she's also incredibly impatient.

I start up the car, throw it in gear, and head towards my hotel to change from these stuffy clothes into something a bit more casual for her. By the time I've changed and grabbed a quick — albeit unsatisfying — bite to eat, the sun is beginning to set and there are twelve new messages on my phone from Ann. I should probably learn to keep my phone, at minimum, on vibrate. I have this awful habit of slipping it on silent at all times, mostly because I hate to be disturbed by the constant ring of calls and texts.

Grabbing my purse and keys, and head out of the hotel towards the address Ann sent in her very first text, then reply with a quick 'On my way.' before tossing the phone into the bottomless void of my hand bag.

Chapter 3

In addition to my submissions to LA*ddict*, I was lucky enough to land a more stable, part-time teaching job at the local college when Riley and I first moved to here. It was there, that I met Ann. She's a former coworker that I met during my first semester teaching.

Ann carries herself with an air you'd expect from someone who's grown up never wanting, however, I do admire her ability to stay semi-grounded. She's not the type who will look down on someone for not having what she has; she just doesn't know how to relate in certain social aspects, almost as if she lacks the graces you'd expect from the general population. It's just another one of those slightly annoying qualities she possesses, and her impatience is less than charming.

I walk up to a pair of large, intimidating mahogany front doors and with a single knock, they fly open. She's standing before me; her eyes, a sunlit forest of jade, and her hair is reminiscent of the red and black of smoldering coals.

"Oh! Thank goodness you're here. Come in, please!"

She reaches across the threshold, grabs me by the wrist and drags me through the expansive parlor until we're standing hip to hip in the doorway to the office.

"I'm really sorry for calling on you, but since you were in the area, I…"

"Really, it's not a problem. I was finishing up a meeting not too far from here, actually, so it's not an inconvenience. Perhaps, next time, I could do without all the messages." I smile.

Her eyes are absolutely enchanting.

With crimson cheeks, she stares down at her feet, clearly embarrassed by my statement, and I regret saying it immediately. I didn't mean to offend her, but spamming me with messages isn't going to make me come here any faster.

"I'm sorry. It's been so long since I've seen you. I just wanted to make sure you were still coming, I suppose. I'm sorry..." Her eyes are still downcast, and I wish I could pull my previous comment out of the air and erase it from existence.

"It's okay! Really. It's no problem at all. However, I'd hate to be a disappointment. I'm not perfect, and I'm certainly not a professional editor, or anything. There will be things I miss, and different people may see it in different ways. If you're certain on going forward with this, I really do encourage you to seek out a second opinion to give it a more in depth review."

"Don't be ridiculous." She states pointedly as she ushers me into the room. "You're far better than I am, at least, and I would really love your opinion."

Ann pushes me toward the desk as my eyes sweep over every inch of the room. It's spectacular; something I could only dream of having as an office.

A rich, espresso wood spreads across every inch of the floor, naked if not for the lush cream carpet beneath a solid cherry wood desk. The walls are a shimmer of white, but can hardly be seen amongst the towering white bookshelves, which are pushed into every corner of the room. The ceiling is an ornate pattern of leaves and vines stamped out in polished copper panels. Each bend, curve, and twist in its surface reflects the dim light from the chandelier, which dangles from the center of the room as if it were a ladies prized pendant.

The light fixture mimics the trees scattered throughout the lawn; a jumbled lump of white washed oak branches, copper stamped leaves and rose quartz flowers which hang delicately among the branches. A soft glow is refracted in the gems, casting dappled pinks on everything residing within its touch.

Ann's hand releases mine and rips my thoughts back to the original reason she called me here. She requested my presence to look over a story she had been working on for almost a year, now. It was something that started as a small idea, then grew till it completely consumed her every waking moment, and the joy in her voice from completing something of this length was palpable.

"It's there, on the desk." She grins, a note of pride dancing on her tongue. "Please, take your time. I really appreciate you coming, and if there's anything I could do or bring you…"

"I think I'll be just fine. Is there anything in particular you want me to watch for? Or anything I need to know before I begin reading?"

"Well it's not done…not really" her eyes drop to the floor as a blush stains her cheeks "and it's a little intense at times."

"It's nothing to be embarrassed about. I'm not one to judge. This is your world; your creation. You should never feel the need to apologize for expressing yourself."

Smiling with relief, she walks from the room, beaming as she mumbles something beneath her breath.

The door shuts with an inaudible sigh, and I'm left alone in the expansive, beautifully furnished office. The wind picks up, howling outside the large window behind the desk and causing the leaves and branches of the trees to scratch against the glass.

Collapsing into the large, leather chair, I wiggle myself into a comfortable position; my fingers idly flipping through the stack of papers. I pull out my red pen, which always seems to become my make-shift hair fastener, and let my hair spill over my shoulder. My weapon of choice finds its mark against the neatly typed pages, weaving its way between letters, words and sentences without remorse. The sanguine ink bleeds across white flesh. Mark after mark soaks the page as it relentlessly seeks out each misspelling, fragmented sentence, run-on and missed punctuation.

A soft cough interrupts my thoughts, though perhaps it's been a bit longer than I originally thought.

She wasn't wearing that outfit earlier, was she?

"You should wear your hair down more often." She whispers from her place just inside of the door.

I was so absorbed in my work that I hadn't noticed her return till she spoke. She enters the room holding a small cup and saucer, and places it on the desk, then pulls an empty chair over and sits by my side, staring at me as I attempt to work.

Does she expect me to continue with her here? Having someone constantly looking over my shoulder is unnerving.

I place the pen down on the desk and sip at the tea she's brought, but I can't seem to refocus my thoughts on the story. She looks stunning, and a deep hunger pulls at my thoughts, dragging them into darker shadows.

"Thank you for the tea." I stutter, struggling to catch my pen as it launches an escape from the desk.

"I just went to straighten up. I could've sworn I said something before I left. Anyway, dinner is done, and I was hoping you would join me. Have you eaten yet?"

"No, I haven't." An embarrassing growl originates from somewhere deep in the pit of my stomach, and my cheeks blush immediately. I wish I could control that.

Standing up, I twist my hair and refasten it with my pen. How long had I been wrapped up in her story, that she was able to come back transformed into such an exquisite being?

Her hair flows down her back like the trail of blood tinged oil on the surface of water, and each movement of her lithe body is so fluid, it's unnatural. Her eyes glow from within with a glint of playful mischief that I must've missed before; just visible behind a feigned innocence. Her lips are almost as red as the highlights in her hair, juxtaposed against her pale skin.

She's come back to me dressed in a dark green silk shirt that shimmers gold when she moves, and is just thin enough to hint at the pattern of her bra. A stiff black skirt stops just above her knees, and upon her feet are simple pale gold heels.

I hope she didn't go through the trouble of changing just for me.

"Will anyone else be joining us?" I ask, hiding the intimidation brought on by her change of clothes. I'm wearing a pair of jeans and a black cotton tank top, and feel completely underdressed.

"No, it's just us for the evening. I hope that's okay."

She flashes a wicked smile and walks from the office, and I'm left questioning her motives for calling me here. Why the sudden change of clothes? Was her reason for calling me here really just to look over this manuscript, or did she have something else in mind.

She leads me toward the dining room with her head held high and her back straight and stiff. She has become a completely different being, as if the girl I met at the door, and this new one, were two separate entities.

The hallway leading to the dining area is just as simple and elegant as the office. There are windows on either side that kiss the floor, and reach their fingers to the ceiling. They were thrown open as the day cooled, allowing the howling wind outside to force its way indoors, creating a wind tunnel throughout the small space.

One side of the hallway gave a view to the inner courtyard, which was littered with flowers of all colors and several stone benches. On the other side, the glass faced a wrought iron fence, and a pristine lawn within its bounds that hugged against the walls of the house; creeping up its sides with tendrils of green vines that stretched up the sides in an effort to reach the heavens.

The dining room opens up before us, yawning like a monster waiting to swallow us whole. It's an imposing room, with a ceiling so tall that the light of the fireplace is too fearful to prod its depths. It's sparsely decorated, consisting only of a large, artfully distressed wooden table with six chairs, and an imposing fireplace that occupies the opposite wall. The fireplace cuts an impressive figure with its white face and dark oak mantle. It's so large, in fact, that if I were to hunch my shoulders and duck my head, I could walk right into it.

A blazing fire crackles within its maw, filling the room with the warm light from its flames.

I pull out a chair opposite to Ann. Her green eyes focus on me, a reflection of the flames dancing within them. She smiles with one corner of her mouth, and pours red wine into the glass before me.

"So, it seems like you've gotten through the first bit of my story. What do you think?"

Don't others normally start dinner conversations with useless dribble such as 'How was your day?' and 'How are things going?' All the better, I suppose. No one really cares about the answers to such broad questions anyhow.

Delicately holding the wine glass by its stem, I draw it to my lips, inadvertently swallowing more than I intended. It's strong, and the scent of fermented grapes assaults my nose as mixtures of sweet, cherry notes wash over my tongue. It hits me instantly, and every inch of my body flushes and tingles, as if Zeus himself electrified every cell with a single snap of his fingers.

"Well, it's really not that bad..." I murmur, as I take another sip for courage. I wasn't too fond of what she wrote, but it may just be my personal preference. I'm really not the best person to do this for her.

"Not bad? When someone reads something and says it's not bad, it means they're too polite to admit that it's awful." She laughs, and it's like listening to wind chimes dancing in the breeze on a warm summer day. She's always been one to speak her mind.

"No, not at all. It's really not bad. There are just a few things that should be addressed, from the small bit I was able to read."

"Such as?"

"Little things, such as the few grammatical errors I have found, and I'm not overly fond of you using the name of your story to refer to your main character over and over again. I'm sure it could be worked in there somehow, but I think what you've done is excessive. I've marked everything out on the pages for you to review whenever you get around to it."

She smiles, visibly pleased by my response then drains her glass of wine in one movement, which is quite out of character. Her eyes begin to gloss over as she sighs heavily and looks over into the dancing flames of the fireplace.

"Well, thank you for coming here. I really love seeing you, and it was a nice distraction for me. It's been a bit of a long day, and it gets lonely in this house when I'm left on my own. You know, it's been so long since we've hung out. We really should make this a regular thing."

She turns back to me, a grin twisting into her lips like a snake, replacing the worried look that had been so clear on her face just moments before. The alcohol is beginning to take hold of her. She drifts into a near dazed state, and giggles happily for no apparent reason.

After one drink? What a light weight.

Leaning over the table with a mischievous grin, she brushes her fingertips lightly over my hand.

"You know," she moans, her voice soft and sultry "I could use a bit more hands-on experience for my story. For the sake of research, of course."

Her red lips slice through my chest, drawing that ever-present ache of desire to the surface. My blood rushes through me, no doubt displaying the hints of blushing cheeks to my new found predator.

"Of course..." I return, as I draw my hand away reluctantly. "I wish I could help with that. I'm sure there are a lot of online resources..."

The look in her eye clearly states her intentions, and the fire flickers as if to solidify the fact that she has no desire to back down without a fight.

"I find online resources to be lacking a certain…intimacy."

"Well yes, but very rarely is research intimate." I cough, embarrassed, and take another sip of wine, which probably wasn't the best idea given my current circumstances. "It's getting a bit late, isn't it? I really should be going. I have a lot of work to finish up before bed, and I really don't need Angela chewing my head off for being late with yet another article."

Standing from the table, I bite down hard on the inside of my cheek to clear my thoughts from the effects of the wine, and Ann's lust-filled eyes.

"I don't think you're in any condition to drive, Cass…"

"My hotel is just a few blocks down the road, and I've had one drink. I'm sure I can handle myself, Ann, but thank you for your concern. I really shouldn't neglect my work…"

Displeasure flashes across her face, then sadness. I know she's lonely, but I can't be the one to help her. I can't mix myself up with her for the sake of quick satisfaction. I swore to myself…I can't give in to such temptations, especially not with someone I know.

She looks up and stares into my eyes as she moves closer, desire mixed with the scent of wine streaming from her lips.

"I have a spare room…"

"Ann, I'd love to but…"

"…then you could finish reading over it in the morning."

"I really should go. I need to. I'm sorry. I wouldn't want to impose, and really…my work. It can't wait until morning. I don't have my laptop here or anything, and all my work is in my room. I promise, if I don't make it back here tomorrow, you can email me the rest and I'll try and take care of it."

"Oh, alright…" she sighs, crestfallen.

She manages to crack a small smile, and I'm glad for it. I'd hate for her lapse of inhibitions to cause a tension in our relationship. As much as my body may want to, mixing ourselves up in something like that would be devastating. I'd have to cut her off afterwards in order to maintain my sanity, and I cherish the relationship we have too much to risk that on a whim.

I walk back toward the office to grab my keys from the desk, and let her show me to the door.

"Thanks again for dinner. It was wonderful."

"Yeah, sorry you couldn't stay for dessert." She mumbles beneath her breath, then catches my eye with a horrified look on her face.

"I mean, pie! I made pie…" she coughs, shifting her weight uncomfortably. "Perhaps another time."

We bid farewell then the doors close, and I'm left alone on the quiet street. The daylight has all but faded, the sun relinquishing its' throne to overcast clouds that jealously shield the moon from view.

I relish in the night air as it washes through me, and aids in suppressing the throbbing desire in my body, even if it's only a temporary relief. It feels good to be out in the night with the whisper of the wind playing over my skin. Being inside with Ann was beginning to make me feel a bit claustrophobic, and the heat from my body was becoming unbearable.

Slipping behind the wheel, I make my way to my hotel with the memory of her lips haunting my thoughts.

Chapter 4

Entering the front doors of the hotel, the light from the lobby envelopes me in its golden glow. Every surface serves only to accentuate the light spilling from the oversized pendant lamps, which dangle precariously from thin steel strands that cascade down from the ceiling.

I feel out of place immediately, standing there with no make-up and my hair tangled from the harsh winds that I braved just moments before.

With a deep breath, I slip through the lobby amidst the disapproving side glances of the more elegantly dressed, and catch the elevator to head to my room on the fifth floor. Pulling my phone from my pocket, I begin thumbing through the contact list as another guest slips through the doors just before they close. I don't bother to look up, choosing instead, to concentrate on finding an evening lover to help with my flustered state.

"That was a close one!"

His voice is right in front of me, filling my ears like the deep rumbling of a dragon. The gentle, abysmal tones resonate to my core, and does nothing to quiet the desire clawing at my insides.

"What was?"

I try on a tone of nonchalance in an attempt to hide any tremble in my voice. I can feel his eyes on me, taking me in as if he were the mythical creature itself, and I was his prey. Glancing down past my phone, I catch my reflection in his polished black shoes. I look so much worse than I original thought. How embarrassing!

"The door to the lift. It nearly ripped my foot off!"

I roll my eyes. What a drama queen.

"Ah. Well it's a good thing it didn't. How would you walk?" I mutter, my finger sliding over the screen. What do I feel like tonight? Hm…

"I imagine I'd resign to hopping around from place to place on one leg; almost like a bunny." He sighs, dejectedly.

The ridiculous thought of this man with the deep, growling voice of something ancient and terrifying, growing fluffy ears and hopping around is too much for me to bear. Damn my overly active imagination.

Within seconds, the elevator fills with my poorly stifled giggles.

Glancing over my elevator companion, he's dressed in a dark brown pinstripe suit, a powder blue collared shirt, and a dark, chocolate colored silk tie. He looks to be in his mid to late 30's, but his face seems older, worn harsh by the years. Worry lines converge on the corners of his eyes that deepen with his laughter.

Glistening eyes hold a boyish, playful light that swims along the ebb and flow of the blues and greens held within their depths. His dark hair is slicked back, and matches the color of his shoes. Parted on the side, it flows with the hint of delicate waves and curls restrained by hair product.

"Ah, so the mobile isn't glued to your hand after all. I had feared a trip to the emergency room would be in order for you." He grins.

His beautiful, hypnotic eyes paired with his silken voice, are enough to leave me staggering for breath. "It's a pleasure to meet you, miss. I'm Ethan. And what may I call you?"

I shuffle through my thoughts; where have I heard that name before? It sounds so familiar, but I'm certain I've never seen him. I would've remembered a voice like that.

He holds out his hand expectantly, and I place my hand in his. Lifting my hand to his lips, he places a delicate kiss on the top, his eyes never leaving mine. His lips are soft and warm, and my skin prickles with goose bumps as a chill rushes through me from head to toe. As I reluctantly pull my hand back, I can still feel the remnants of his kiss.

"Are you always this suave with the ladies?" I ask amidst a chuckle.

"Only the pretty ones." He smirks

Oh, so he must be blind. I'm standing here, vaguely resembling a troll, and he's seen fit to refer to me as pretty.

"I'm Cass."

The elevator stops and the doors slide open onto the fifth floor. I move past him with a polite smile, and step across the threshold onto the plush, royal blue carpet.

"It was a pleasure to cross your path, Miss Cass. Are you staying in the area long?"

"Just the weekend."

"Well, I do hope our paths cross again."

He flourishes his hand and bows low as I leave, with an air that makes it seem as if he was born a few centuries too late. Blushing with the memory of his lips on my hand, and a flutter in my heart, I walk to my room.

Chapter 5

The room is lavishly furnished, and looks out on to the river. If I'm going to spend a weekend in this city, I'm glad it's in a nice room. The carpet inside matches the hallway, and feels harsh beneath my bare feet. The bed is dressed in champagne colored satin sheets and cradles my body within a cloud as I sprawl out on its surface.

Gliding my fingers over the code to unlock my phone, I begin swiping through my list of potential guests. They're meticulously categorized into their height, eye color, hair color, body type, location and a list of their fantasies. Matching up what I want for the night with a candidate who can complement that, is important, and will ensure enjoyment for both of us. Now it's all just a matter of finding what it is I want.

Scrolling to the M's, I select a contact simply labeled as M.L. In the contact info is the first and last initial, description, phone number, and a list of interests. I select the number and type out the text.

*Busy? *

Not tonight.

Want to be? I could use some company while I'm in town.

*Oh! You're in town? Where? *

At La Bohème, 5ᵗʰ floor, room 518. Think you can be here in an hour or so?

Sure thing! I'll see you in a bit.

I list the address of the hotel in my last message then shut down the phone; I won't need it again tonight. Securing the phone, my purse, and other identifying items into a small safe, I hop into the shower, pull on a short black dress, and apply my make-up. Smokey eyes, fake lashes, blue contacts and blood red lipstick make their appearance. As I pull on my heels, I hear a knock at the door, and sneak a peek through the peephole.

"Cass?"

Her voice slips through my door, soft and sweet, and as I open the door, my guest glides effortlessly into the room. She turns to face me with a seductive smile as I close and lock the door.

Her dark, tanned skin is wrapped in a loose fitting white dress with matching sandals on her freshly pedicured feet. Vibrant, almond shaped eyes with a color reminiscent of espresso accent her soft, rounded face. Her hair falls in straight, silken tendrils, framing her face and resting just below her shoulders. It mimics the color of her eyes; a deep, rich brown that draws me in.

"It's so good to see you. It's been a while. Here on business again?" she asks. Her voice teases the air; gentle and sultry, like the feel of velvet against my ears.

Moving closer, her fingers caress my arm from elbow to fingertip. Her eyes are hungry, and a smile curls against her lips. She wraps her arms around me and hugs me tightly; her face burrowed against my hair as she inhales deeply, taking in my scent.

"Yes as usual. You do make these trips worth it though." I smirk, as I pull back from her embrace.

I came across my lovely companion for the night, only one time before, and with the same excuse; that I often come to Louisiana on business. We met each other at a local bar in the capitol city, and the lustful look in her eyes was too hard to pass up. She never questioned me about the nature of my trips, where I'm from, or what it is that I actually do. It's what makes our arrangement work out so well.

I felt a certain chemistry between us immediately, from the moment I caught the lascivious look in her eye. We knew each other well enough, after the hours spent, speaking of our lives, or at least, the parts of our lives we wished to share.

I learned her ambitions, her desires, her wishes, fears and needs, and amidst the coy laughter and whispered flirtations, she became mine. We shared her bed that night, and I woke just before dawn. Scribbling a hasty note accompanied by a kiss to her forehead, I left her where she lay, fast asleep. No goodbyes. I'm honestly a bit surprised she was willing to keep me company tonight. Not that I'm complaining.

She giggles at my comment, her brown hair fluttering in a nonexistent breeze. Placing her hands on my cheeks, she lifts herself on her toes, and brings her eyes level with mine. They sparkle in the dim light of the room, dancing playfully as she cradles my face within her hands and brushes her luscious lips against mine. Smiling against her kiss, my hand slips through her hair, delicately running my fingers through the silken strands.

Breathing deep, I draw her in, and the light scents of jasmine which coat her skin and hair, soon fill my nose and mouth. Tracing my fingertips along her jawline, I relish in the softness of her supple skin. Her breath catches as my fingers slip to the front of her chest, leisurely unfastening each button.

Her luscious body is quivering beneath my touch, and she grins playfully as she pulls away from me inch by inch. Dropping her fingers down my arms, her light touch tickles my skin, and she pulls me toward her until the back of her knees hit the foot of the bed. Gripping the front of my shirt, she pulls my body flush against hers. Her petite breasts press against my chest; her hardening nipples pushing through her clothes, begging for my touch.

Her eyes flutter as I let my hand drop to a hardened nipple, deliberately rubbing it through the thin white fabric. Leaning in, my lips trace along her neck. The smell of her skin is absolutely enchanting, and I can't help but let the tip of my tongue slide along her flesh to sneak a taste. Lightly blowing on the moistened skin, a visible chill rushes through her body, shuddering through her small frame. Her arms wrap around me, steadily sliding up and down my spine as I bending down, scooping her into my arms.

Carrying her from the bed, I move toward the love seat just under the window, but the muscles in my arms are screaming. Picking her up definitely seemed like a better idea in my head, than it is in practice, but dropping her would completely ruin the mood. Besides, she seems to be enjoying it. Thank God she's so tiny.

She giggles as I rest her on the arm of the couch, and my lips trail down the middle of her chest. My fingers finish unfastening her dress, tugging it off her body. Gripping her shoulders, I turn her to back to me and marvel at the smooth, silken skin of her back. She tosses a glance over her shoulder, a devilish grin on her lips as I press my palm against her back, pushing her forward over the arm of the couch. I inhale sharply at the sight of her naked body; each gentle curve of her body outlined in the moonlight, which peeks innocently through the window. I press my lips against her shoulder, then down her spine in lingering kisses as my hands rub over her smooth backside.

Her grin haunts my eyes as she wiggles her hips from side to side. I know what she's waiting for, and I lift my hand, bringing it down hard against her ass. Her head tilts back as she gasps in pleasure, her skin rippling from the impact of my hand. She squirms below me, her hands gripping the couch cushions as I draw my hand back and allow it to collide again against the opposite cheek. Her skin reddens and grows hot beneath my touch. .

"Such a sweet, dirty girl." I moan as I press my lips against her lower back and against her quickly heating skin.

"Harder…" she groans, wiggling against the arm of the couch. "Harder, please."

I find it hard to resist such a sultry voice, and so, I give in to her desires. I bring my hand down harder, again and again, in response to her whimpers and moans. The palm of my hand stings against her skin; her nails grip the cushion so tightly, that I fear she may rip them to pieces.

I slide my tongue lightly over her hips, then the curve of her behind as my fingers slip between her thighs. Pulling her legs apart, I kneel between them and can hear her voice trembling with longing, as she whimpers and moans for me. She begs and I smile, breathing deep and taking in her sweet scent. I tug her panties to the side then push my lips against hers. She writhes against the arm of the couch, her breathing heavy and labored as I slip my tongue from my lips and press it flat against her, drawing it sedately along her slit as my hands hold her thighs spread. Her back arches, and her hand slips down her back till it's tangled in my hair, tugging lightly upon it from behind.

Shifting on my knees, my tongue darts between her lips, the top lightly teasing her clit before plunging deep into her. It traces lazy circles inside of her, becoming quickly drenched in her excitement as it deftly works its way around and inside of her. She collapses forward once more, panting and pressing herself back against my mouth as I grip her hips and push my mouth firmly against her. The taste of her floods over my lips and tongue, sparking flames and heated desire through my veins.

I pull away slowly, my tongue trailing over my own lips in an effort to relish every drop of her. She groans and pleads with me, begging me to continue, and I grin in response. Oh how I love when she begs. Lightly nibbling on her upper thigh, I snap a quick smack against her ass.

My fingers work down to her ankles as my lips follow their trail, licking and smothering her soft skin with well-placed kisses along her thighs.

My lips glide to the other leg, running my tongue slowly along her heated flesh as I slip back up her body.

Pulling her from her position, I hold her in my arms and guide her to the edge of the bed. Her body shifts, writhing in excitement, anticipation, and sexual frustration as my hands trace along the back of her thighs, resting on the underside of her knees and massaging gently. I can feel her pulse through my fingertips, pounding against them as I press my nose between her legs and kiss the dampening cotton. She collapses back on the bed as she feels my tongue probing playfully against her panties, her thumbs hooking into the waist of her panties as she wiggles herself out of them and tosses them playfully at me. She giggles as I catch her panties and place them on the corner of the bed.

Gripping her hips just above her thighs, I pull her closer to the edge of the bed. Her knees drape over my shoulders as I run my fingers along her damp slit. My lips lightly kiss along her groin, but refuse to move any closer. Not yet, at least, though her scent is intoxicating. It's enough to make it near impossible to keep myself away, but oh how I love to make her squirm.

"Please…please don't make me wait too long" she whimpers; her body twisting on the sheets.

Her lust-filled voice makes me ache, and after teasing around her sweet spot with the tips of my fingers and tongue, I give in to her begging. One finger slips into her and her back arches, her head pressing back against the bed as her hips rise up to grind against me. I drive my finger deeper as I press my lips between her legs; my tongue dancing its way around her sensitive little clit while my finger curls and twists inside of her. I draw moan after moan from her as she squirms and trembles on the bed.

Her voice rings out, begging for more, and I find it impossible to hold out against her for long. Her moans draw the ache from hours of pent up unsatisfied desires to the surface. I slip in a second finger, sucking and licking her wet lips. Her moans quickly turn to screams of pleasure, as her head tilts back against the bed, and her body begins to tremble. Her muscles tense; each sound from her lips draws that ache from my body closer and closer to the surface, and I soon find myself wiggling as I kneel down between her thighs, a free hand dipping between my own thighs and forcing its way beneath my soaking panties.

She's caught in a beautiful agony, begging for release her and I work with renewed vigor. She's so close…so close. Her screams of pleasure ring through the room, gaining in volume and intensity until her body falls limp, twitching and trembling against the bed. Her breath comes in short gasps; her body drained of every ounce of energy.

I crawl onto the bed, my body tingling at every touch from the silken sheets as I wrap her in my arms. Unhurriedly, I place kisses along her jawline and stroke her arm until she gains control over her shuddering body. She smiles up at me, her hand reaching up and gently tucking my hair behind my ear.

"It's your turn now…" she whispers breathlessly.

"Oh, sweetie; I question your strength to accomplish such a task." I grin. "Don't worry about me, why don't we sleep?"

"Oh I insist…" she growls seductively.

She presses her palms against my shoulder and forces me onto my back, then straddles my waist as she begins working my dress off my body. I can still feel her thighs shaking as she presses them against my hips.

"Madalyn…"

"Shhh…" she whispers, "just lean back and enjoy."

Chapter 6

"Housekeeping!"

I wake with a start, my heart thumping from my chest as my body trembles in anticipation; fight or flight responses cranked to the very edge. It takes a few seconds to remember that I'm still in my room at the hotel, but who the hell is at my door at this hour?

"Housekeeping!"

They're knocking so hard against my door, I swear I can hear it creaking and splintering beneath the assaulting fist. The voice that rips against my ears is harsh, deep and near deafening. Is it really necessary to be that loud this early?

knock knock knock

"HOUSEKEEPING!"

"Okay, okay. Give me a minute!" I shout. Did I forget to put the Do Not Disturb sign on my door? I could've sworn I took care of that last night.

I stumble out of the bed, nearly slamming myself face first against the wall as my feet tangle themselves in the sheets. Freeing myself from my bonds, I make a mad dash for my robe and pull it on hastily. A quick glance around the room, and it's pristine; no evidence of my activities from the night before, as if she had never existed. It's easier this way. No good-byes, no follow up calls, and no expectations.

The smell of her lingers on my skin, on my lips, and all over the bed sheets. Taking a moment, I breathe deep…letting myself drown out the room to reminisce over the memories I've allowed to resurface for a single, bittersweet moment.

The incessant knocking breaks me away from my thoughts prematurely, and the obnoxious voice continues to slam against my ears. I grab the door handle and wrench it open, the full might of every known foul word, and perhaps a few made-up ones, anxious to fly off my tongue.

Standing before me is Ethan, the man I met on the elevator last night. He's grinning so widely that his eyes are naught more than two thin slits, and the apples of his cheeks are saddled high on his finely crafted cheekbones. My words die on my tongue, and slip out silently through parted lips. Jostling my mind back from the shock, anger from being woken so unceremoniously now takes the lead.

"What on earth…how did you…what do you want?!"

"Well, aren't you the picture of perfection in the morning. You do realize it's just past 10, yes? Now, Miss Cass, you mustn't give in to sloth-like tendencies."

A scowl plasters itself upon my face as I stand there barefoot, hair resembling a very large bird's nest, and with blackened rings under my eyes from the runoff of eyeliner. When you're exhausted from a night of passion, you often forget to remove your makeup.

And yet, he's here, beaming like a child who was just given a puppy for his birthday.

"Coffee?" he asks innocently as the grin on his face tones down, taking on an amused smirk. "You look like you could use it."

Biting my tongue, I resist the urge to slam the door in his face. This is not how I imagined waking up this morning, and to be honest, I didn't think I'd ever come across this man again.

"Fine" I relent.

I really could use the coffee.

"Give me a few minutes, and you're buying!"

"I'd have it no other way."

Closing the door, perhaps a little harder than I originally intended, I run to my suitcase and shuffle through the few clothing options in my bag, settling on a pair of jeans from the night before and a grey t-shirt. I douse my hair in the sink to tame it, shaping the curls quickly with my fingers, then grab my purse and am back at the door.

"Ah! The queen emerges!" he exclaims, a twinkle in his color-shifting eyes.

"Shut it."

Laughing, and obviously far more entertained by his own humor than I am, he leads the way down the hall to the elevator.

"I'm glad to see you're still here."

"How is that a shock? I told you I'd be here all weekend. And how did you know what room I was in?"

"Oh. That. Yes, well, I knocked on eighteen other doors before I found yours…"

"In the same manner?"

"Of course!"

What could possibly possess someone to knock on a bunch of strangers doors in an effort to find someone you met for a couple of minutes the night before? It's kind of creepy. I hope he has no plans to slice me to bits and hide me in the floorboards of some abandoned building.

"I'm sure the occupants weren't amused. I'm surprised they didn't have security escort you out."

"Oh, they were a lovely group of people, and I found out that I'm pretty quick! I dodged all but one ice bucket."

His hand slips into his hair, rubbing the side of his head and ruffling his waves as if suddenly remembering the blow.

"Ah, anyhow. Coffee, yes? It's a bit too strong for my taste, but I can understand the allure of it. The smell is far better than the taste is, in my opinion."

"Yes, please. I could definitely use the extra kick this morning, maybe with an extra shot...or three."

We take the elevator to the lobby and exit the hotel, and the air smothers us the minute we leave the doors. It's already 90 degrees and climbing. Why did I move down here, again?

Reaching over, he takes my hand and leads me across the street and about two blocks down to a small French country style café.

It's a beautiful little place tucked into a nook on the street, and flanked by two larger buildings. The floors are the mixed shades of rustic stone, the walls are covered in brick and the ceiling is a white washed arch with patterned leaves painted along its edges. The tables are quaint, round, and covered with an emerald glass mosaic that shimmers in the light streaming through the large front windows. Each table is paired with a set of worn, white iron chairs.

The café is fairly empty this morning, with only three other patrons occupying the small, intimate space. He picks a table in the front corner by the street, and pulls out a chair for me.

"M'lady."

He smiles, his eyes sparkling as he holds the chair for me, waiting patiently. Embarrassed by his gesture, I sit down and shoo him off to his own chair as our waitress comes to greet us. Thankfully, the chairs are more comfortable than they originally looked.

"Peppermint mocha, please, and can you add an extra shot?"

"I'd love some tea. Earl Grey, if you please."

He flashes a smile at the waitress, and she catches his eye, blushes then rushes off to fill our order. Ethan settles in and holds me in his color shifting eyes.

"Why did you find me this morning?" I'm genuinely curious and wary about his possible stalking tendencies. Does he do this to everyone?

"You looked stressed and wound tight last night. It seemed to me like you deserved a bit of relaxation, so I was hoping to make you laugh this morning. You know, to loosen you up a bit. Maybe give you an excuse to cast aside your worries for a day."

"So you're just a regular white knight, trying to save stressed out women from their burdens?"

"Oh, nothing like that, Miss Cass." He chuckles. "It's more akin to seeing someone who could use a smile in their day, and wanting to help. I hardly consider that something deserving of knighthood. I see it more as one human being helping out another. We all need a bit more joy in our lives, these days."

I smile at his stirring response as our waitress places our drinks in front of us. She asks if we need anything further, lets her hand linger for a few seconds on Ethan's drink as her eyes take on a look of longing, then she rushes off to tend to the other customers.

"What is it you do? If you don't mind me asking?"

"Well I'm currently staying here with some mates for a work-related conference."

"That doesn't tell me anything about what you do." I grin.

"I'm a nurse, if you must know. Well, technically, at least. I'm here in New Orleans for an annual conference at the request of my employer." He leans back, sipping on his tea. "I travel around quite often, and it can be stressful. It's nice to meet new people from the various walks of life, and from the wide array of cultures that span this country. It's refreshing."

"You hardly know me, though, and you've invited me out to coffee." I tease. "You know, I could be a secret axe murderer or something."

"Oh, my dear, I'm a big boy. I think I could take care of myself. I do believe I could ward off any attacks from a woman of your...stature." He stifles a laugh, hiding his grin behind his cup.

"Is that a short joke? I don't think you're giving me enough credit. I'm fairly certain I could take you down. You shouldn't underestimate those of us who are vertically challenged..."

"I don't underestimate you at all. I'm just confident in my ability to bat my eyelashes and make you swoon." He grins.

I wrap my fingers around my drink and sip cautiously at the scalding liquid, my thoughts wavering back to my phone. Should I call Delacroix today about that meeting? I think he wanted me to call him today...or did he say he'd call me? Damn my shitty memory.

"What can you tell me about this city? I haven't had a chance to wander around yet, but I like the feel of it. It's almost buzzing." He asks, his deep, sultry voice spanning the space between us and flowing like honey between my ears. His eyes wander out the window as he speaks, and he seems to lose himself in his own thoughts.

"Honestly, I don't think I can tell you much. I moved to this state a few years ago with a friend, but this is the first time I've actually set foot in New Orleans. I'm just as new to this city as you are."

"It's a shame you've never been here before, though I guess I don't have much of an excuse either. I have a brother that lives fairly close by, but whenever I've come to visit, we never ventured out here. It feels a bit rough around the edges; this city, but it strikes me as a bit of a creative haven. Have you heard the street musicians? They're wonderful!"

"I suppose they are."

"Well, what brings you here then?"

"My editor pushed me to come here and conduct an interview, which I failed. I didn't get much that I can use, though I'm hoping to gather a bit more before the weekend is over so my editor doesn't string me out of her office window by my ankles."

"So you're a writer then?"

"Maybe, in so many words, though I don't really know if that suits me. I just write the occasional article for a magazine based out of the city I live in, and write some things for my own pleasure that never see the light of day. I don't know if anything I create is really that good...certainly not good enough to label myself as a writer. That seems like such a prestigious title to me." I laugh

"That sounds fascinating. I have never had the talent to write, myself, though I'm quite the avid reader. I'm sure you're being too hard on yourself. We're all our own worst critics."

"I suppose. It helps pays the bills at least, though not very well. I don't always get to write about subjects I'm interested in, but I get by. So, you're a nurse? Here, in the states? You sound like you're from..."

"I'm from Britain, originally. I have still managed to keep the accent. It really helps with the ladies." He winks.

Laughing, I shake my head.

Yes, I'm sure it does help you with the ladies.

Whether he was making a simple jest or not, his accent mixed with the deep tones of his voice are difficult to hold out against. His voice is definitely having an effect on me.

"What brings you to this side of the pond, then?"

"My brother and I moved here about seven or eight years ago when we were teens. My father relocated to this country for work and I saw no real reason to go back afterwards. My brother found work here, in Louisiana, and I briefly moved up north just outside of Boston, Massachusetts. My parents live along the eastern border of the country, on the coast of Virginia."

"I see. So you have a brother that lives here?"

"I do. Not here in New Orleans, but yes, in Louisiana. He's maybe an hour's drive away. Maybe a bit more. We've always been close growing up, and I usually stay with him when I make trips here. He's not exactly close to this conference, however, and it was easier to stay in a hotel than it would be to rent a car and drive the distance."

The conversation slips into him speaking more of his childhood, his family, and his work as we sip our respective drinks. I seem to have this curse where people find themselves immediately comfortable around me, and spill the secrets of their lives within minutes or hours of meeting. A blessing, and a curse, I suppose; as it often helps with potential partners when trying to figure out their desires.

His eyes shift from blue to green and back again as they seek out mine, but I can't seem to keep myself focused. My eyes slip from his, over his prominent cheekbones and down to his soft lips that I had the pleasure of feeling on my hand the night before. There's something about him; something odd that makes him stand out of the crowd, and as my ears pull the sound of his voice from the air, my mind wraps lovingly around each syllable. Each sound from his mouth melts through my body, trickling down my spine to rest between my thighs.

I'm aching unexpectedly, and I don't know how to make it stop. The conversation has gone so well and it's nice having something so casual and non-sexual, but my body is rebelling against me. I absently nibble the corner of my lip as my eyes trail down his neck and take notice of how the buttons on his royal purple shirt strain against one another, begging to burst free and reveal the pale skin hiding beneath.

I shift uncomfortably and find him staring at me with his head tilted ever so slightly to the side.

"Are you feeling alright?"

"Yes, sorry. My mind wandered a bit. I'm still trying to wake up, I suppose. You were saying?"

"Oh. Yes…right. I was actually saying that I've kept you quite long enough, and I should be heading back as I must attend yet another meeting. Part of the convention, you understand. I do thank you for the company. It has been a wonderful experience, and I'm honored you agreed to join me."

"Of course, thank you for the coffee." I reply, trying to hide the disappointment in my voice. I'd love to sit here and do nothing other than listen to the delicious bass tones that resonate out of those soft, parted lips.

"Not at all, miss. Perhaps, if you're free, we can explore the city together later on."

His eyes rest on mine and I'm transfixed. The shifting colors demand my attention, and I regrettably tear my gaze away from him.

"I would love to, but I'm supposed to meet up with someone tonight to finish the interview I mentioned earlier. I'm sorry, really."

"Ah, well I'll leave you to your day, then. Some rather boring people will be awaiting my presence shortly, and I mustn't keep them waiting. Perhaps we will see each other again?"

"I would love that."

I smile sweetly, take my purse and stand. After I thank him again for the drink and offer him a handshake, I head back to the hotel alone. My phone rings the minute I step into the lobby and startles me. So rarely do I leave my ringer on, that I have forgotten what it sounds like. The call is from Alexander Delacroix.

"Miss Roman."

"Speaking."

"I've made some free time tonight. Shall we meet around 7?"

"Sure. That sounds great."

"Any preference on a venue?"

"No. I'm not too familiar with this area, so wherever you'd like to meet is fine with me."

"Wonderful. I'll text you the address."

He hangs up instantly with a snap of the line, and I peek at the screen in time to see a text pop up, stating the address he's chosen for us to meet.

He's decided not to volunteer the name of the establishment, just an address and the time he expects me. I roll my eyes and head to my room for a much needed shower, a change of clothes and to prepare myself as much as possible before tonight.

Chapter 7

The clock on the desk flashes 6:30 as I pull on my heels and make one last check in the bathroom mirror. I run my hands over my hair in an attempt to smooth down any wayward strands, and marvel at the style I've whipped up. I managed to pull off a pretty clean French twist, which is normally impossible for me. I'm still unsure of how I managed it, but I'm not about to step on the toes of the good-hair-day gods.

Being unaware of what kind of venue he has chosen, I decided on a simple, tasteful black cocktail dress and a plain silver necklace with a teardrop shaped sapphire hanging from it. I rub my hands together to calm my nerves. Everything will be fine. There's no need to be nervous.

This time, I've gone through the trouble of writing down every single question I plan to ask him. I have absolutely no intention of floundering over my words this time. I'll make sure I come off as clean, crisp and professional; the ideal representation for Angela's pride and joy, and I'll make damn sure that I get enough from him to spin a good article for her.

I take a look at the address and type it into the GPS on my phone. After seeing that it isn't too far from the hotel, I take the elevator to the lobby and catch a glimpse of the back of Ethan's head from the open door of the conference center. He's the center of attention, playing the room with the elegance and grace of a trained ballroom dancer, and I smile at the memory of our early morning coffee. He's a nice guy, and I find myself drawn to him, but I abolish such absurd thoughts from my head. He's too sweet, and I'm too fucked up to ever mesh well with someone like him.

Stepping out the door, I slip behind the wheel, letting the GPS chime in and lead me down a street to my right, off of Canal Street. As I turn down the road, my outlook of the city shifts. The roads thin into a nerve-wracking series of one-way streets overflowing with people. They're everywhere; milling around on every corner and surging out in front of cars in large groups without a care. My fingers grip the wheel as I slowly nudge my car through.

He wants to meet *here?*

The skyscrapers fall off and give way to short, thin buildings that I had seen during my trip to the café, crammed together side by side. I notice cables strung between the buildings, and a thicker one following the same path as the road I'm on. Looking down I notice a track in the middle of this asphalt hallway, and as I follow the road around a corner, a streetcar blocks my path. An honest to god street car! I didn't realize there was still such a thing, much less one that was still up and running regularly.

My fingers grip the steering wheel tighter; can I pass it? Do I wait? The tight confines of the roads, mixed with the crowds of people, leaves me anxious, and my mind racing. I feel permanently overcharged with nervous energy, both for this second chance, and because of the slight case of claustrophobia that's creeping its way up the back of my spine. My nerves feel worse now than they were for my initial meeting with him, and I can't decide if it's the area, the tight space, the suffocating streets, the quickly depleting daylight or a combination of all of the above.

A few more turns and the GPS announces 'You have arrived.' Arrived? Great, but the street is packed to the brim with surging bodies and cars parked along every edge. I glance around and notice the street sign. Bourbon Street…wonderful. The address he gave me apparently shares a common corner with this notorious street, and it only serves to further heighten my anxiety. I've heard my fair share of stories of this place; everyone has, and they're always a mix of crazy and dangerous.

Driving around eagle eyed, I search for a place to park and finally settle on the only parking garage in the area with vacancies. Unfortunately, it is several blocks away from the venue.

After grabbing the parking ticket, I head back to the address, once again searching around for him. I'm hesitant to call; I'd hate to be a bother, but it's hard to pick him from the hundreds of other people currently occupying the road. I pull out my phone and zoom in and out of the map, trying to pinpoint the exact building, but they're all melded together and I see no sign of a building number on any of them.

I walk along the block, then cross to the other side of the street, hesitant to place even a toe on the corner of Bourbon. After several moments, I come across what I believe to be the place. It's a small building tucked between two larger establishments, and adorned with thin, dark wood French doors. I finally spot his auburn curls just behind a group of five revelers, and approach cautiously.

"Good evening."

"Ah, you've made it! Wonderful." He smiles broadly as his eyes sweep over me. I feel so vulnerable here; so exposed. I'm sure it's just the area…

My mind is frantically working to fill my thoughts with every worst-case scenario possible, and I'm trying my hardest to keep my hands from trembling in nervous fear. I'm not used to being in this area, nor am I accustomed to being around such large groups of people.

"Shall we?" He asks as he opens one of the doors. I slide through and am greeted by a green tinged light that spills out onto black and white tiled floors. It vaguely reminds me of a New York subway bathroom sans the trash and stench of urine.

He steps in front of me, and I follow him toward a desk where two young women are dressed in black pants, crisp white shirts and black vests. They nod before he makes it to the desk, and motion toward another set of French doors to their right. He ushers me through.

The room is long and narrow with high ceilings and muted light spilling from ornate glass wall lamps. The bar itself occupies two thirds of the far long wall. It's a gorgeous, gleaming dark wood with a small woman standing behind it in an old-style bartender's uniform; black vest, black bowtie, white long sleeved shirt underneath, and black pants. Her sleeves are rolled up to her elbows, and there's a clean towel tucked into her belt. She's petite with shoulder length light brown hair, and greets us with a pleasant, chipper voice. A tall, husky man with an impressive mustache waves at us from the far end of the room nearest the street, then walks to meet us in the middle and begs us to take a seat.

"Can I get your usual?" he asks Alexander.

"I'm not sure tonight, Charlie. I'll let you know after we settle in."

Alexander leads me to the side of the room that faces the street, and eases me into an ornate, lion claw loveseat positioned right beneath a large window with wooden shutters that obscure the view of the street, and thankfully, the crowds.

He pulls up a chair and positions it at an angle with a small table between us. The female bartender comes up and hands us both menus then asks if she can get us anything. I stare uncomfortably at the menu; I'm not well versed in cocktails, and have no idea what any of these are. I'm much more comfortable pouring some rum in a glass of coke and calling it a night.

He speaks softly to her, placing his order, then looks over at me with a spark of amusement in his eyes.

"And what would you like?"

"I…I don't know, honestly." I stutter, embarrassed. "Do you have any suggestions?"

He glances back at the waitress and smiles.

"Why don't we get her something on the sweet side, with a bit of citrus thrown in? Thanks, Rebecca."

"Right away." She replies, and scurries off to start the drinks.

"I'm sorry about our earlier meeting, so drinks are on me. I'd show you around, but honestly, I'm in a more sedentary mood tonight."

"It's fine…" I respond, as I nervously glance at my phone to check the time. "I don't know how comfortable I would be walking around here at this hour, anyhow."

"That's silly."

Leaning over the table, he looks through me with soft brown eyes.

"I wouldn't let anything happen to you while you're in my care."

Smiling, I press my lips together to stifle any impending laughter, as the idea of this man taking down some armed assailant is preposterous. He's not exactly the body builder type, and with his lean build, I doubt he could take down a grandma coming after him with a box knife.

Rebecca brings our drinks and places them on the table along with glasses of water. With one sip, the bubbles dance along my tongue and tease my nose, but it was his eyes and silver tongue that intoxicated me long before the first taste. As he launches into a conversation about his recent perusing of an exhibit that had come to the local museum, I feel his words delicately weaving themselves around my body. German artwork, I believe, is what he's speaking about...but the low murmur of the bar patron's melds with the blood pounding in my ears, and I find it hard to concentrate on his words.

The drink tastes like a mix of champagne and sugar with a lemon wedge sitting peacefully in the center of the glass. I chastise myself for not eating before this meeting. The alcohol goes straight to my head as the heat from my blood pools into my cheeks.

What was he saying?

It was an engaging conversation that I was actively participating in, but I'm having trouble really grasping what's spilling from my lips.

What did I just say?

Words are sliding unrestrained from my mouth before I've finished fully forming the thought. I hope I don't sound like an unintelligible mess.

"Are you enjoying it?" he asks, with a small glance toward my drink.

I nod, smiling broadly. I can feel his gaze slip from my eyes to other aspects of my body; feel them piercing through me. Everything in the lounge has taken on a soft haze, and I'm drunk on the atmosphere.

"It's quite good. I've never had anything like this."

As I take another sip, he leans back in his chair, resting one ankle on the knee of his other. He lights a cigarette, takes a drag from it, and lets his arm dangle languidly over the edge of his chair. He regards me with warm eyes, never taking them off of me as an infinitesimal smile tugs at his lips.

"It's an awful habit, I know." He sighs, as he glances down at the cigarette resting precariously between his fingertips. "I haven't gotten around to kicking it yet. Does it bother you?"

"No, not at all." I reply, though in a normal setting, I can't stand the smell of cigarette smoke. It makes me cough and gag, but something about the smoke spilling from his lips seems to draw me into a trance, and I find myself craving the sight and smell of it more and more with each passing second.

"This is much more comfortable for me. I'm quite fond of this establishment, and I'm glad we were able to work this out. So, tell me more about you."

I take another sip to calm my nerves and it surges through my body, sending liquid courage into every inch of my being. Parting my lips, the words materialize before me with no regard to keeping myself aloof. I scramble to grab them, to hold them close to my chest and bury them deep, but it's no use. They're drawn to him as if he were a hypnotic flame, coaxing them closer and closer to their death.

I open myself up completely, spilling my hopes and dreams on the table for this man to scrutinize.

What has gotten in to me? I'm never this open, and certainly never this honest. What happened to my composure? Where was that professional and distanced personality that I was due to wear this night?

Regarding me intently, he leans forward, his eyes holding mine. His fingers reach across the table and rest on my arms, which have crossed in front of me in an unconscious attempt to hide myself. I have this terrible hate of my own body; a hate that's only ever shed in the dim of night while wearing a personality that isn't quite my own.

Gently stroking my forearm with his fingertips, he pulls my arms aside, exposing my body to him.

"You don't have to hide yourself from me." He says tenderly, his eyes piercing through my veil.

I blush, my words floundering on my lips.

"I'm sorry... It's a bit of a habit." I stutter. "I didn't realize I was doing it..."

"I understand. Continue. Tell me about your work."

"It's, well honestly, I'm not very good at describing things in general. I haven't prepared or rehearsed anything…"

He smiles and strokes the back of my hand with a single long, slender finger. The sensation turns my blood to ice in my veins then pours napalm on my skin. Everything is thrown into a heightened state. I can smell the faint aroma of cigars on the air mixed with the scent of wood, and feel the electric current jumping from his fingertips to my skin.

He waves for a member of the staff and orders a second drink for us, though I don't remember when I finished my first. I glance over and see the lemon wedge sitting alone in its glass; the only trace of the cocktail is on my lips and tongue.

The night slips by in a flurry of colors and scents, the flame burning ever hotter between my thighs as he coaxes a confession about my secret little blog and previous work experience, for the sake of research, I assure him.

I don't remember the second drink, nor can I place its taste or texture, or the way it coursed through my blistering veins. Every ounce of my attention is solely on him as his voice lulls me into a trance-like state, leaving me unable to break myself away. I don't want to break away. I'm his puppet; his play thing.

"My dear Miss Roman, you have yet to tell me your first name."

"It's Cassandra, or Cass, really." I stumble over my words as I reach out my hand in an awkward attempt at a hand shake.

He chuckles and takes my hand in his, stroking his thumb over the top of my hand.

"It's a pleasure, Miss Cassandra."

Hearing my name slipping sensually off his lips sends me teetering off the edge. He's charming and intelligent. Every word that has come from his mouth is a finely crafted symphony of tones and inflections, purposely created to coax me under his spell. And it's working. I barely know this man, and I've exposed my soul all too willingly.

The second drink is gone, nothing more than an empty glass on the table. I try my best to sip from the overfilled glass of water placed by the staff to try and sober myself up, even the slightest bit, and in my clumsiness, a single drop slips down the front of my dress. His breath catches, and his eyes follow the bead of water as it slides down my skin and between my breasts. He smiles, and leans in close, his hand slipping beneath the table to rest on my outer thigh.

My brain is hazed…I can barely think; the release of my wound up nerves and the alcohol has resulted in me becoming a babbling mess of truth and lowered inhibitions. His hand squeezes my outer thigh gently and the fire roaring through my body explodes into an engulfing inferno. It's only been two drinks. I really need to get ahold of myself, but I'm aching. All I want is more of his touch, his words, his smile, and his eyes holding me firmly in their grip. I need him.

With a deep, shuddering breath, I squirm in my seat at the feel of his hand as it slowly slips up my thigh, bringing with it the smoldering heat of his fingers against my leg.

Breathe. I just need to breathe.

My eyes flutter as I struggle to concentrate on something other than him. Anything, just to steady my thoughts long enough to hold on to some small part of me that isn't completely overwhelmed with a consuming lust, but my thoughts come up short and leave me abandoned in a roaring tempest of desire.

"I should really move my car. The parking attendant made it sound like I couldn't leave it there long…I should go…" I manage to stutter. I came here on business. I mustn't mix them…I can't, but can I even figure out the stick shift in my condition? Maybe there's a hotel in walking distance where I can crash for the night, or I can grab a cab. Surely there are cabs around…

"Alright…" He responds hesitantly.

Giving my thigh one final, impassioned squeeze, he slips his fingers away it reluctantly, and I stifle a groan of disappointment. Why did I have to interrupt? How far would it have gone, if I hadn't? I'd give anything to feel his hand back on my thigh…

"Let's go then." He says without any further hesitation. "I'll have a talk with them."

He pays the tab in cash and helps me out the door, his fingers lacing between mine as we step out into the dark night and stifling humidity. Is this charming gesture simply to help stabilize my unsteady steps, or is it out of affection? Either way, it's a welcomed feeling that draws an ache from my chest. When was the last time someone held my hand like this? Actually, no one has held my hand like this.

We wander up and down the various one-way roads, my mind grasping at landmarks, trying to remember which parking garage I left my car in. Aided by alcohol and the steadily increasing desire pulsating through my body, the memories of the landmarks I'd convinced myself to remember beforehand, are running into one another.

"I think it's down here." I state, uncertainly, and lead him down a road where the towering skyscrapers of the business district meet the smaller buildings of the French Quarter.

He stops in his tracks halfway down the road in front of a large shattered hole in the sidewalk, his fingers gripping mine tightly and causing me to jerk back against him. I lose my footing, and he reaches out to hold me fast. When I look up, his face is inches from mine.

The scent of alcohol and musk of smoke mixes with his words as he cautions my steps. It's an intoxicating mix that fills my nose, my mouth and smothers my body.

My mind blanks; my body a bubbling cauldron of hormones and booze ready to boil over. I hold my breath as he stares into my eyes, then in one fluid movement, press my lips against his. And in that moment, nothing else exists. The couple walking by us no longer exist. No one on the side walk, no cars and no buildings. No cracking, fractured asphalt, no stifling heat, no brilliant lights or noise wafting through the streets from Bourbon.

The world around us falls away, each sound and scent and touch melding into a single moment filled with everything and nothing at all. A blank canvas splattered with the swirling colors that dance beneath closed eyelids.

Pulling back, my heart hammers against my rib cage as my cheeks flush the color of blood.

"I'm so…I'm so sorry." I stutter as my brain wrestles my thoughts and body under control. This is supposed to be a business meeting. You don't make out with the guy you're interviewing. It's unprofessional!

So is getting drunk…

He reaches behind me and rubs my back gently, his eyes blazing. His hand moves up further and further until his fingers are touching the base of my neck. Pushing his body against mine, his muscles tense against me as he looks down into my eyes.

I move my hand away from him, drop my eyes and try to step away, embarrassed at my behavior, but his hand reaches along the last inch of the back of my neck and grips my hair firmly from underneath. Tugging my head back, my eyes are now forced into his. An animal has now taken the place of this well-spoken, well-mannered author I had met with just a short time ago.

Pushing my back against the brick wall of the building behind me, he holds my hair firm, and presses his lips passionately against mine. I relent, every muscle in my body surrendering to him. His hand tightens in my hair as his tongue hungrily seeks passage through my lips, and as he deepens the kiss, his free hand roams down my side.

Strong fingers grip my hip, then slide their way down the front of my thigh and beneath my dress, teasing along quickly dampening panties. I groan against his kiss, my knees trembling and growing weaker by the second. The need to maintain the line between the two sides of my life becomes thinner by the second, but my god, this is incredibly hot. I'm finding it hard to navigate through my murky thoughts.

I manage to break from his lips, our noses and foreheads still touching.

"We shouldn't...not here...there are so many people around." I whisper breathlessly.

What am I saying? Am I honestly considering this?

He smirks, the devil dancing in his eyes as he strokes his finger between my thighs once more.

The moonlight shimmers against his glasses as he takes my hand. His fingers slip between my own, and his thumb softly strokes the top of my hand.

"As you wish."

We manage to walk, carefully, another block before finding the parking garage. He grips my hand and leads me up to the desk.

"How much would it be to leave the car overnight?" he asks as he approaches a woman behind a desk enclosed in glass.

I can do nothing but stare at him, my jaw hanging open. Overnight?

He looks over at me and reads my expression.

"Well you're certainly in no condition to drive tonight." He muses.

"I suppose you're right."

I can barely stand up straight. Even driving the short distance down the road would be incredibly dangerous and idiotic.

"It would be $25." The woman behind the counter yawns.

He pulls out his wallet and hands her the money and I ask for the keys. I'm certainly not going back to his place without at least a change of clothes. Thankfully, I stash a bag in the trunk of my car for such emergencies.

She prints the receipt, and hands them over.

"Your car is up on the 5th floor."

"The 5th floor?!"

I'm having enough trouble walking in these heels with the alcohol coursing through my veins, as it is. I don't want to imagine how much of a challenge it would be to walk up five flights.

"It's not as bad as you may think. Trust me! The stairs are right there behind you."

She smiles, a sly spark in her eyes as she looks over us. I'm sure she has seen this dozens of times before. We shouldn't be an anomaly.

I place the keys in my purse and turn around. The stairs are dangerously narrow and steep, and my pulse is racing just thinking of all the terrible things that could happen.

Squeezing my hand in reassurance, he leads me to the first step.

"After you, Miss Roman. I'll walk behind you in case you lose your footing."

"How comforting…" I mumble dryly.

My hands rest on the railings and my heart picks up its pace as a wave of claustrophobia crashes against my body. The railings are far too close to my hips for comfort, and I feel as if they'll take on a life of their own and strangle me between them. How does anyone manage to squeeze up these stairs?

After braving the first eight steps, we've reached the 2nd floor and after another four, we're at the 3rd.

"I guess this isn't so bad."

"Not at all. Besides, I have a great view of your ass."

I can hear the smile in his voice as he speaks, and feel his hands reach up to grab my ass, then smack it playfully. Stifling a moan, I grip the rails of the stairs just a bit tighter to keep myself steady. Someone could be watching us, and I love the thought of it.

We quickly reach the 5th floor, and my car is conveniently parked right in front of us. Popping the trunk, I reach in and grab the bag which he offers to carry for me, then we make the precarious trip down the stairs of death.

Going down is significantly worse than coming up. I can't push the thought of tumbling headfirst, all the way down, out of my head.

The trip to his place is a long one, and halfway through what feels like a 10 mile hike, my feet go feel numb. Damn these heels. Had I known I would be walking this much, I would've shoved a pair of sneakers in my bag.

He pulls me into an 'Irish Pub' on the corner, only in name, of course. It's a pretty dingy place, with a few pool tables and some girls huddled in a corner watching two guys play. He pulls out a chair for me, and goes to the bar to get a drink.

"I vaguely remember you mentioning being partial to rum and coke" He smiles as he approaches the table, and places a drink in front of me. I don't ever remember mentioning I'm a fan of it, but I'm nervous, sore, tired, and my hormones are raging. The smoldering fire I try so hard to keep at bay on a daily basis has become a blazing, overpowering volcano on the edge of blowing. I want him.

He reaches over and plucks my purse from my lap, where I was clutching it protectively, and lays it on the chair next to me. I didn't realize I was holding it.

"Remember, you don't have to hide from me. I realize it's a bit of a security blanket, but you don't have to worry when you're with me. Relax and enjoy yourself."

He's mesmerizing. He's left me exposed with nothing to hold on to and I feel like a flailing fledgling thrust from the warm nest of safety with the ground rushing up to meet me. But that fear is quickly replaced, and all I see are his eyes, his lips, his naked body on top of me, pinning me down to the pool table with everyone watching.

His hand grips my thigh and it clears my thoughts, leaving me unsatisfied and aching.

"Finish your drink. We're not far, now." He smiles as his fingers dance over my exposed skin, leaving lightning in their wake.

Smiling sheepishly, I drown myself in the rest of my drink. How unladylike.

We continue the trek to his home, passing several couples and a horse drawn carriage with the driver spouting, what clearly sounds like bullshit, about the various structures in an attempt to impress the tourists in his backseat. I draw my eyes upward, happy and content walking hand and hand with him as we discuss the various architectural features found on the homes of the French Quarter. They're so intricate and beautiful, each iron wrapped balcony joined with the first floor by elegantly curled scroll brackets. Each one unique and beautiful.

We pass by a store front with neon lights flashing in its window, advertising its chapel services right next to a window with voodoo charms, and his hand is in my hair again. His mouth finds mine, his tongue slithering across my lips seeking entrance, then running, twisting together with my tongue in a forbidden, exotic dance.

"You're incredibly sexy" he whispers against my lips, each word searing my skin, oozing against my ears with a carnal need. "I want you."

My body tenses as I press against him, my fingers finding the small of his back and gripping tightly, feeling the lean, tensed muscles beneath his shirt. I want to rip his clothes off right here and now, and beg him to have his way with me.

"We really should get indoors…" I whisper breathlessly, trying in vain to keep my voice from shaking, and to control the runaway desires battering against my body.

"Not so comfortable out here?" he teases. "I'm sure no one would bat an eye at us."

"No! I'm not comfortable…" I frantically check the windows of the surrounding buildings and scan the faces of the people on the street. Several couples are eying us, whether it's out of curiosity or some twisted amusement, I have no idea.

Taking my hand, we round the next corner. The humidity of the night has left a sheen of sweat on every inch of my body, and I'm oddly aware of how disgusting I feel in clothes that must be soaked through by now. I really could use a shower.

"We're almost there."

He leads me to a set of large deep red arched doors, twists the lock, and pulls me through a white stone corridor into an outdoor courtyard. It's completely sheltered by the surrounding buildings on all sides, but open to the clear, star-littered night sky. It's a world cut off from the French Quarter surrounding us; like a secret oasis meant only for us.

Squeezing my hand affectionately, he leads me around a large, stone fountain in the center of the courtyard. The three tiered basins play home to thin silver threads, which dance, twist, and play in the bright moonlight.

I'm led to a pair of large white washed French doors set against an impressively thin three story home. The second and third floors cradle balconies wrapped in the same wrought iron reminiscent of the French Quarter homes we'd passed just moments before. I had no idea a house lay just beyond those wooden doors when looking from the street, and certainly did not expect something as impressive as this.

"After you" he smiles, stealing a kiss to my hand as I slip through the doors.

I step inside his home and am completely overwhelmed by books; they're absolutely everywhere. I feel as if I've stepped into heaven itself, led by my own personal angel.

The dark wood floors stretch out from the foyer, bleeding into the kitchen on my left, and an office on my right. A ladder props itself against a wall littered with bookshelves in the office, and leads to a small loft tucked against the high ceilings. It's shrouded in shadows, but I can see the hint of additional bookshelves just on the edge of the loft space.

He leads me toward the back of the house,

past a winding staircase leading to the second floor, and through hallways with walls purposely scraped down to expose the blood red brick beneath. The house is much larger inside than I had thought while standing in the courtyard.

A couch rests directly in front of me facing a fireplace, which is pushed into the far wall, and an arm chair situated to the left of the couch. There are books on makeshift shelves against the wall, piled on top of furniture, stacked on the floor in front of the cold fireplace, and carefully arranged upon the its mantle. There are several stacks on the coffee table, so much in fact, that I doubt it's possible to use the table for anything else.

He pulls the armchair until it is sits parallel to the couch then turns to me, wrapping his arms around my waist and gazing deep into my eyes.

"Can you trust me?"

Trust him? I barely know him! I met him yesterday, but the memories of those sweet hand holdings, and light touches to my hands wraps me in its warm blanket.

"I…yes. You're not going to kill me, are you?"

He laughs, running his fingers lightly

through my curls, then kisses my lips gently.

"No, I'm not going to kill you, or hurt you in any way unless you ask for it. Have a seat, and don't move." He commands, motioning his hand to the armchair.

"I...you know, I'm feeling sweaty and gross. I could use a shower..."

He grins, his eyes sparkling with amusement. Grasping either side of the chair, he presses me into it, his lips an inch from mine.

"A shower? I rather enjoy you just as you are, Miss Roman."

I sit, obediently, and try my best not to squirm under his gaze. My mind swims, trying to grasp at passing thoughts that flit around my head like hummingbirds. His nose brushes against my neck, his lips leaning in for a quick bite that stirs my body into a swirling, throbbing mess of excitement. God, I want him.

"You have so many books." I blurt, instantly regretting the statement. It's so random; I must sound like an absolute fool, but the words are past my lips before I can restrain them. He pulls back, laughing with such genuine joy that it's infectious, and I giggle, rolling my eyes at my own comment.

"You should see the loft, then. In the meantime, as I'm sure you wouldn't make it up a ladder in your condition, I'm going to mix us another drink."

He disappears into the kitchen, the sound of tinkling glasses and closing cabinet doors wafting over the gap between us.

I look around, giddy at the sight. A complete collection of Sherlock Holmes rests on top of the mantle. The stacks on the floor are made up of books I've never heard of, but would love to read either way. And yet, amidst my wonder, my body can't seem to sit still in the chair. I'm shifting against it, grinding myself against the fabric. He's wound me up so much that every muscle is twitching in anticipation.

He walks back into the living room several minutes later with a drink in each hand, and hands one to me. Settling himself into the couch directly across from me, he rests his drink on the floor, and pulls my chair closer to him, then leans back, casually placing his ankle on his knee, and sips from the glass.

"Now," he grins, a hungry glint in his eyes, "let's discuss the rules."

I'm aching under his gaze, my mind

screaming and hammering against the confines of my skull, begging.

Take me, please, just take me.

Leaning forward, and careful to stay seated as per his request, I grin wickedly, unable to keep my voice from dripping with desire.

"I only have one rule. No marks...for now."

A seductive smile dances across his lips, and I can no longer stand the screaming of my own body. Placing my hands on his knees, I lean forward and press my lips hungrily against his.

He returns my kiss, gently at first, then harder and more impassioned until he's scraping and biting his teeth against my bottom lip. I crawl onto the couch, straddling his lap as I wrap my arms around the back of his neck, my lips never leaving his. I'm hungry for the taste of his tongue.

He moans against my lips then draws back, careful to stay mere centimeters from my mouth. I feel his hot breath, labored against my skin, as if he's struggling against himself to pull away.

With a deep, shuddering breath, he places his hands on my shoulders, pushing me down his body.

"Oh Miss Roman; you're not the demure woman you present to the world after all, are you. What a bad girl, and you've gotten out of the chair." He purrs. "We will have to punish you for that soon, but for now, on your knees."

I fall before him, fueled by two parts desire and one part alcohol, and there's no doubt in my mind that I'd obey him whether the alcohol was involved or not. Perhaps just not in this way.

The two lives are mixing, and under normal circumstances, I would be scorning his advances with my nose held high. But this isn't exactly a normal circumstance, it seems. And oh, I want him so badly that my mind is happily driving me toward the edge of madness.

He takes my hands in his, and then places them on either side of his growing erection, guiding me to rub back and forth on either side on the outside of his jeans. I can feel the desire growing in him, stiffening beneath my palms, and it adds to the wetness between my own thighs.

"You're so much more sexual than I imagined." he moans. "Stand up for me."

I stand, a bit shakily at first, but I manage to hold my balance even in these heels.

"Take off your dress, fold it, and place it on the table."

I hesitate, shifting back and forth on my feet. I've never taken off my clothes for anyone while the lights were still on. It's usually a pretty strict rule of mine with my partners, and brought on by my own self-conscious tendencies. However, it seems I'm not really the one in control this time.

The shutters that guard the large windows against the outside world, are open into the backyard, exposing me to the night air and any curious eyes.

Slipping off my dress slowly, I fold it in front of him, turn and place it on the table among the towers of books as per his command. And I stand there, exposed and vulnerable, in a black laced bra, matching panties, a sheer pair of nylon stockings and my heels, as he appraises my body.

He smiles slowly, deliberately, and stands, beckoning me to come closer. He takes my hand and guides me to the chair, then has me kneel on it with my breasts dangling over the back. Reaching down and pulling my breasts from the confines of my bra, he lets them hang free, then lightly tugs and teases my sensitive nipples.

"You must be spanked for disobeying me

earlier. Are you ready?"

Spanked? Oh yes. This is better than I could've ever hoped for. I've never been spanked, though I've done it to others, and spent countless times fantasizing about how it would feel.

Nodding, I bite my lip, so hard in fact, that I'm dangerously close to tasting my own blood on my tongue.

I want this, I need this.

"I want you to count every one of them. Do you understand?"

"Yes…" I whisper, meekly

"Yes what?" he demands.

He leans over my body, his chest pressing against my back. He tangles his fingers in my hair, tugging back roughly. Another pulse through my body leaves me wet and aching as I revel in the feeling.

"Yes I understand." I groan.

He tugs harder, making me whimper in pain, but the pain quickly turns to an overwhelming pleasure that spikes my blood with dragon's breath.

"That's not the response I was hoping for.

You don't look like such an innocent girl, Miss Roman, kneeling here near nude. I'm sure you know what I want to hear."

"...yes, Sir, I understand." I whisper, the wetness between my thighs nearing a full blown flood. I had no idea he could be so dominant.

"And you will not come without my permission."

"Yes, Sir."

"Mmm, good girl." He moans.

Slipping his hand between my thighs, he lightly rubs the outside of my panties, and coaxes my thighs as far as they will go. As he moves his hand lightly over my ass, he taps his fingers against my skin three times, then smacks.

My head leans forward as I moan at the feel of my skin, warm and tingling, beneath his palm.

"One..."

Smack

"Two..."

Smack

"Three."

The wetness from my body seeps through my panties, soaking them…running down the inside of my thighs. Each smack brings more and more force, and it feels heavenly. I can't think; my mind is fogged, and I feel nothing other than the sting of his hand against my skin, and the overwhelming desire it's bringing me.

I have never felt more alive than I do at this moment.

He continues smacking his hand against each cheek, then rubbing the spot lovingly afterward, working the sting into my skin. Even with the warning, each hit is a shock to my body, drawing out more of the primal desire I normally keep behind careful lock and key.

Four…Five…Six…

He manages to hit the same exact spot on each cheek with every slap. My skin is burning beneath his hand, but I don't want it to stop.

More. I need more.

Seven…Eight…Nine…

He hesitates…and the tenth doesn't come. Instead, he pulls my panties aside slides his fingers against slickened skin, seeking and finding my sensitive clit. He pinches it lightly then rubs it between his fingers, drawing louder and louder moans from my body as my hips writhe and rotate at his touch. I want him. I need him.

He rubs faster and harder, bringing me right to the brink of orgasm. Every muscle in my body tenses; my eyes flutter as my breath comes in short, quick gasps. I'm so close…

"Not without my permission." he commands. I hear the smile in his voice; he knows he has me.

He thrusts a finger inside of me, turning my moans into screams that have no doubt penetrated the windows of his neighbors. My fingers grip the back of the chair as I struggle to control my body.

Not yet. I'm not allowed to.

"Do you wish to come?"

"Yes, please."

"I'm sorry, I didn't quite get that. What did you say?"

"Yes please, Sir. Please. I need to come."

"You *need* to? You only need to do what I command."

"Yes, Sir." I manage to say between moans.

My voice is shaking…my whole body is.

"Beg."

"Please Sir, please. Please let me come. I'll do anything, just please. Please let me come."

He leans over me, his fingers continuing their assault on my overly sensitive, soaking body.

"You'll do anything? Quite a high price to pay." He whispers against my ear, as his lips brush lightly over my neck. "Come for me, my dirty girl."

The heat of his breath curls around my ear, setting my nerves ablaze.

My whole body shudders; trembling, writhing, and twisting beneath him as I scream until my throat is raw and sore. I clench around his fingers, soaking them completely as I orgasm once…twice…and still, he doesn't stop until I slump over the back of the chair, weakened by his onslaught.

He slips my saturated panties off of my body, tells me to open my mouth, and slides them between my lips as a make-shift gag.

"I do love your screams, my dear, but I also like the thought of you tasting yourself. Now, if you'd like, you may clean yourself up, but keep those in your mouth as you do."

He smiles, kisses my forehead, pets my hair gently, and walks out the back door with a cigarette in hand. Stumbling my way to the bathroom just off the kitchen, my hands grip the walls as my trembling legs struggle to keep me upright. I wipe down the sweat and fluids from my body with a washcloth; feeling the faint breeze from an open window play across my damp skin. When I walk from the bathroom, he's still outside, so I crawl onto the couch and wrap a throw blanket around me to fend off the chilling currents blasting from the air vents.

He finally comes in, the scent of smoke wafting off his body. Why do I find it so incredibly exhilarating?

Smiling, he walks up to me and holds out his hand. As I slip my fingers into his palm, he pulls me up and leads me down the hall and up the spiraling staircase. Further and further we go, my blurring vision causing the walls to shift and spin around me, but he holds me firm as we climb to the top floor. The entire third floor is a massive bedroom, with a large bed situated in the middle. On the right is a large, wooden dresser pressed against a wall. Behind the dresser are tall, arched windows that look down onto a backyard garden, complete with its own three tiered stone fountain. To the left is a large black desk with papers scattered across its surface, and a desk lamp hidden behind a few more books. The desk is also pressed against windows, but these look down on the front courtyard, and over the wall that shields his house from the world. They offer a fantastic view of the surrounding French Quarter, glittering in the night like diamonds scattered on the ocean.

He guides me toward the bed in the middle of the room, slips off his clothes, and crawls between the sheets, drawing my naked body in beside him. The bed is warm against the increasingly chill room, and incredibly soft, like crawling in to take a nap in down feathers after running yourself ragged all day long. I sink into the mattress, and pull the covers over my exposed body.

I really do hate seeing myself naked.

Cuddling close, I feel the soft flesh of his body against mine as his fingertips lightly brush over my cheek.

"Shh," he whispers as his eyes peer through mine "stop hiding yourself from me…"

Gathering me in his arms, he cradles my head against his chest and wraps his arms around my shoulders. His head tilts down, heated lips pressing lightly against my forehead. Long, delicate fingers move a stray curl out of my face, then press beneath my chin, tilting my head up toward his as he removes the makeshift gag from my mouth. Placing his lips lovingly on mine, those same fingers trail lightly down my neck, and stroke down my side, playing their way along my hip.

Turning me onto my back; his hands stroking the inside of my thigh, drawing delicate circles along my skin. His soft, gentle lips move down the center of my chest as he slides a finger inside of me once again, deeper…deeper. I gasp, my body shuddering as my eyes roll back. He adds another, roughly assaulting my already sensitive and aching body.

What started as something so loving has slipped into something primal and forbidden as he draws moans and screams of pleasure, unrestrained, from my lips. I gaze down at him, my fingers gripping his curls as my back arches. One final, air splitting scream rips from my lips and he smiles, relishing in his conquest.

As he feels the energy slip from my body, riding on the waves of each orgasm he pulled from me, he rolls onto his back, propping himself against the headboard of the bed, and pulls me on top of him.

"Do you trust me…" he whispers against my lips, lightly tracing them with his tongue.

"Yes..."

"And you will tell me if you ever want me to stop…"

"Please don't stop."

Leaning off the side of the bed, he rummages through a side table, and draws something metallic sounding from the depths of a drawer. His lips seek mine once again, wrapping me in his spell. The smell of him, the feel of him; I'm hopelessly addicted.

Shifting my body on him, my legs straddle his thighs and he reaches behind me, gathering my wrists together. The cold snap of handcuffs bind my wrists to one another, and I look down at him, surprised.

"I really hope you have the keys to these…"

"Oh don't worry, my dear." he laughs, "There's a quick release switch."

He eases me down his body, which is a bit awkward without the use of my hands, and I struggle to keep myself from toppling over to my side.

Handcuffs; another thing I've fantasized about but never had the pleasure of experiencing. They're a bit more awkward than I had imagined.

His long, firm erection presses against my belly, then slips between my breasts as he pushes me further down his body. His hips are grinding up against me, and I want nothing more than to feel my lips wrap around him.

"Would you like to taste me?" His tone is a heady mix of lust and need, wrapped in fire and passion.

"Yes, please, Sir."

I have to admit, I had feared the worst, but it was more than I had imagined. I'm starving for him, craving the touch of his cock pressed against my tongue.

His hands grip my hair as he guides my lips to the tip. Parting my lips and hungry for a taste, he presses against my eager mouth and eases the length of it over my tongue. Pushing down slowly on the back of my head, he drives it deeper until the tip begins to brush the back of my throat. I open my eyes, cautiously, and notice there's still several inches of it left, as I fight to suppress my reflex to gag. There's no way I can fit it all, but damn, if I won't try. I want to please him, and the only thought in my mind is of his complete and total bliss at my hands, or rather, my lips.

I suck on the length of it with renewed vigor as he guides my head for me, gyrating his hips against my mouth and sliding it in deeper, half an inch at a time. It's hard to breathe, and my head is swimming, but my body is burning with an unquenchable thirst. Faster and faster he guides my lips, driving it deeper each time. His moans growing louder, and my body is electrified, tingling from my lips to my toes. Hearing his moans and feeling him pressing down my throat feeds the flames, and my body threatens to bring me to orgasm just from the thought of it all.

The muscles in his thighs tense beneath my body, and he holds my head down one last time as he empties himself down my throat. He breathes a sigh of relief, his face a mask of euphoria, as his head leans back against the headboard, and every muscle in his body grows slack.

He reaches behind me and removes the cuffs from my wrists, drawing me up and placing another kiss upon my lips.

"You've done so well. You are incredible." He whispers, nuzzling his nose against my own.

"I'm not as coordinated as I would be

otherwise..." I murmured apologetically. "I still want to feel you. I want to feel you inside of me."

"My lovely girl, you will soon enough." He coos, as he runs his fingers over my tousled hair. "For now, we both need our rest. It's been a long night, and I need to be up early."

He rolls me onto my side, and curls up close behind me, bare skin against bare skin. His arms wrap around me as he presses his chest against my back, his legs tangling themselves in mine.

I turn my head back towards his and stare into his eyes...

"Do you snore?" I ask, deadpan.

He laughs unabashed, and in the dim light, it's hard to tell his emotions.

"Only slightly." He responds, a smile curling its way into his words. "Now, sleep, my dear."

Chapter 8

I toss and turn in his arms, awakening at an ungodly hour from a fitful sleep. I barely notice the light, occasional snore coming from him. It's so small, it's almost adorable. Well, as adorable as a snore can be, I suppose.

The room has gotten so cold that, even under the plush comforter, I'm shivering uncontrollably. His arms wrap around me tightly, his hand softly running up and down my arm in an unconscious attempt to soothe me, but my body simply will not warm up.

Slipping out from between his arms, and being careful not to wake him, I rummaging through my bag, pulling on socks, a pair of pants, and a tank top. Sadly, it does very little to warm me, and I'm still shivering. As I pad lightly and soundlessly down the winding stairs, pausing briefly on the second floor to glance over the numerous closed doors, I slip into the living room. It looks so different at night, every object casting long, twisting shadows across the midnight floor.

I curl up on the couch with my phone, and pull a throw blanket around my shoulders, gazing out across the room as my eyes adjust to the darkness. It's peaceful and quiet. The chair where I sat earlier is still parallel to where he had been, but has now dried from our previous fun. It seems like a dream, like it didn't really happen, as my shadow dances with his, reenacting the scene. It's like something out of some romantic porn; girl meets guy at a bar, guy makes out with her against a wall while tugging her hair, girl goes mad with lust and they screw all night. Things like this don't just happen, do they?

I want to remember every painful, pleasurable, stirring detail, but I can only seem to recall a tangled mass of limbs and fluids, mixed with screams of passion and moans of pleasure. I remember his lips, the scent of him, and the warmth of his body, but all else is a muddled mess.

My eyes flutter, remembering the scent, oh…the scent of him. It's on my clothes, on my skin. I can smell it everywhere. It draws my thoughts to his kiss, his eyes…his touch. That wonderful, delicious, overly sensitive area between my thighs is still aching from him. The small twinge of pain is a gentle reminder that yes, it did happen, and I want it to happen again and again.

Several minutes, and a glass of water later, I crawl back into bed beside his slumbering, sweltering body. He immediately rolls towards me, his arms and legs wrapping my chilled limbs close against his body once more. Smiling, I gently run my fingertips over his arm, and drift to sleep.

Chapter 9

The sun has already begun its morning climb in the sky, its golden whispers streaming in through the windows and painting its light across the floor. Alexander is already sitting up in bed, propped comfortably against the headboard.

I groan with the gift of a hangover, and attempt to tie my hair up, as it has taken a life reminiscent of a bird's nest.

The bed and blankets are so comfortable that I find myself hesitant to slide out of them. I wish, fleetingly, that I could lie here forever and watch him work, then push the thought from my head. It's ridiculous. I barely know him. Am I going to gush over a near stranger because of one good night of...can that even be considered sex? My body seems to think so, but my mind is grasping for a reason to disagree.

He glances over at me, the gentle smile slipping over his mouth. For the fraction of a second, the hunger from the night before flits quickly through his eyes then vanishes as if it had never existed, and I wonder whether I had imagined seeing it in the first place.

"I need to get some work done this morning." He says with a blank expression as his eyes move back to his phone; his thumb casually scrolling across the screen. His voice no longer holds any of the sentiment of the night before, and it leaves me stunned.

"Oh, okay. Of course. Is it okay if I use your shower, first?"

He nods, his eyes never leaving the screen.

"You can use one of the towels hanging in there."

Slipping from the bed, and thankful for dressing in the middle of the night, I grab my bag and wordlessly slip into the bathroom.

The water takes ages to warm up, but once it does, it feels heavenly against my chilled skin. Even with the heat and humidity outside, his house has become an icebox overnight, which he credited to a broken air conditioning unit.

There's a large window that sits from my shoulder to the ceiling in the shower stall, and I can't help but feel self-conscious. How easy would it be for someone to peek in on me, and there's no curtain to shade me from view!

That's ridiculous. I'm on the third floor; who's going to be looking all the way up here?

With my normal shampoo and conditioner keeping my hotel room company, I'm forced to detangle my hair with my fingers and water alone, which quickly becomes a nightmare. I browse over his shower products and squirt a small bit of basil-scented body wash into my palms. It sounds ridiculous, and I fear that I'll come out of the shower smelling like I rolled around in spaghetti sauce, but I lather it between my hands anyhow and run it over my skin. I'd use anything just to feel clean again.

Soon, the smell fills the bathroom, carried on the swirls of steam undulating all around me, and it's divine. The scent brings memories of the smell I caught on his skin last night, mixed with the hint of smoke from his cigarette, and now I'm scrubbing every pore of my body with it.

I lean my head back against the shower stall

as the water gently washes away my sins, and mentally chastise myself. I don't mix work with this side of me. Never. It's an unspoken promise that I made to myself, and a promise that I need to keep in order to maintain some level of sanity.

That side of me doesn't exist. It's smothered and choked off every morning when I wake and don the face of the innocent girl. I'm professional, untouchable, and yet he broke it. He shattered my illusion; fractured the face I presented to him and every member of the waking world, and now, this monster; she bleeds through. The sinful, lustful beast, which foams at the mouth every moment she comes across even the prospect of an intimate encounter, endangering everything I've built.

She's an abomination meant for nothing but destruction, and yet I'm still aching; still sore, and I can't help but let my hands linger for just a moment longer on my sensitive breasts. From there, they cascade down my stomach and between my thighs on their own accord, threatening to bring her back to the surface.

No. She doesn't exist. The sun is up, and it's time to slip away from that monster; that…embarrassment.

My fingers dip down to grace my sensitive clit.

Stop. It's over. It's done.

But I can't. The nails of my free hand dig into the soft, smooth flesh of my thigh, and I can't stop. I'm sore, but it feels so good to slide my fingertips against my aching clit.

My breath grows ragged as the tips of my fingers tenderly massage it, rubbing in lazy circles. My eyes flutter as my fingers work; faster and faster and yet, still just barely touching.

I tense and shudder, the mix of pleasure and pain bringing my body to its peak faster than I'd expected.

So close…so close.

My lips part as my breathing hastens, my back arching against the cold tile wall as I cling to the edge of absolute ecstasy. The air catches in my chest, refusing to rush past my lips as I rub faster, pushing myself off the edge of an orgasm.

My legs tremble, threatening to throw me to my knees in his shower, as I feel the rush of my orgasm seep from between my fingers.

Oh god, what have I done.

A light knock at the bathroom door disrupts my thoughts, bringing my surroundings rushing into the foreground.

"Cassandra? Are you alright?"

"Yes! Yes. I'm fine, thank you. I'll be out in just a moment." I stutter, praying that my faltered words weren't too obvious.

I finish rinsing my body, dress, and try to make myself presentable. Walking out into the bedroom, I'm greeted by an empty, perfectly made bed. Gathering my things, I make my way down the staircase, and as I walk towards the living room, I find him settled on the couch in the very same place he sat the night before. His laptop, nestled in his lap as he furiously types away.

"Almost ready?" he asks, never glancing up from his work.

"Yeah…I'm ready whenever you are."

"I'll get you to your car, then."

He rests his laptop on the floor and leads the way out, pausing briefly outside of the door to offer a hand with my bag, then follow him out into the street as he rounds the corner onto Bourbon.

The French Quarter has lost its luster, beauty and excitement once day broke. The sun is harsh and unforgiving, and the close proximity of the buildings stops even the smallest breeze from penetrating. It's stifling, and I feel as if I am swimming my way through the streets in a near boiling pot of water. Now I know how the crawfish must feel.

I quicken my pace in an attempt to keep up with his long legs, which gracefully and effortlessly weave in and out of the near abandoned road. The stench of this place has become damn near overwhelming; a mixed scent of urine, vomit and dog shit baking in the unrelenting sun.

"You know, they do a pretty decent job of cleaning this place up in the morning."

He must be joking, though I can discern no hint of jest in his voice. I dance along the fractured asphalt, trying my best to avoid the puddles littering the roads and sidewalks. It didn't rain the night before, and with that in mind, I'm wary about getting whatever is in those puddles on my shoes.

The conversation between us is nothing more than fragmented comments about the area as we rush past, and a very short, agitated comment to a man who was trying to beg for money, but balked when Alexander cast a sidelong glance at him.

Everything looks desolate and abandoned without the pounding music and flashing lights as we near the shared corner of Bourbon and, what I assume is the street with the parking garage. There aren't throngs of throbbing human bodies surging into every crevice; there is no loud music or bright lights. Most every store and bar is closed, save for one we pass that's filled to bursting capacity. How could anyone stomach alcohol at this hour?

We make it to the corner and he hands me my bag, guiding me in the direction of the garage. We exchange a quick good-bye and part ways. No hug, no kiss, no flirtatious knowing glances.

"Sorry," he offers "but I really do need to run back and get to work."

"It's fine. I understand. Thanks for walking me this far. I probably wouldn't have found it alone."

He catches my eye for a second, and I entertain the thought that there's a hint of a smile hidden in there somewhere, before he turns from me and walks back towards his house.

I walk up the road to my car and don't look back, but try as I might, I can't stifle the smile that creeps onto my face from the memories of last night. Did that really happen?

The parking attendant takes my ticket, and

saunters off to retrieve my car. The world around me feels blurred...unreal...as if I'm pushing through a lucid dream, with all the sounds and images fading into each other.

There's a tap on my shoulder, and a tall, elderly black gentleman in a pair of blue-gray coveralls, hands me my keys.

"Thank ya, darlin'. Have a safe trip, now!" he says happily, and flashes me a brilliant white smile. Palming my keys, I slip him a sweet smile accompanied by a "Thank you" and a small tip. I'm not one to be rude, after all.

I'm instantly grateful that the attendant has already turned on the air conditioner, as I slide into the car, and pull my phone from my pocket. I scroll through the missed text messages and missed calls. Three out of the five missed calls are from my roommate, Riley, and the other two are from Angela. Angela can wait. I'll bring her what she wants, and I really don't feel like hearing her shrill voice at this hour.

Slipping the Bluetooth into my ear, I ease the car out into the street and make my way back to the hotel room, thankful that the streets are far less crowded during morning hours.

Once I'm cleared of the asphalt paved

hallways, I dial up Riley. If she doesn't hear from me soon, she'll give herself a stroke.

"Cass?" she answers

"Hey, Riles."

"Hey? HEY!? I haven't heard a peep from you for three days, Cass. Three fucking days! Do you have ANY idea what I was thinking?"

Her tone is deafening, and my face involuntarily scrunches as my ears try to accommodate her volume.

"I could only guess. Riley, I told you I had some work to do down here and would probably be busy…"

"But it's dangerous, and you never called me when you got there! You've never been there before. What if you got lost, mugged, raped or murdered!"

"Awe, you're so sweet. You really do care!"

"Hmph, care? I don't think so. I just don't want the hassle of trying to find another roommate. You know, a roommate who will bring home wine to apologize for making me worry so much all weekend. I hear those are *really* hard to find."

"Is that a hint?"

"Of course it is, idiot. You're still coming home today, right?"

"Yeah. I'll check out and head home in a bit. Two, maybe three hours tops if there's traffic. I need to drop by the office, first."

"Alright. Good. I'll cook something and you, of course, will bring the wine."

"Yes, ma'am."

She hangs up, and I'm once again assaulted by my thoughts.

Was I just a one night stand? Me? No…that's impossible.

I park and make my way to my hotel room. Hanging from my door, is a carefully folded note with my name elegantly scrolled across its face. I grab the note and slip in the door.

"*Cass,*

If you're still here to receive this, I'd love to see you again. I enjoyed our little coffee meeting yesterday morning, and tried to catch you tonight but I guess you were out. Please consider joining me for dinner later, if you're still around.

Sincerely,

Ethan"

Sighing, I roll my eyes toward the ceiling. Of course he'd ask me to meet tonight. I guess I wasn't entirely clear with him on when I planned to head home, or maybe he was hoping I wouldn't leave this early.

I stare at the desk in my room, and the hotel stationary carefully placed upon it. I'll just write a quick note; it'd be rude to leave him without a response, and I don't like the thought of hurting him.

Hastily packing the few things left in my room, I start toward the door with my hastily scribbled note. It explains that I'm heading home today, and enjoyed meeting him. I wish him the best for his further trips, then sign my name without leaving any sort of contact information. It's for the best.

I leave the letter with a man standing behind the front desk, then head to my car, and as I settle into the driver's seat, I'm pleasantly reminded of last night's activities by the soreness present between my thighs. Smirking, I grind myself against the seat, and relish in the ache. I pull out my phone, checking it before I begin the drive, and find a text from Alexander Delacroix.

I have some homework for you, if you're interested.

Homework? I wasn't aware you had become my teacher.

I'm well qualified to become that for you, if you wish. Considering your appetite, I'm assuming you have some toys stashed at home. If you're interested in my little homework assignment, then I want a full list and accompanying pictures of them. Gather it together, and I'll tell you when I wish for you to send them.

Swallowing hard, I stare in disbelief at the text. A list of my toys? I don't think Riley has even seen them; and we have practically gone through every inch of one another's belongings at some time or another. My body aches at the thought, and a persistent throbbing settles between my legs, as I start the car and head home.

Chapter 10

I drive the hour and a half back, and stop in to the office to finish up an unrelated assignment I promised I'd have done last Friday. Hopefully, Angela won't rip me apart in the morning. I'm really bad at deadlines. It's a miracle she hasn't kicked my ass out the door yet.

By the time I make it home, the sun is just beginning to set. The various shades of purple and orange splatter against the sky like water colors on a child's canvas.

I pull into the driveway and the door flies open, revealing Riley in the doorway. Her hands grip her hips firmly, as if that gesture would somehow curb her desire to beat me to a bleeding pulp. The look on her face is vehement; her eyes burning so fiercely that they evaporate the normally cool, calm ocean from their depths and turn it into a churning grey maelstrom of death.

I avert my eyes; she's pissed. I can feel the air between us trembling with her rage.

I gather my things from the car, being sure to grab the bottle of wine I picked up. As I move closer, I grip the bottle by the neck and hold it out before me, cowering behind it as if it would somehow provide a shield against her inevitable assault.

"Peace offering?" I whisper meekly.

"Hmph."

She snatches the bottle from my hand and meticulously inspects the label. Her eyes light up.

"Ohh…."

"So am I forgiven?"

"Hardly." She laughs. "I'm not that easy."

She flashes a smile and turns on her heel. Flipping her long, ginger locks across her shoulder, she marches into our house.

Our shared house is nothing spectacular. It's a two-story, three bedroom home that we rent from an elderly couple who moved to Florida last year. The house sticks out like a sore thumb in a neighborhood filled with squat, one-story ranch homes. It's blanketed in brick, with round, white columns that stretch from the ground to the roof.

Once I walk across the threshold, my nose is filled with the savory smell of Riley's lasagna. Now, it should be noted that this isn't some frozen tray of premade crap that she threw in the oven for a few hours. No, this was a labor of pure love and dedication for the art of cooking. It was a carefully crafted masterpiece that would bring tears of joy to Bottura himself.

Everything was made by her hand, from the sauce to the noodles. All of the vegetables were lovingly plucked from the greenhouse she tends in our backyard.

She has become my domestic goddess, and I'm eternally grateful for it. My version of dinner is normally a grilled cheese, or a granola bar and a cup of coffee while I pour over my work.

I follow Riley through the hall, then climb the stairs to my room to empty my bag and clean up.

"I have company joining us!" she yells up the stairs.

"Oh? Who?"

"Tom, of course, and Ryan."

"Ryan?" I groan. Why couldn't it be just Tom?

"Yeah, sorry hun. It couldn't be helped."

Tom is Riley's boyfriend, and Ryan is his slightly less attractive friend from work. Ryan is Tom's opposite in every way. Tom is, well, in a word, gorgeous. He's tall, somewhere around six foot two or three, which dwarfs poor Riley who comes in at just under 5'3", and has deep ginger waves, which roll gently over the top of his head coupled with pale blue eyes. He's eloquent and refined, with a boyish charm, impeccable sense of humor, and a silver tongue that could talk the pants off of the most stoic individual. If that wasn't enough, the way he moves his hips when he dances, would put any Hispanic man to shame. It truly was a sight to behold.

Oh…those hips make even me swoon in desire, though I guess that isn't really saying much.

Ryan on the other hand, is completely overshadowed by his colleague. He's just shy of 5'5" with unruly, dark brown hair which hangs like straw around his face. He's a bit on the heavier side, but not terribly so. Physically, he could look worse, but his personality definitely leaves something to be desired.

For whatever reason, he has clung to me like a starving tick on a deer's ass. It's borderline obsessive behavior. Not one day goes by that I don't receive a call, a text, or an email from him. On holidays or my birthday, he makes it a point to send something. Though that would normally be a sweet gesture, his gifts often take on the appearance of being something expensive and a tad inappropriate. Jewelry, shoes, clothes (how he knows my size, I'll never know, nor do I want to). It's sad and creepy, and the complete stink of desperation is off-putting.

Though I spurn his advances, I think in some twisted way, he finds enjoyment in it, and like an overly affectionate puppy, I find it impossible to bring myself to be outright cruel to him. I've tried the 'let him down easy' approach. Either he's completely blind, refuses to accept it, or thinks persistence is the key.

I step into my room, dump the contents of my bag into the hamper and slip into the shower. I close my eyes as the steaming droplets coat my body. White noise from the gushing waters block out the clashing sounds of dishes and silverware from downstairs, as Riley prepares for our guests.

As I work shampoo and conditioner through my hair, filling the entire second floor with the scent of peppermint, my thoughts stray back to the night before.

I can see him, smiling at me behind closed eyelids, and instead of my hands in my hair, they're his. They trail up my spine and grab my hair from beneath, tugging lightly. He coils himself around my body; his long, slender fingers probing the deepest, darkest desires of my soul. His labored breath coats my neck as he pushes against me. Every cell of my body aches for him, crying out for another touch, another kiss; another scream of blinding pleasure ripping from my lips by his skillful advances.

A soft knock on the door interrupts my daydream. The door whips open immediately following the knock, exposing my soap covered body to the cold air from the hallway, and Riley's face.

"Riley!" I scream, immediately covering my body with my arms. Riley sighs exasperated, rolling her eyes as she steps into the bathroom. Closing the door, she settles her rump on the closed toilet seat by the shower.

"Oh, please. It's nothing I haven't seen before. Get over yourself."

I sigh and dunk my head under the shower

stream, rinsing the soap from my body and conditioner from my hair.

"Cass, what really happened this weekend?"

"What do you mean?" I ask in my best innocent voice.

"You normally don't go that long without checking in. Geez, Cass. I sent a text to make sure you got there; I called Friday and Saturday night, and got nothing. No text or call or even a damned smoke signal. Would it have killed you to let me know you at least got there okay?"

I wanted to snap at her. Who does she think she is? She's not my mother, or my keeper. I don't owe her any explanations of any kind on where I go or what I do, but I look at her, and those thoughts die where they sprouted.

Her voice is shaky near the end of her statement and her eyes begin to water; tears threatening to break the dam she's built to hold them at bay. The sight of her like this wrenches at my heart. She's normally so calm and collected, no matter what. In fact, in the many years I've known her, I have only seen her cry once.

I turn off the shower, grab my towel, and kneel down in front of her, then look up into her quickly reddening face.

"I'm sorry, Riley…" I murmur gently. "I wasn't thinking. I let myself get distracted and caught up with everything I had to do. I'm really sorry."

Leaning in, I hug her tight, my still damp skin soaking through her clothes.

"Ah! Get off! You're getting me all wet!"

"All wet, huh?" I smirk.

She laughs, reaches over and playfully pinches the top of my breast.

"Don't ever put me through that again. Now get dressed. They'll be here any minute. And *please* try to be nice to Ryan."

With an exasperated sigh, I roll my eyes and get dressed. Oh how I hate playing nice.

When I come downstairs, Riley is already seating our guests.

"Cass, why don't you grab the wine glasses?" she asks as I reach the bottom step.

I head into the kitchen and, after rummaging through the cabinets for glasses, turn to find Ryan standing right behind me.

"Need help?"

"Uh, yeah. Sure. Thanks."

He beams at me, as if accepting his help was the pinnacle of his day. I pass the wine glasses to him, grab the bottle of wine by the neck and usher him back towards the dining room while dodging his unwelcomed advances. I settle in next to Riley with the two guys sitting opposite us.

Riley is still stuck in what I like to call the 'honeymoon phase'. It's normally the first 3-6 months — and sometimes up to a year — of the relationship where your partner is absolutely perfect, though Riley's phase has gone on for the entire time she's been with him. The significant other can do no wrong, and your complete and total love for them is so overwhelming, that you can do nothing other than grin stupidly like a lovesick school girl whenever they are around.

Perhaps, that's just how normal relationships are. I haven't really had relationships to compare against hers. I mean, I've had relationships, but they've all been complete washes. Maybe I'm just not good at them.

I have to give Riley some credit though. When Tom does piss her off, the entire neighborhood can hear the swear words flying from her mouth, as if she were raised by sailors. Riley isn't the type to take anyone's shit, whether she's hopelessly in love with them or not. I often think it's the reason Tom stays with her. He loves her fiery passion in all things, her head strong nature and her overly compassionate heart. She is both sides of the coin. The two competing extremes of her personality somehow complement one another, like chocolate and chili powder.

As Tom, Ryan and Riley laugh over the events of their last few days together, I lose myself within the glossy surface of the sanguineous liquid resting in my wine glass. I watch helplessly as the liquid swirls, forming into a picture of Alexander standing over me. I can hear the crack resonate through the air as he brings his hand down, hard, on my backside again and again.

Biting my lip, my cheeks grow hot as I grow damp from the memory. My body tingles in response to the excitement drawn from my memories as my heart pounds against my rib cage.

I force down another bite of Riley's delectable lasagna and chase it down with a mouthful of wine. I can't get him out of my thoughts. Even after two showers, I can still smell him on my skin, oozing from every pore. I'm sure I just need a few days to let the memory fade.

Just a few days…

"What do you say, Cass?" Tom asks as he beams at me from the other side of the table.

"What? Sorry, I haven't slept well lately…I wasn't really paying attention…"

His question clears my thoughts; even if it's only for a moment, it's a welcome respite from the face of Alexander Delacroix. They're all staring at me expectantly.

Damn, what where they talking about?

"I'd like to treat us all to a movie after this exquisite dinner Riley has prepared for us."

Tom's eyes are piercing, and his boyish grin stretches straight up to his ears. The way he looks at me makes me shift in my seat, as if he can somehow see my thoughts, and is grinning at the knowledge of all the dirty secrets he's coming across.

"I uh…I'm sorry. I really have a lot of work to take care of from the weekend. I have an article I need to piece together, and it needs a lot of polishing."

I haven't the slightest idea how I'm going to build an article around a short coffee meeting and a night of drunken debauchery.

"Awe, Cass! C'mon. Take a break. You've been working all weekend!" Riley whines.

"I'll make it up to you, I promise. Rain check?"

"Sure." Tom says, as he reaches over and squeezes Riley's hand.

Ryan looks crushed, like I ran over his heart with a semi. He looks up at me with sad, puppy dog eyes, and it's absolutely nauseating.

"You can't just put it off till later?" he whimpers.

"No, I really can't. Sorry." I'm not sorry. Anything that he's involved in instantly makes me sick to my stomach. I want to be as far away from his as humanly possible.

God knows what he'd try if I actually went. I'd have to swallow down the urge to shrug out of his arm on my shoulder, or turn a cheek to ward off his kiss. At the end of the night, I'd have to scrub my skin from my bones just to feel clean again.

We finish dinner, clean up, and the three of them leave for the theater. Ah, sweet silence. The entire house is mine for the next two hours. Three, if they decide to stop for a drink after.

I take a moment to pity Ryan; he really needs a girlfriend, or at least a good lay. Not that I'm volunteering. Something about him makes my skin crawl.

Climbing the stairs to my room, not bothering to close the door, I collapse face first into the bed. Pulling out my phone, I stare expectantly at the screen. No calls, no text. Nothing at all from him. Not even a few words to ask if I got home safely.

Rolling onto my back, I stare at the stark white ceiling, groaning as I push my thighs tightly together. Behind closed eyes, he's towering over me on the bed, his fingers plunging into me as he draws scream after scream from my lips.

I slip my fingers into my panties and trace lightly over my throbbing clit. The light touch sends a shock of instant pleasure followed by an ache and more wetness.

More…I need more.

I glance at my phone again as I trace lazy circles around the sensitive little button. No, it's too late to find someone, and I'm far too tired to go out anyhow.

I stare at the screen longingly, as if my force

of will would somehow, subconsciously, convince him to text or call, then dropping the phone on the bed in frustration, I grip my hair, tugging hard as I force my eyes closed.

I need to get him out of my head! This pining is so pathetic!

Groaning in frustration, I move — or attempt to move — my thoughts onto someone else. Anyone else. Taking a deep breath, I conjure an image of a pale man who vaguely resembles Ethan. Smirking, I clothe him in a royal purple shirt. The buttons at his chest are straining; on the verge of ripping apart, and exposing his smooth, white flesh to my fingers and lips. I bite my bottom lip and moan; my fingers adding pressure as I picture him moving between my thighs, slipping down my body and tracing his lips over my skin. His tongue flicks between them, causing a ripple of fire to course through my body.

As the scene dances through my mind, my fingers twirl between my thighs; stroking, rubbing and lightly pinching in order to draw me closer and closer. I'm teetering on the very edge; every muscle in my body tensing as my breath catches in my chest. Swirls of reds and blues dance behind my fluttering eyelids then burst into a scintillating collection of stars as I reach my peak and toss myself from its edge.

As every ounce of strength seeps from my body, my breath shudders in my throat as my heart struggles to regain a regular rhythm and I sigh, satiated, as all the worries and stress from the last few days fade away. Turning to my side, I cuddle my pillow and drift peacefully to sleep.

I wake to River perched on my back, kneading at my skin, and mewing against my ear. I lift my head and my eyes cross, focusing on a pink, heart-shaped post-it that's been stuck hastily to my forehead. Pulling the note from my head, I glance over the scribbled words.

"Cass, I didn't want to wake you because you looked so peaceful. I'm staying at Tom's tonight. I just didn't want you to worry (because I CARE). See you in the morning."

It was signed with a smudge of her lipstick. At least she didn't have him stay here. All their moaning and groaning surely would've woken me.

It's already 6 a.m. I must've been more tired than I thought if I slept through the night. River's incessant mews remind me that the poor thing hasn't had her food bowl refreshed since the night before, and if even one small silver spot is visible in the dish, she acts like it's completely empty.

Sometimes I wonder whether I'm her owner, or she's mine.

I make myself busy caring for River then prepare for the day ahead. Checking my phone reveals a glaring text from Angela. I'm sure she'll want me in to discuss the pile of crap I left on her desk yesterday. On my way in, I'll be sure to ask the barista for an extra shot or two in my morning mocha. I may need it to deal with Angela.

Chapter 11

Several days passed by without another word from Alexander Delacroix, and my thoughts have moved from regarding that night with fond memories, to questioning myself about the validity of the events. As the ache in my body begins to fade, so does my recollection of everything that happened. The bar, the drinks, his scent, and the feel of his lips against mine seem no more real to me now than an old dream struggling to tug at the edges of my memory.

My meeting with Angela earlier this week wasn't as bad as I thought it would be, but she made it a point to harass me about finishing the article about him. I have nothing, and she's riding me for the article on Delacroix on a daily basis. Surely I can spin *something* from the time I spent with him, and mix it with a bit of internet magic.

I'm reminded — by a quick peek at my email — that amidst the flurry of activity this past weekend, I completely forgot to stop at Ann's on my way home. She has sent her full 500 page manuscript to my inbox with texts every other day asking whether or not I've finished going over it, coupled with apologies over her actions the night we had dinner together. When am I going to have time to read through 500 pages? I should demand money for this shit.

By Friday, I'm dragging. I've emotionally and mentally put myself through hell, bouncing back and forth on my thoughts about Delacroix. I've been fighting off the urge to text him, and scolding myself by trying to convince my lust addled brain that he's not worth another thought if he doesn't have the decency to check on me.

Coupled with stress from Angela, and having to balance the part time teaching gig, I find it hard to keep my eyes open, and it's only 9 a.m.

The tinge of obsessiveness tugs at me. For heaven's sake, I met him once! It was some random fling; something that will never happen again, but oh, how I wish it would.

If I can just get through today, I'll take the weekend for myself to relax. Maybe I'll go get a pedicure or something, you know, like girls do.

Maybe I can convince Riley to go with me so I don't feel so awkward with some stranger scrubbing my toes and massaging my feet.

I gather my things and head to the local college for class. With a stack of graded papers under my arm, I march into the classroom with my head held high. This will be a great day. I demand it!

As I slam the papers, my purse, and the class book down on my desk, I lift my head and take a look around. I'm greeted by five pairs of eyes. In a class of 20 students, only five have bothered to show up today. Well, better than no one at all, I suppose.

It seems to happen more and more each passing semester. New students join this course, convinced they can breeze through and not show up to actually learn anything. Then, they hand me a paper worse than that of a 10-year old, and expect a passing grade. If your idea of an essay is one long run on sentence that explains how a sport is your life because it's 'cool', it'll make me want to strangle you and hide your body beneath a library in hopes that in your next life, some of the knowledge from those books above your rotting corpse will have implanted some semblance of intelligence.

As I struggle through the frustration of

teaching college students the finer points of period usage, and the reasons why 'I like football.' isn't a sentence worthy of a college student, I feel the memories start to slip further beneath the surface.

The walk down Bourbon Street, how his body felt pinning me against the wall and the first step into his book lined home, have all but disappeared. They're nothing more than a soft whisper on the wind.

That is, until my phone begins to vibrate violently on my desk.

The class grows silent and stares at me, as I stare at the trembling phone; my thoughts temporarily lost in the moment as I see his name flash on the screen. He's sent a message. It took him five fucking days to send a message.

I wrap up the class, dismiss them fifteen minutes early, then fall exasperatedly into my desk chair and stare maliciously at the phone. With the smallest bit of hesitation, I pick it up and unlock it just to be greeted with six simple words.

Was fun. Will do it again.

I stare at the phone, dumbfounded. Was that it? It was fun? I hit reply, choking down the anger bubbling inside of me.

Yeah it was. I'd love to do it again sometime.

I rest the phone down on the desk, repeating over and over. I will not send more than one text. *I will not.*

Hours pass by, and I make my way home to crawl into more comfortable clothes, which consist of a pair of black pants and a tank top. I toss my phone casually onto the bedside table; it has yet to receive another message from him, so I attempt to bury myself in more work.

Rifling through my filing cabinet, I pull out yet another article that I had begun several weeks ago, but didn't finish. There's dozens of them littering my desk and filling the cabinet in the corner of the room. A dust covered collection of scrapped ideas that never achieved what I was hoping for, or that I simply lost the desire to finish.

I try to concentrate on the half-hearted written words, forcing out ideas to twist and meld with the previously started work, but it does nothing to ease the deep ache of desire that's taken hold of me. Those small six words brought every minute detail from my night with him, rushing back to the surface, as if it had taken place mere hours before.

And all at once, we were together again, seated in the cocktail lounge as the cigar smoke danced in ribbons on the musky air. As the carefully crafted words spilled from his lips, I found myself willing to do anything he asked so long as he didn't stop talking. I felt like a desperate woman, starved of the nourishment afforded by such decadent conversation, that I couldn't get my fill of it.

I want more, I need more.

The desire for him has become so deeply ingrained, that it negates the sole physical desire for him. That night, he satisfied something in me that I wasn't aware existed. He had, in mere fleeting moments, spun an enchanting web of words into every fold of my mind and impregnated that salivating beast with an intense, insatiable hunger for him and him alone. I was exposed all too freely for this man I barely knew. I bared my soul, seeking his approval or scorn, and was greeted with kind eyes. The soothing touch of his hand against my arm, the reassurance that I needn't hide, the comfort that I could tell him anything and never fear the harsh sting and subsequent heart-ache of rejection.

What has he done to me? I've always found it so easy to hide away and purge the thoughts of my encounters. There was no attachment to them. Nothing that would draw my mind, unwillingly, back to memories with them. It was so easy; they simply ceased to exist the moment the night was over. If we happened to come across one another, no glance was shared, no touch was experienced. There were clear cut rules and regulations that were always followed; plans that were always in place. We knew what we were to each other when we were tangled in one another, swaddled within the hushed whispers of the night.

So what, then, was he? I so freely cast aside my rules for him. I couldn't place him neatly in a box to be tucked within the darkest recesses of my mind and called upon whenever I felt the need. He was not *just* another one of my lovers. I had no control over this man. I could not read him, or predict him, and he's wrestled the control from my hands with naught more than a few words. He's unknowingly driving me towards the edge of a precipice, and I can't help but feel hopelessly entangled.

I lace my fingers behind my head; breathe deeply and smother down the memories until they twist and pale from asphyxiation. I struggle to gain some semblance of control of my mind and body, willing my racing heart to calm, my breathing to become deep and tranquil and my thoughts to grow as still as a secluded lake on a breathless night. I cannot allow any man or woman to invade my thoughts so completely. This is how mistakes are made. I've already made the mistake…

I must understand. Why is it, after all the experiences I've had and after the men and women I've known, that I have found myself enamored with this single man above all others? Physically, he was nothing incredibly impressive. No chiseled chin or hardened body. No abs of steel, if you will. Was it the way he looked at me? No. I've seen that hunger in many eyes. However, there was something more in them. Something my poor, intoxicated mind couldn't grasp at the time, and can't fully remember.

Maybe it was his touch. That small, reassuring gesture as he touched my arm. It made me feel safe; like I belonged there with him at that very moment, and nowhere else. He had come off as witty, sweet and respectful at first. Perhaps that's what held me so firmly. It wasn't the hair tugging or the stinging of my skin following a spank from his hand. At least, it wasn't only that. This man found a way to cater to my entire being; to both sides. He found a way to earn my trust, then found a way to stimulate both my public face, as well as finding submission in my darker side. He forced a melding between me with my personal monster, and relished in the experience. How could I have been so foolish as to let that happen?

Chapter 12

The days and weeks slip by, with each hour bleeding into the next until they're indistinguishable from one another. Every morning I'd wake up and go about my mundane life; work, home, Riley. The mindless drumming of every passing minute ripping blackened, decaying pieces away from my body; and yet, I still heard nothing of note from Alexander Delacroix. I'd occasionally get a single text asking how I was, and once I replied, I wouldn't receive another response until exactly seven days later. All the while, the slavering beast which coiled about my beating heart, whose tail wrapped between my aching loins, clawed my flesh from my bones in a mix of frustration and desire. It's insatiable, and holding it at bay this long has drawn every ounce of reserved strength I could muster.

I glance down at my phone, running my fingers idly over the single button at the bottom as my heart chips away at my rib cage with a pick.

It's been a week since his last message to me, and I've grown to expect a note just to know he was still there, and still thinking of me. This desire…this need to hear from him, gnaws at me, causing my body to physical ache in wanting. It's agonizing.

I exhaustively set my head in my hands and grip my fingers in my hair. A knock at the front door interrupts my thoughts and draws me back to the stark, corporeal world.

"Riley! Door!" I yell, irritated from being ripped so violently from the obsession which permeates my brain.

Was she expecting guests? I certainly wasn't. Is she even home? I wrack my memory, trying to recall the sound of the door closing or a quick word from her that carried a hint of where she had gone, but can't remember a thing. Just his lips…his touch, his scent.

I'm going mad.

The knock comes again and there's still no sound of Riley's footsteps rushing to the door. A third series assaults the door before I grudgingly convince myself to walk down and answer it. It's probably some solicitor; oh how I hate them.

I place my hand on the knob and peek through the peephole. Staring back through is Tom, looking as handsome as ever as he rakes his fingers through his ginger-tinged hair and flashes his naturally soothing smile. His voice wafts through the door, and another, deeper voice speaks in response. It's not Riley, obviously, unless she's had a sex change that she neglected to tell me about. She'd never knock anyhow, though she does often forget her key.

No, the voice I'm hearing is so much deeper, and familiar. I shrug, dismissing my thoughts, and open the door.

"Cass! Where's Riley?"

"Riley isn't h…"

I'm greeted by two figures, one of which is Tom of course, and the other…

"This is my brother, Ethan. He's decided to pay a visit and I wanted her to meet him."

Tom steps forward and wraps me in his strong, albeit platonic, hug as my eyes fixate over his shoulder, on his guest.

"Uh, she's not here at the moment. I don't remember you mentioning a brother…" I murmur, trying in vain to hide my face from his brother beneath a torrent of my curls. Tom hunches down and tries to catch my eye in his quizzical gaze.

"Oh, I'm sure I've mentioned him loads of times. You do have a habit of drifting off, though…maybe you've forgotten. Of course, I'm older by a year, two inches taller and far more dashing than he is, however. Perhaps you were simply distracted by my debonair presence."

He pauses briefly, placing both hands on his lapel and grinning, thoroughly pleased with himself. Ethan rolls his eyes at his brother. If I had to choose one, Ethan's voice would get me every time. Those deep tones vibrate every cell of my body, and set butterflies swarming in my belly.

Tom glances down at me and perks an eyebrow.

"Are you feeling okay?"

"Yeah I'm fine." I cough, and try to look at anything other than Ethan. "Why don't you two come in? I'll give her a call to see where she's run off to."

I step aside to let the two men pass. Tom

heads immediately to the living room and settles on the couch, flipping on the television to find it set to a rerun of the Doctor Who show I had watched the night before. Ethan pauses just inside of the doorway, staring into my eyes.

"I know you…" he whispers, his deep purring voice reverberating through my body.

My brain is frantic, scrabbling at the corners of my mind to explain this coincidence away, but coming up empty handed. I stare at him, unable to speak as I feel everything tangible begin to unravel and coil lifelessly at my feet.

"Yeah…it seems that way. Small world, huh?" I laugh weakly. My voice is failing me; I never thought I'd see this man again, and to think I had used his image a handful of times for my own pleasure…

I'm grasping for some untapped well of strength, but I'm blindsided. My attempt to keep my thoughts organized is unsuccessful; it's like trying to hold onto moonlight with my bare fingers, and I'm failing miserably. He steps closer and I can smell the sweet, musky scent of his cologne wafting off of his skin, and mixed with the sound of his voice, I'm left breathless.

"I was hoping to see you again before you

left, and was disappointed that I missed that chance. I'm glad fate has seen fit to steer us in this direction."

A key scrapes against the lock, then turning, the door flies open. Riley rushes through with half a dozen bags in her hands, and almost crashes straight into us.

"Riley!"

Tom jumps up in pure joy and rushes to the door to help, completely oblivious to Ethan and I. I manage to pull from his eyes, and walk to the couch, but he's at my heels and settles in just opposite from me. He leans back comfortably on the couch, crossing his legs and regarding me with calm eyes, which glitter just below the surface with a hidden sense of amusement.

"So, why is it that you go by Cass?"

I can hear Delacroix's voice in my head, my full name slithering from his lips and causing my body to shudder in excitement.

"I don't normally go by my full name. I haven't for many years."

"And you prefer it that way?"

"Yes, I do. It's short and uncomplicated."

"Because a name is complicated?"

"It could be."

He holds his tongue, sharing a look that seems to convey the idea that he thinks I'm odd, then switches seats to be closer to me. His body heat radiates off of his skin, and I glance over the buttons of his fitted black shirt. They're straining against the fabric as he rolls his shoulders and makes himself comfortable. I try my best to beat down the twitch of excitement, but I can't smother the flames.

Deep breaths. Calm down, I'm just fine. I will *not* let myself fall to desire.

He's gorgeous. An absolutely beautiful specimen of the male form, and it's no surprise that he and Tom are related. I can see the resemblance in their eyes and their breath-taking smiles. How did I not notice that before? If I had taken just a second to really take a good look at him, I could've made that connection earlier. Then, maybe, I could've prepared for this.

He crosses his leg, resting ankle to knee, and turns to face me, draping one arm casually along the back of the couch. He's let his hair go unrestrained today without a drop of product. His mop of curls gently fall over his forehead, as if a crown of silken chocolate twirls had been draped over his head. Without the hair products, his hair resembles a deep, near ebon hue; a stark contrast against his brothers' ginger locks.

Riley's voice is rising to a frantic volume upstairs, and Tom's voice rolls down the stairs in response, as little more than a low murmur. No doubt Riley wasn't forewarned about Tom's visit with his brother, and dragged him upstairs to bitch about her displeasure.

I turn away from Ethan as Riley runs down the stairs with Tom in tow. She rushes into the living room and Ethan stands to greet her.

"You must be Tom's brother. Ethan, is it? I've heard so much about you!"

I can tell she's lying; her face resembles a tightly pursed peach, muscles strained into a fearfully fervent smile as she forces the words for the pure sake of being polite. I've never heard about this brother of Tom's, and I'm sure this is the first time she's hearing of it too. Though, even if he did mention it, I doubt I would've remembered it. I've been so preoccupied lately.

"Yes, ma'am. And I've heard quite a bit about you as well. Tom doesn't stop talking about you."

I can see the anger rushing to her face, contorting into a mix of emotions as she tries to reign in her desire to slap Tom. After all, why would he tell Ethan all about her but not tell her a thing about him?

"Well, it's wonderful to finally meet you, Ethan. Please excuse the state of the house; I wasn't aware we would be entertaining company this afternoon. Can I get you anything? Would you like something to eat or drink?"

"A drink would be absolutely fantastic, thank you."

Without further hesitation, she rushes off to the kitchen, flashing a dagger-filled look in Tom's direction. She's not exactly a fan of unexpected company. She thrives off prior warning, so she can plan the entire evening, and make sure the house is pristine. The arrival of our unexpected guests has completely thrown her off, and she's attempting to make up for it by playing the perfect hostess to keep her mind off the rising anger.

I turn to find Ethan staring at me, a sly curl upon his lips.

"What?"

"So this is what you look like in your natural

habitat?" he laughs.

I'm suddenly self-conscious of the fact that I'm wearing a pair of black pajama pants with Superman emblems all over them, and a faded AC/DC shirt well passed noon. I hadn't planned on doing anything other than staying home, writing, drinking and maybe a bit of channel surfing, so why should I get dressed?

I crack a smile as I debate running upstairs and trying to make myself look a bit more presentable, but toss the idea away. What use would it be in making myself look better now that he's already seen me like this? It would be a waste of time, and I'm not really looking to impress anyhow.

Tom collapses into the seat opposite from us, leans forward and rests his elbows on his knees. His fingers press together to form a steeple on which he rests his chin as he regards us intently. He smiles gently; he always seems to be smiling about something, as if he were privy to all the worlds' secrets, but kept the information for his own personal pleasure.

"So, have you two met before?"

"Kind of." I answer meekly. "I was in New Orleans a couple of weeks ago, and he was staying at the same hotel. We just sort of bumped into one another one night."

"Small world, isn't it!"

"Yeah…small world…"

Riley rushes into the room in a flurry of pink chiffon skirts, with a tray held in her hand, as she precariously balances four champagne glasses filled near the brim with golden bubbles. Accompanying the glasses is a plate filled with some sort of spinach stuffed puff pastry. When the hell did she make these?

She places the tray on the coffee table, passes out the drinks, then settles in near Tom. He kisses her cheek affectionately, murmuring a soft "I love you" sweetly into her ear. If there were any trace of anger still present in her body, it evaporated at that moment. She instantly relaxed, and the hint of a smile curled on her lips to accompany her love-filled eyes.

Sensing that her rage had faded, Tom came up with the idea of taking a trip into the city of New Orleans the following weekend in order to give Riley, and his brother, a proper tour.

Since Riley and I moved here, we still have yet to fully explore our own town, much less the city of New Orleans, so when the weekend crawled upon us, Riley was absolutely ecstatic. She spent an hour in front of her closet trying to pick the perfect outfit, and another hour doing her makeup and hair. I wasn't about to go out looking like I just blew in off the streets, so I pulled on a pair of black slacks and a sleeveless gray blouse with a slouched neckline that rests peacefully upon the top of my breasts.

It has just begun to cool, which is surprising, even with the calendar slipping into October. I've become accustomed to the weather sitting in the high 90's until December, but the cool front brought a bit of respite from the normal heat and humidity. I decide to leave my hair down, with no worry of it turning into a frizzed mess by the end of the night.

Tom and Ethan were already waiting outside by the time Riley and I meandered downstairs and locked up the house for the night. As we all clambered into my car, Ethan caught my eye and smiled. The skin at the corners of his eyes fracture, like snowflakes on a cold winter's day, with the hint of a dimple just barely visible on his left cheek.

Since Ethan and Tom left last week, him and I had exchanged numbers and found ourselves texting each other on a daily basis. Our conversations covered everything from talk about politics, to speaking about his childhood in the UK and about his parents. He talked extensively about his work, and on how his mother becoming ill during his childhood, spurred him to pursue a career in the medical field. He wanted to help others during their time of need, and try to ease their suffering with his bleeding heart. It was a noble calling for him; one that made him proud to wake up every morning and go to work.

I managed to keep myself rather tight-lipped about my past, and instead, encouraged him to share pieces of himself with me. By the time our trip to New Orleans came up, I felt like I knew him better than I knew my own family, and it helped to ease my anxiety and nerves.

Having him this close to me plucked the tightly wound strings of my heart. It made me ache with longing for a simpler life. I'm not the best with relationships. Not really. I'm a solitary creature, and often find it so hard to express myself, unless I'm sitting in a fading room with poison on my lips, spewing out my desires in a drunken haze. It's at those times that I can stagger over, wrap Riley in a giant hug and whisper, 'I love you so much!', and I do mean that in the most platonic way possible... I think.

And yet, here I am, with Ethan sitting by my side, enticing me with thoughts of that evasive white fence and a beautiful wedding. With wishes and fantasies of an ivory dress and matching beaches, while walking amongst crystalline waves in the fading sunlight. With his arm around my shoulders, and his whispered promise of love forever...forever. Who is to say I don't deserve it? Doesn't everyone deserve a happy ending? Is there such a thing as a happy ending?

No, that's silly childhood fairytale bullshit.

The drooling beast is there in the darkness, pulling at me...ripping at me till my mind is sent screaming as it pummels my memories with thoughts of Delacroix. He will always be there, with coiled rope and cold, metal cuffs. Those brown eyes swallow me, drowning me as I relish in it, crying out in exaltation at the feeling of helplessness against his touch. Instead of being with him, I'm trapped in a metal box with a man I couldn't possibly have. He's too good for me. Too perfect.

He moves to the driver's side door and holds it open for me to climb in, then settles in to claim the passenger's side seat. Riley and Tom slip into the backseat, and honestly, I don't want to know what they plan to do back there. As long as the clothes stay on and the windows don't fog, I'm more than happy to concentrate on the road. Sometimes they are hard to distinguish from teenagers when they're together.

After an hour and a half, we finally cross the line into New Orleans. Moving through the side streets, we take in the sights. My phone is resting in the cup holder between Ethan and me, when it begins to vibrate wildly. I turn the car down another road littered with bars and restaurants that sidles along Canal Street, and pull off to the side to check my phone. Flashing on the screen was a missed call and subsequent text message, the name that followed was Alexander Delacroix.

I can feel Ethan's eyes fixated on me, my cheeks blushing as I read the name. Taking a breath, I stumble to unlock the phone.

It's been two months now since I've heard from him. I had already pushed him to the furthest reaches of my mind, and buried him beneath several hundred boxes of false memories. No matter what I may have told myself, I know I hadn't forgotten completely. I had cast aside my addiction to touch, and forced myself to suffer the absence of sex in the vain hope of him calling upon me again.

How pathetic.

The contacts in my phone had collected dust, and thinned, as I went through once every few days and deleted another couple of names. I had pushed myself through months without sex; it's not something I ever thought was possible, but I found if I just ignored it…if I could pretend it wasn't there gnawing at my flesh, it'd go away and I could live as any normal person would.

Sometimes, ignoring it worked. Other times, it didn't, and I would drown the monster with a bottle of wine or far too many shots of vodka till I paled and fell sick to the floor. I wanted to forget. I wanted to rip apart the loop that went 'round and 'round my head, and stomp it down until it exploded into cloud of dust specters that slipped beneath the floor boards.

I struggle to keep my face in a relaxed state, choking down the pounding of my heart as I read over the text message.

*Meet me at the following address. Now. *

What is it that he wants with me? What excuse could I possibly give for ducking out on Riley and the guys? I don't know what he wants, or how long I'll be, and I don't really care. The memories I thought were fading with each sunrise, had rushed in and overcharged every part of my body, and I didn't care.

Am I actually considering going?

My mind is a jumble of thoughts and scenarios rushing by, colliding, and merging with one another until I'm left with a runny mix of splattered ideas. I'll just fall back to the tried and true excuse; work.

"I'm sorry, it looks like Angela needs me to meet up with someone for the magazine. I shouldn't be more than hour or two, I promise. Why don't I drop you guys off here, and you can start having drinks on me? I'll be back before you know it."

I grab my purse, careful to avoid the scrutinizing gazes from the three of them, and pull out my credit card. I hand it to Riley, a look in my eye that pleads her not to ask any further questions.

"I'm really, very sorry." I offer apologetically. "I promise not to be more than an hour. Two at the most."

Riley is tangled deep in her 'I'm with Tom and not pissed at him, so everything is perfect' frame of mind and smiles, taking my credit card and slipping it into her wallet.

"Well, if it's on you, I'm sure we'll get by. See you in a bit?" she leans forward and kisses my cheek, then leaves the car with Tom.

Ethan glances over at me, his eyes searching

my face for some kind of hint to my true feelings.

"Are you feeling okay?"

I reach over and squeeze his hand reassuringly, leaning over to kiss his sexy, dimpled cheek.

"I'm just fine." I smile. "You're very sweet to ask. Things like this just crop up now and then for me, but I'll see all of you in a bit. Keep an eye on Riley for me, okay?"

He returns my smile and slips out of the car, following Riley and Tom down a few doors to a restaurant and lounge on the corner. I return my attention to my phone, plug the address into the GPS and follow its directions. Does he know I'm in the city, or was he taking some off-the-wall chance? Or, perhaps, he expected me to just make the hour drive.

As my car slips down the series of one way side streets, and turns down roads that feel more like hallways than anything fit for a vehicle, the GPS brings me to the corner of a tree lined street. Branches from the oak trees hang over the road, joining fingers with the trees on the other side. They blend their branches into one another, joined by delicately hanging moss. It's a gorgeous sight; the sun dappling the road, filtering through gaps in the canopy as I drive between the living archways.

The address is about six blocks away, and takes me five minutes to reach. Before me is a five story building which may have been an old factory in a previous life, but has now been turned into some sort of small museum, with loft style apartments occupying its top floor. I park on the street, surprised that I'm actually able to find a space, and make my way into the building.

The bottom floor is littered with glass cases, which hold books and documents that look as if they would turn to dust if anyone so much as breathed on them. I pull out my phone and stare at the message again just to confirm the address. Why would he want to meet in some random place like this?

The phone vibrates again in my palm and another message pops up on the screen.

When you arrive, come to the top floor.

I feel my heart face with nervous energy. Is he watching me? Moving to the stairs, my legs begin to climb slowly. Gripping the side rail tight with one hand, I drag myself up one step at a time. With my nerves flashing, flitting from juncture to juncture, I soon find myself easily agitated at the difficulty I seem to be having convincing my body to keep going.

I take a deep breath, round the next set of steps and approach the fifth floor landing. There's a man with his back turned towards me, fumbling with the lock on the door of a loft. His long slender legs shift as he rummages through his pocket and pulls out another key.

"A…Alexander? Mister Delacroix…I mean…" I whisper all too weakly.

He turns to face me, the silver frames of his glasses glinting in the setting sunlight that's streaming in from an adjacent window.

"Ah, my dear Cassandra. You can call me Alex, you know." He smiles. "I'm glad you came, and much faster than I had expected. Please, come in."

He slides the correct key into the lock, twists, then holds the door open for me. I step into the loft, where a bed sits with its headboard flush against the middle of the far brick wall, framed on either side by large floor to ceiling windows. Sitting adjacent to the bed is a desk pressed against another window, and a laptop. The walls are lined with shelves filled to capacity with varying types of books and periodicals that have been worn by the years; with faded lettering and fraying bindings.

These are not for show; these have been loved and tenderly read for many years.

He tosses his keys and briefcase onto the desk and turns to face me. As he steps closer, a smile tugs at his lips, his eyes glinting flecks of gold in the deepening orange light. Closer and closer he comes, until his fingers move to my face and brush aside a curl. His chest presses against mine as he wraps one arm around me and pulls me close.

My eyes flutter as I catch the intoxicating scent of cigar smoke, mixed with the musk of his cologne, steaming off of his skin. He presses his forehead against mine, locking our eyes. His touch sends an electric pulse from my skin through my body, sloughing off the days, the weeks, the months of decay and longing that had built itself up around the memories in an attempt to bury them.

"It's been too long." He purrs, "Why didn't you tell me you'd be in town?"

"I hadn't heard from you in a while. I thought you'd moved on and so, I stopped contacting you. I didn't want to be a bother…"

"Silly girl." He muses. He pushes against me, causing me to take a step back, then another until my back is pressed against a wall.

"Alex…" I whimper as I feel his lips press against my neck. The cells of my body are on the verge of combustion, threatening a complete meltdown. "I can't stay…I'm not here alone. My friends and I came to spend the day here and just…I just left them at a bar."

"Then they'll be fine. They'll get drunk and lose track of time." He murmurs against my skin. His hand tugs forward on my pants, slipping between the gap of clothes and flesh.

"I…I can't just leave them there. How did you know I'd be here?"

"Is that important right now?" he whispers. His tongue trails over my neck and cheek until his lips press passionately against mine.

My mind is wiped clean with his succulent kiss. The void left by the hasty retreat of every thought and memory held confined within me, is now filled with his scent; his touch. I need him.

His fingers slip beneath my panties and he pulls back from the kiss, grinning.

"Oh Miss Roman, why didn't you tell me you were so excited? You're dripping."

"I…"

"How long has it been since you've pleased yourself? How long since you've had sex?"

"I…I haven't had sex since you and I…"

"Oh my dear; an addict like you?" he chides, his fingers lightly tracing over my clit. "Look at you. You're absolutely soaked. Let's save you the trouble of having to find a new pair of pants to go back to your guests in, hm?"

His kiss steals my breath once more, his tongue slipping between my lips as his fingers deftly remove my pants and toss them carelessly over the back of a chair. His hands travel up from my hips; slender fingers gripping my shirt as he breaks the kiss and tugs my shirt from my body. He tosses it behind him, letting it lie lifeless on the floor.

His desire is overwhelming; the gold and brown eyes, replaced by an inferno, are fueled by the setting sun. Unzipping his pants, they fall from his sensuous hips. Grips the back of my knees, he pins me against the wall, guiding my legs around his waist.

The passion in every inch of his body is a shock that courses through my veins, merging our two bodies into one. Every touch is charged; every kiss the taste of sweet nectar on my parched lips and tongue.

Peeling my panties to the side, he slides into me, slowly, inch by agonizing inch. My fingers grip his back; my nails biting into his soft, unmarred flesh. With a heated moan, he deepens the kiss. The feel of him finally inside of me is overwhelming; my body bursting with pure, unadulterated pleasure. Every inch drives into me, and I'm lost in complete bliss.

His hand slips up my side and ventures into my hair, teasing the curls around his fingers and tugging…hard. He picks up his pace; sliding in faster, harder. Every inch of him invades my body, and pushes deeper than I had ever thought possible. His muscles tense against me, helping to pin my body firmly between him and the wall.

"Scream for me." He growls, as his teeth find my ear and tug.

My body is quivering in ecstasy at his touch, at his taste, and as my back arches against the wall, my thighs tighten against him. A light moan escapes his lips, wrapping me in its silken sound as my own moans of pleasure grow louder and louder.

"Scream for me!" he commands, his lean muscles rippling along his chest and arms as he takes my body and mind, claiming them as his own.

My head tilts back, guided by his hand ripping at my hair, and my vision blurs; the room fading to black, as my body drinks him in from every sense. His scent fills my mouth and nose; his touch overcharges every nerve in my body until it sings with a single need — him.

My lips part, and the air is cut with my screams of pleasure. Over and over, my screams ring out until the strength from my body drains, and I'm left slumped between the wall and his body, panting heavily in an effort to catch my breath.

He slips from inside of me and picks me up in his arms, holding me close to his chest as he moves to the bed. Laying me down gently, he walks to the bathroom, fetching a dampened wash cloth and towel to clean us up. Once he finishes, he sits on the edge of the bed with his back towards me. I slip my arms under my head, a smile painted against my lips as I watch him sitting in the fading light.

"What is this? Is this a surreptitious relationship with you?" I ask hesitantly.

I'm not sure if I want to know the answer; I'm afraid of what I may hear, but I need to define it somehow.

"I don't know. It could be. I don't really know what you're asking, here. I can't be anything like your garden variety boyfriend, if that's what you're looking for."

His elbows rest on his knees as he gazes out the window. The light catches his hair, scorching his curls, turning them into a delicate tangle of spun gold and coiled fire.

"I can't come and spend birthdays with you, or sit by the fire under a decorated tree for Christmas. I can't commit to a Valentine's Day dinner, and can't promise I'll ever remember important dates. My work is my life; it's my child."

"I'm not asking anything like that. I've never been good with titles, anyway. I guess what I'm saying is…I don't really know what I'm asking. I feel like I need some idea of what we are; of what this is, so I know how to treat it. We had this great night together that I haven't been able to get out of my head, and then it feels like you dropped off the face of the earth. I tried to forget about you…I tried to move on, then got roped back in. I want to know what all of…this…is, and what you expect of me."

"What do you want me to be? What do you want *us* to be?"

"I don't know…"

He chuckles and turns towards me, brushing

his thumb against my cheek.

"So you wish to know what we are, but don't know what you want." He smirks, crawling into bed beside me and wrapping me in his arms.

"Yes, I suppose so. Sounds foolish, I'm sure."

"Not too foolish. I enjoy the pleasure of your company, and I would love to indulge in it further, however, work tends to get a bit out of hand for me at times and things slip my mind. I am too easily lost in what I do."

"You simply forget to respond? It takes ten seconds to type a text and hit send."

He sighs, clearly trying to hide some smidge of annoyance, and rolls onto his back, staring at the ceiling.

"Yes, and if I'm in a meeting, I'm not going to respond. Once I get out, chances are I've gotten other messages, and responding to everyone seems impossible. I won't pretend to make excuses; I'm just telling you how it happens. I can't always be around to talk to you and reassure you of my feelings, and regrettably, I can't always be here to cater to your insatiable appetite, as much as I may want to. I just don't have that kind of time."

His words would cut if they weren't so delicately spoken. It's like being slapped with a down pillow, or sliced open with a piece of chocolate. It should hurt so much more, but instead, it's just a dull ache centered somewhere in the vicinity of my heart. It's just enough to let its presence be known.

"I don't really want to do this with anyone else..." I murmur, my eyes fixed on an exposed beam in the ceiling.

"Are you even capable of handling that? It seems like it would drive you a bit mad; not getting satisfied as often as you need to be. I've had a taste of that appetite, Miss Roman. I know it can't be satiated on a meal given once every week or two."

"I'd like to try. I like to think I'm stronger than my urges. You've satisfied this part of me; not just physically but more...I don't quite know how to describe it, honestly. I feel so comfortable with you, and that isn't something I can say about many others that have come in to my life. I want to see what this is, what it could be, just so I can be certain. And if it doesn't work, then at least I'll have the satisfaction of knowing I tried, and can find some kind of closure in that knowledge. Not knowing will do nothing but bore holes in my bones."

What the hell am I saying? Shut up, Cass! He doesn't need to know any of this shit…

"Well then, I suppose we can give it a try. I make no promises that you'll be completely happy with me, but you already know that."

I bite my lip as I think back to Ethan and his deep, sensual voice. There's the potential for something there, isn't there? Am I willing to give up those every changing eyes and the sound of his voice melting against my ear? I guess I'll just have to see…

"So, how did you know I would be here? Now that you can't distract me with a kiss…"

"Oh I'm still quite capable of distracting you, but if you must know, it was Riley's doing. She loves to post pictures and status updates every time you two go out." He chuckles.

"So you've been stalking me via social media?" I laugh.

"Hardly. She's putting it out there for everyone to see. It's public. What I saw was no different than what any other random person would see if they stumbled upon her account."

I open my mouth in protest, but my words fall short as I think back to the times I've searched him on the internet, and the many times I've visited his webpage just to get some sense of connection again.

He leans toward me and places a soft kiss to my forehead, then slips his arm under my head. His fingers stroke over my arm and leave goose bumps in their wake. Tilting my face toward his, he kisses the tip of my nose.

"You are so easily distracted. You seem to have forgotten something very important, my dear."

I cuddle close, draping my arm over his bare abdomen and nuzzling my face against his chest. I breathe deep, savoring his scent mixed with the sweet, stimulating fragrance of our lovemaking.

"What might that be?"

He laughs, softly teasing my hair.

"My silly girl, you've forgotten all about your guests."

Chapter 13

By the time I had showered and raced out of Alex's loft office, the sun was barely visible, slipping behind the horizon as the stars began to illuminate the night. I hop in the car, trying to fix my hair in the best way possible, given the circumstances, and speed back to where I left Riley, Tom, and Ethan. As I pull into the parking space and race up to the door, Tom catches sight of me through the window and jumps up to open the door for me.

He's always such a gentleman.

I flash him a quick smile as I pass, and he grabs my arm, forcing me to face him.

"Riley was worried." he hisses, his brows knitting together. "It's been almost two hours and you weren't answering your phone. Is everything okay?"

"Yes! Of course it is. I just got caught up and lost track of time." I stutter.

His eyes do an overly-critical once-over of my body, and he squints skeptically.

"Are you sure? You look a bit...disheveled..."

"I was rushing to get back, that's all. I'm sorry I kept all of you waiting so long."

"...is your hair wet?"

I pull politely away from him, smile again, and make my way to the table with Tom at my heels. I pick the chair next to Riley and opposite Ethan, as Tom settles back into his place at the table. Ethan's eyes are burning into me with the intensity of a southern midsummer day. His emotions are plastered against his eyes; a silent 'Where on earth were you' pleading against my heart.

We glance over our menus and Riley and I leave our orders with the men as she grabs my arm, much too tightly, and drags me to the restroom to 'Powder our noses,' in her words.

Once the door to the extravagant restroom

closes behind us, and Riley peeks under all the stalls to make sure they're unoccupied, she turns on me like a hellhound that's clawed its way out from the mouth of the underworld itself. Molten fires are swirling beneath the surface of her eyes, as her words spill from her lips in a near incoherent fashion.

After what feels like a lifetime caught between a wall and a raptor, and the incessant slew of obscenities quells, her body deflates, and the fire in her eyes turns to nothing more than ash.

She slumps against the wall, and sighs heavily. She's utterly spent, as if she'd run a five mile sprint while holding the combined weight of two full grown men.

I want to explain, to comfort, but I can't lie to her and I can't bring myself to break the silence that has so precariously balanced itself between us, as fragile and transparent as a thinly pulled piece of sugar.

"It wasn't work, was it?"

It wasn't exactly a question. No, it was more of a complete, irrefutable fact.

"No…"

I didn't bother to find an excuse, or try to

say anything other than no. She would've seen right through it, and I would've lost more than just her trust. At this point, I'm surprised she is still talking to me at all.

"Who was it?"

"Someone I met a few months back while working."

"Did you use protection?"

"Riley…"

"Answer me!"

"Of course I did! I'm not an idiot."

It's not like we had sex anyway. Well…not at first.

"Sometimes I wonder." She huffs. "Got it out of your system, then?"

I'm being chastised in the most passive aggressive way possible. Perhaps it's best to not say anything that may send her teetering off the edge.

The lust in my body wasn't quelled by my random romp in the loft of Alex. If anything, it only added to the flames which were destined to engulf me and leave a burned, charred husk in their wake, still twitching with the aftermath and yet, craving more.

"Yes…" I answer hesitantly, though I don't see Alex *ever* being out of my system.

She turns to the sink and splashes cold water on her face, then touches up her make-up to the best of her ability. As she pulls a few stray strands of hair back into place while she stands in front of the mirror, she says those few words that every person hates hearing.

"We will talk about this more when we get home."

I'm five years old again, being scolded by my mother for talking back and saying 'No' in the middle of the store, and I hear those same three words. Though I'm sure a conversation with Riley won't end up with a belt to my ass and me crying in the corner, I have no doubt I'll feel just as miserable afterwards.

"For now…" she sighs, then tries on a fresh smile in the mirror to check her new face "let's try to enjoy the rest of our evening, okay?"

She stares into the mirror for just a second more, puckers her lips to slather on one more coat of lipstick then ushers me back towards the dining area.

She can't even stand to look at me…

We settle back into the tail end of a conversation between Tom and Ethan about the importance of music in films, then it somehow segues into the age old debate about whether Batman or Superman would win in a fight against one another.

For the record, Batman would win every time.

As their debate intensifies, the waiter — a tall, stringy man with his hair gathered into a neat ponytail — places our plates before us. He then flourishes a bottle of wine, though I haven't the slightest idea where he pulled it from, and tops off our glasses before rushing off to tend to other customers.

The conversation between the two men dwindles, and Tom refocuses the spotlight on me.

"How did everything work out with you and your client?"

I swallow and glance frantically at Riley. She doesn't look my way, but I can see the corner of her mouth curve into a roguish grin. She wants to watch me burn.

Both Ethan and Tom are staring, waiting

patiently for my response, and with a deep, exasperated breath, I try to plaster an annoyed look on my face.

"It went fine, I suppose. She wanted me to look over a few more things and it clearly couldn't wait until I got home." I sigh, rolling my eyes to portray how completely inconvenient my meeting with this 'client' was. "She has a tendency to over-exaggerate, and made it seem like life or death circumstances. Otherwise, I would've made her wait."

The grin on Riley's face wavers, and it's hard to tell whether she wanted me to get caught in a lie, or is satisfied with the fact that I dug myself out. I clear my throat and casually take a sip from the wine glass in front of me.

"So, did you guys get a chance to explore the area in my absence?"

"Oh!" Riley exclaims.

It's as if the events of our little bathroom pep talk had been completely forgotten as she to excitedly rambles on about everything she had seen while walking around the city. The words spill from her lips, and I wonder how she manages to speak so much without taking a breath.

She describes the Mercedes-Benz stadium in intricate detail, and then moves on to speak of the street vendors and the street car they had passed. It takes a bit of mental reshuffling to remember that this is her first time here, and though it was only my second, the city had already lost its shine after my first night with Alex Delacroix.

"Cass! The streetcar was so cool! Like, from that one Disney movie! I never thought I'd actually see one in person!"

Her eyes sparkle with the complete, unencumbered joy of a child.

"Sadly," she pouts, "Tom wouldn't let me ride it."

"Darling, it was filled to the brim." Tom coos gently. "We can ride it another time. I promise."

He reaches over and squeezes her hand. Riley's lips crack a smile as she sips at her glass of wine, and launches back into her one sided conversation. Amidst their chatter, my mind wanders back to that tall, slender man with the silver rimmed glasses and curls.

The ride back home is a quiet one. As I'd only had a few sips of wine, I was dubbed the official designated driver for the evening. I don't mind. After all, I wouldn't let just anyone drive my car.

As a slow, haunting song spills softly from the speakers, Ethan lazily reaches over and places his hand on mine, which was resting on the stick shift between us. His soft fingers trace over the back of my hand, caressing their way back and forth along each of my fingers. The faint touch sends a chill down my spine and goose bumps erupt along my arm.

I glance in the rearview mirror to see Riley with her head on Toms shoulder, and his head resting upon hers. They're passed out. I think that third bottle of wine was a bit too much for them to handle, and perhaps, a bit much for my bank account.

Ethan lolls his head to face me, and the shadow of a goofy, alcohol-induced grin slips over his lips. He lifts my hand to his face, and presses his lips against the back of my hand. His lips are like hot fire, burning the very flesh from my bones. His heated breath seeps out from between parted lips, wrapping around my hand and wrist, willing my hand to melt between his fingers so he could drink me in.

"Cass..." he whispers, the low tones in his

voice reverberate throughout the car, assaulting my ear drums with the sweet stickiness of warm maple syrup.

"Yes?"

"I know it hasn't been long since we first met, and I know we've only really started talking this past week, but I'd love if we could, you know…"

I keep my lips sealed as I attempt to concentrate on the music and on the barren road before me.

"We could make a long-distance thing work, couldn't we? I know I move around a lot…"

I try out a fake, but thoroughly convincing, giggle to hide my lack of emotion. He's incredibly attractive, with a face chiseled from pure marble and a voice which will forever haunt me in my dreams, but the pull toward Delacroix is all-encompassing, and I can't hurt Ethan like that. No…he's too good, and I don't know if I could ever wrench myself from Alex's web.

"Oh Ethan," I exclaim, in my best impression of a swooning girl, "I'm flattered! But I think all that wine has gone to your head! Why don't we talk about it more in the morning, after you've had a proper night's rest?"

He smiles, seemingly satisfied with my statement, and drifts to sleep.

By the time I pull in to the driveway, my car is filled with the sounds of drunken snoring. It takes all my will to rouse the men, and all my strength to assist Tom in carrying Riley into the house while making sure he didn't topple over as well. I open the door to a very irritated cat, who absolutely refuses to move her rump from the middle of the entryway, forcing us to go around her.

After some very delicate maneuvering, I manage to get the three lushes into the living room, and settle Riley and Tom into the queen sized pull out couch. I fetch two cups of water and Tylenol for their wake up call, and tuck both under a light blanket. I then turn my attention to Ethan, who had attempted to brace himself against the wall, unsuccessfully, as I tended to Tom and Riley. He was now, a crumpled mess on the floor, desperately trying to grab the bannister of the stairs in an attempt to hoist himself to his feet.

"You're not going to vomit on me, are you?" I ask as I hold my hand out for him to grab.

He manages to crack a smile, then pulls himself up and wraps me in his arms. As he sways unsteadily on his feet, he buries his face in my hair and breathes deep.

"You smell divine." He slurs.

I lightly pat his back and pull away, letting him hold on to my arms to stabilize his unsteady steps.

"Okay, why don't we try to get you settled in for bed too, okay? Do you think you can handle the stairs?"

"Mhm." he groans, as one hand reaches out for the bannister and holds tight. I position myself on the other side, drape his arm over my neck and help him up the best I can, despite the drastic differences in our height. Surprisingly, we reach the second floor without him plummeting head first in the opposite direction.

I lead him to the room, and press him into the bed, with him giggling like a school boy as I struggle to remove his shoes. As I grab a spare pillow and blanket from the closet to make my bed on the floor, he grabs my wrist and pulls me close, causing me to stumble and crash into the edge of the bed.

His mouth presses heatedly against mine; tongue slithering between my lips, wrapping me in a deep, intoxicating, passionate kiss. It's hard to pull away as his hand reaches behind my head, holding me firm against his molten mouth. My legs weaken and give, and my body aches and throbs from the passion he pours directly into my blood.

The several seconds that encompass the kiss, stretch on for hours in my head. As our lips regretfully pull from one another, he presses his forehead against mine. His breath is hot against my skin as his words drip from his lips; breathy, decadent and oozing with primal lust.

"I want you." He whispers, the tip of his tongue tracing my lips.

My body shudders; my excitement building as if I had been starved of sexual contact for years, when in truth, it'd been a mere few hours. I struggle against my thoughts, my brain pounding against the confines of my skull as my hips develop a mind of their own and press firmly against the bed, sending yet another aching shock through my system.

I can't. As much as I want to, I can't. It feels too much like cheating, though I know in my head, it shouldn't.

I push away from him regretfully; my fingers moving to gently caress the soft ebon waves of his hair.

He's so beautiful…

"Ethan…I can't. Not when you're like this."

Curling on the floor amidst the disorderly lump of blankets and spare pillows, legs crossed and head hanging, I spew out a very unconvincing explanation of why I can't crawl in bed, pin his arms down and ride him until he moans and begs for more.

After I've run myself breathless from my 10 minute speech, I look up at him and he's passed out, with his head dangling off the side of the bed. With a sigh, I position him comfortably and wrap myself in my blankets, curling up with my phone as the hard floor presses against every bony prominence.

Unlocking the phone, my eyes focus on the straight, clinical black letters set against the stark white screen, and run my finger over them absently. Alexander R. Delacroix. With hormones rushing through my body from the impromptu make-out session with an incredibly sexy British man, my heart still aches for him.

He doesn't have time for me. He may never have the time, and instead of taking Ethan up on his offer, I'm still too wrapped up in Alex to think straight.

I press his name and bring up a text message, idly scrolling through past conversations and smiling as I reminisce. They were sparse, with days or weeks between replies, and yet just knowing he'd responded…

This is ridiculous. I'm head over heels for a school girl worthy crush.

Scowling, I type up a message…just a simple "How are you?" I don't expect him to reply, and a glance at the clock reveals the ungodly hour of 4 a.m. With the sun only an hour or two from rising, I rest my head on a pillow and reposition my body in an attempt to find the most comfortable position possible on the hard, cold floor.

As my eyelids fall, I see him waiting for me in the darkness, his hands brushing over my skin as his scent smothers me. My heart hammers against my chest, aching, as he lovingly slips a sharpened dagger through my rib cage and gently massages the dull side against my heart.

Chapter 14

I awaken to the groans of my bedroom guest as he stumbles from my bed, nearly crushes my ankle as he steps over me, and crawls his way to the bathroom. As he reaches the tile floors, he collapses face first, groaning in pain.

"Caaasssss…" he calls weakly.

"What…on earth…"

"Can you help me?" he whines "Please? I feel awful. I feel like I've been run over."

Standing, I stretch my back, which unfortunately aches from my night on a freezing hard floor, and wander over to him. I offer my hand, and he crawls up my body like a vine on a tree, then somehow manages to steady himself long enough to run the shower without diving headfirst into the bathtub.

"I think…I'm just going to wash up."

"Mhm. I'll meet you downstairs. Try not to drown in the tub, okay? I'm really not up for burying a body today."

He looks at me with a mix of fear and dread, and with a smirk, I turn on my heel and head downstairs.

Riley and Tom are still cuddled up on the pull out couch, with one of her legs draped over his hips, and his arms wrapped around her. I don't know how they could sleep comfortably like that.

It must be nice to have semi-stable relationship like that, where you could yell and bitch at each other, then still wind up snuggling in bed together at the end of the night. Maybe I'm just not cut out for that kind of thing. I feel torn, as if some force has separated my desires into left and right halves then split me down the middle. Half of me aches for love; the thought of having a house, a husband, a white picket fence and a baby on my hip. The other half can't stand it.

Why should I have to tie myself down to one man? How could a single person possibly offer me everything I want out of life? Is there even a person out there who could keep up with my high sex drive? And if they cannot, would I be able to stay happy with someone who couldn't satisfy me as often, or as completely, as I want?

Slipping into the kitchen, I pull out a pan to fry some eggs, and go about making breakfast as I push those conflicting thoughts from my head. I'm not nearly as good with cooking as Riley is, but how hard could it be to whip up a few eggs, hash browns and bacon for breakfast?

Apparently, it's harder than I originally thought. Half an hour, and several foul words later, the bacon is black, and the fried eggs are more reminiscent of peeling yellow wallpaper.

Riley was rudely awoken by the smell of burned bacon, and attempted to rush to my rescue, but the damage was already done.

With a scowl, she tosses my poor attempt at breakfast in the trash, and shoves me toward the living room where I help Tom pack away the sofa bed, and shove some Tylenol down his throat to help with the headache. As we go about setting the table for breakfast, Ethan decides to stumble down the steps to the main floor. These men really can't hold their liquor. It's almost embarrassing! But being the lady I am, I won't tease about how hopeless they were in their intoxicated state last night.

We settle in at the table as Riley comes out with perfectly cooked bacon, fried eggs, and hash browns for our late morning breakfast. As I reached for the orange juice, Ethan catches my eye, blushes, and looks back down at his plate. I'm not sure if he remembers everything from the night before, but I'm sure a few memories have begun to resurface if he's managed to produce that particular shade of crimson on his cheeks.

Mentally patting myself on the back, I smile inwardly, proud of myself for not taking advantage of him in his inebriated state. That's not to say I didn't want to. Oh, did I want to! His voice alone still sends shivers down my spine and causes those oh-so-sensitive areas of my body to ache in desire. In fact, I'm fairly certain I could get off just listening to his deep, silken voice.

It's hard to take my eyes off of him as I slip quick, inconspicuous glances at him between bites of food. His dark hair is still damp from his hasty shower, and small droplets of water leave a shimmering trail down his neck from a hasty towel dry.

He looks up and catches me staring, and I blush as he reaches across the table to run his fingers over my hand.

Would being with him really be so bad? Maybe deep down, he's a freak just like me. I wonder…

The thought brings a sly smile to my lips. Taking his hand in mine, I squeeze gently, shifting just a bit in my seat as he clears his throat and begins talking to Tom about his upcoming trip to New York City.

Oh that voice… it's like listening to pure sex.

I bite my bottom lip, focusing much too intently on the perfectly fried egg on my plate in an attempt not to think of such dirty thoughts, as his deep voice teases my ears.

I wonder how he would sound when he moans…

Riley glances over, noticing our joined hands, and immediately lets out an overly loud gasp followed by a mocking "Aww!!!" She rushes over and wraps her arms around my shoulders, hugging me close

"So…" she smirks "did you two have a nice night?"

Coughing, I withdraw my hand from his. Nothing happened, we both know that, but the extra attention and mocking from Riley would make anyone uncomfortable. She squeezes my arm and begins picking up the plates.

"Cass! Don't be rude. Come help me put everything away!" she mutters through gritted teeth.

With a roll of my eyes, I follow her into the kitchen, gathering as many dishes as I can carry in the process. I know where this is going. She's going to question me, then encourage me to pursue a relationship with this cute little British biscuit.

As I walk quietly to the kitchen to wash the dishes, she comes and hugs me from behind, resting her chin on my shoulder.

"What happened last night? I don't remember much of anything, but I'd simply *love* all the details on you and Ethan sharing a room."

"Nothing happened, Riley."

"You can tell me! I promise I won't gossip to Tom about the size of his brother…"

"Riley! Comparing sizes? That's disgusting! Besides, nothing happened. I wasn't going to take advantage of him. Who knows whether he would've actually wanted to engage in such activities! He was completely wasted. He probably would've gotten motion sickness, anyhow, and threw up all over the bed. It was bad enough I had to lug everyone to bed, I didn't want to be on cleanup duty as well." I laugh.

"Hmph!" she groans, and lets me go. "That's no fun at all. You should know how he feels about you, by now. He hasn't exactly been subtle. Well, maybe a little subtle. He hasn't exactly thrown you against a wall and kissed you yet. At least, not that I know of…" she grabs me and forces me to face her "has he!?"

"We may have kissed a little last night. He surprised me with it. It didn't go any further than that."

"Oh! So, do you think it *might* go further?" she beams.

"Riley, I really can't deal with that right now. I'm busy, you know, with work and everything. Two jobs is a lot to keep up with."

"And busy with that other guy that you still haven't told me about."

"It's really not all that important…"

"But I'm your friend! And I think I deserve an explanation for your recent random disappearance."

I sneak a peek through the door of the kitchen to where Tom and Ethan are seated. Their faces are stoic; it must be an intense conversation. I turn back to Riley, who is staring at me with daggers in her eyes.

"Riley, I highly doubt it'll happen again. It was just a fluke. I didn't go over there expecting anything to…"

"So you *did* have sex. Don't you think you're leading Ethan on, then?"

"I'm not! I like him, I just don't think I'd be good for him. I don't want to make up that whole 'It's not you, it's me' bullshit, but in this case, I think it may hold true. I don't know, Riley. It's…really hard to explain. This guy has really gotten to me." I shake my head in frustration, turning back to the dishes. "Why are you grilling me over this?"

"Don't sass me, woman!" she exclaims then drops her eyes to the floor. "I just want to help…" she mumbles "You look so unhappy, sometimes. Lonely. I want to see you happy with someone."

"I don't need any one person to be happy, Riles. Besides, I have you!" I smile, and give her a big hug. I can feel the tension drain out of her as she returns my embrace. How long has she worried about me like this?

"You're lucky I love you." She smiles, reaching behind me and pinching my ass as she walks out.

Once the dining room is cleaned up, the two men leave. It had been a long night for both of them, and I can only assume they're going to nurse what's left of their pride from having a woman drag them indoors and put them to bed. Ethan is due to hop on a plane in three days to New York City for a convention on some new medication, and I somehow got roped into driving him to the airport.

Since he was only here a few weeks on a contract with a local hospital, he had been driving a rental car and originally enlisted the services of Tom to get him to the airport. However, Tom had something of his own come up and had to back out, and a taxi from here to New Orleans would be a disgusting amount of money. So here I am, signing myself over to be Ethan's personal chauffer.

Deep down, I know I jumped onboard because driving into New Orleans would give me an excuse to see meet up with Alex to discuss the article I've written about him. Assuming, of course, that I can actually get ahold of him. I've put it off for a month with Angela, knowing I had no real substance for it since all of my meetings with

Delacroix have been somewhat… off subject. I just wanted to see him for research purposes. That's all. Really…

Chapter 15

The days leading up to Ethan's departure dragged by, as if I were struggling through a moat of molasses. I did, however, have some time to grade papers so I wouldn't have to make up yet another excuse to my students as to why I still had no grades posted for them. It was a daunting task to tackle, but it successfully distracted my thoughts from Alex long enough for me to feel some degree of normalcy. I'm sure my lovely students will appreciate all my hard work, though that may be a bit of a stretch. Once the papers are done, I change gears and look over my article for the magazine this week.

I wouldn't go so far as to say I'm 'employed' by L*Addict*; I write articles on whatever my heart desires, and if they like it, they'll buy it from me. It's usually not much in the form of compensation, but I get this sense of pride from seeing my name on the page. Riley, in her desire to help boost my self-esteem a bit and out of her own pride for me, has bought a copy of every magazine that I've had an article in.

The article I've written for this week is essentially my rant on the taboo nature of sex. No one talks about it, unless you live in New Orleans, but New Orleans is practically its own state with its own set of rules. The education on it in schools is lackluster and not just here, but throughout the country, and meanwhile everyone runs around scratching their heads and wondering why STD's and teen pregnancies are running rampant in our country. Sex is a natural act! It should be explained with no more awkwardness than teaching a child how to brush their teeth properly. They need to know what to expect, how to stay safe, and the magnitude of making that kind of decision. By keeping it taboo and forbidden, we're only enticing them to act out of rebellion!

I glance at my phone as I look over the article. No flashing lights, no chimes of a message. I do a quick run through of the article, read it aloud to make sure it has the flow I want, then pack it away in my bag. I rake a pen across a post-it and shove it on the wall above my desk, reminding me to drop it off in the morning. I really can't afford to forget it again, and recently, it feels as if I would forget my pants in the morning if I were distracted enough. My mind seems to be full of distractions these days.

More like one, persistent distraction.

Peering at the phone once more, I fiddle with the home button and unlock it. Maybe I just missed it or cleared the screen without realizing…but there's nothing. No new messages from him. I take a deep breath and lean back in my chair, closing my eyes and concentrating on the gentle sound of the breeze rustling through the trees outside my window, to distract from the pang of disappointment that's settled in my chest. It's been one day. He's gone longer without contacting me. There's no need to start stressing myself out about it, right? I'm too old to be acting like this. It's disgusting.

That familiar ache of longing grows as the memories pull at me. The feel of his hands on my skin, how the sun glinted off his glasses, and the way it set his hair aflame. This beautiful, unobtainable creature has ripped me to pieces and left me wanting more. Wanting…needing; the two have come to mean the same. My desire has become a need, and my body calls out to him as if he were oxygen to my starved lungs.

I run my fingers over my phone as I recall

every exquisite detail. Did it happen? It seemed so surreal. How has this single man found ways to make me squirm and ache in ways I didn't think possible.

Chapter 16

The act of sex itself has always been a very carnal act to me. It's this need that has been driven by the desire to feel another's touch. The clothes that are stripped away reveal a true beauty within every curve and every small imperfection. Every skin discoloration and birth mark; every stretch mark and scar is a natural, raw masterpiece that has been bound in human form and forced to cower behind a cover of clothes and polite conversation. But when you're behind closed doors, and that cover has been stripped, you fall into this all-consuming dance. You cease to be a lawyer, a doctor, a secretary or grocery store clerk and become a passionate, primal being. Your bodies find a certain common rhythm within one another; moving and beating as one. Every individualized thought is extinguished in the presence of passion, and when the dust has settled, those memories have always been so easy filed away for me. There is no tie to them. No expectations. This person has bared their soul and released their inhibitions for a night of release; a single night in which they are not judged for the passions of their heart, then it's over.

I often think of it as a favor. I'm allowing them to express themselves in a way that is best done in the company of another. Remembering the desires of one night is not conducive to my everyday life, however. It doesn't fit into the 'norm'. How seriously would I be taken if I blatantly expressed myself to those I interact with every day? I highly doubt Riley would want to hear my thoughts on being so openly sexual.

Society has bred a race of humans with a sense of embarrassment. We're embarrassed to love, to feel, to become excited and flustered. We are pressed into boxes and force fed ideas of chastity and life-long love, then bound together with one person 'till death do we part'. What about those who don't fit into societies perfect boxes? Are they doomed to feel some sense of loss and shame for not seeing themselves flawlessly pieced into the ideal relationship? The picture perfect relationship where the woman is a virgin, and any thoughts of sex other than to reproduce strictly in a missionary position, are abhorrent? Those who are labeled freaks? Those misunderstood monsters that are slaves to their passions?

And yet, there are times when I want to be in that box. A part of me wants to be dressed in white, with family and loved ones around me as someone takes my hand and pledges their undying loyalty and devotion to me. Are they my own desires, or is this growing beast within me, a reminder of my body's own rebellion against forced ideal standards of life?

Another day has passed with yet more restless sleep, and I find myself sitting at my desk again, gazing out the window as I watch the sun sashay across the sky. Minutes. Hours. I don't know anymore. I feel like Riley hasn't been home all day. Maybe she hasn't. The house is deathly quiet, and each creak and groan from the house picks away at my sanity.

Shaking my head, I rest it in my hands, then glance at the phone. The light in the corner is flashing blue, and my heart skips several beats. I unlock it, my fingers shaking in anticipation as my heart pounds against my ribs, shattering pieces like crumbling cement.

Sadly, my hammering heart is disappointed, as the text is from Ethan and not from Delacroix. He was confirming the time he'd come by tomorrow, and reminding me of the time his flight leaves. Thankfully it's a desolate morning hour, and so, the traffic should be near non-existent.

I reply to confirm, then check the time. It's five in the evening already. Where did the first half of the day go? When did I wake up? At least it's not too early to pour a glass of well-deserved wine. After all, I managed to grade my papers *and* proof my article within the last couple of days. I'll write that off as the beginning of a fairly productive week; and productive weeks call for a treat.

I steal away to the kitchen to pour a glass of wine, and grab some leftover spinach tartlets from yesterday. The wine isn't the good stuff I'd brought home as my apology to her, but it'll get the job done just the same.

My new bottled friend accompanies me to the living room, and I light the fire in the hearth. A cold front has come through, and left the evenings and nights well into the 40's. Riley loves opening the windows when the weather cools down; it's a nice respite for us northerners to not be smothered by humidity and heat once in a while, and there's nothing quite like a bottle of wine by the fire.

The house is quiet except for the crackling of charring wood, and I can't remember where Riley told me she was going. My mind struggles to sort through an ever-thickening haze. Was it to

Tom's again? Or Melissa's? Or was it Tonya? Did she even tell me she was going somewhere? I don't keep up with all of her friends.

I set the glass on the coffee table and curl up, flicking the remote to stream some music from the speakers in the corner. Slow, sensual notes spill from them and pour out over the floor, filling my head and giving me a much deserved break from my ridiculous fixation.

Stretching across the couch, my eyes close as I let the music fill me. I can feel everything; the heat from the fire, the breeze whispering through the windows. I can hear the silence broken by the crackling fire and the sweet song of the wind as it twists with the music. Breathing deep, I relish in the rhythm of my heart as it beats slow and steady, swaying along to the notes pouring from the speakers.

It's not long before my sweet relaxation is cut with the buzzing of my phone vibrating on the coffee table. I peek over at the lighted screen and see my mom's name. I can't ignore it, or she'll keep chain calling me and leaving frantic voice mails, thinking that the reason for me not picking up is because I got shot or mauled in some way.

Reaching over, loathing the thought of having to get off the couch, I clumsily grasp the edge of the phone with my fingertips, and work it into my hand.

"Mom?"

"Hey, sweetie! How are you? How are things? How's Riley?"

"Fine. Everything is fine, mom. Do you need something?"

I love my mom, I do, but every time I hear her voice, it grips my heart in a vice. She was great, really. She did the best she could, but she was a single parent, and became very ill when I was young. The stress of her job drove her to a breaking point, and I was left alone to pick up the shattered pieces at the tender age of 10. I took care of her, but I don't think she ever recovered. I don't think I ever recovered either. Whenever she visits, or calls, it's hard to listen to her because she's still so broken, and it brings up so many of those bad memories. Seeing her fracture like that tore something from me…something I never gained back, and though I may try to hide my frustration and fill my voice with love every time I speak with her, it hurts. This painful ache in my chest makes it hard to speak. The sound of her voice retells the story of when she fell apart every time I hear it, and try as I might, I can't smother down those thoughts with anything other than avoidance. I'm not proud of it; I just don't know how else to handle it. Sometimes I'm afraid she'll hear a hint of it in my voice...

"Yes! Sweetie, do you remember Emmanuel, your second cousin? He and your great-aunt are coming for a visit! It's been so long since we've all been together, and I was hoping to get everyone to come over for their visit! I'd love if you came. It's been so long since you've been home."

Our family is pretty extensive, with great aunts and second and third cousins scattered all over the globe. They tend to keep in contact with each other and will sometimes get it in their heads to have these huge family reunions. Usually the reunions are just holiday meet-ups for Thanksgiving or Christmas, and solely consist of my direct aunts, uncles, cousins and grandparents. No seconds or third or fourths, just the people I primarily grew up around. I like it that way, as I don't know the distant family nearly as well as my mother does.

My last encounter with Emmanuel was something I've tried to purge from my memory. We were thirteen, or rather, I was thirteen. He was seventeen or eighteen at the time, and much taller. He was like a giant to me; well over six feet at his age, and I was just barely reaching five feet. He was big, intimidating, broad shouldered and built like a linebacker. He took advantage of my innocence, and my shy, withdrawn disposition. I'll never forgive him. Hell, I wouldn't douse him with piss if he were on fire.

"Uh, actually, I really have a lot of work to do. When is this whole get-together supposed to be happening?"

"I was hoping for next weekend. That's when they'll be up. Can't you bring your work with you? I know Emmanuel would love to see you. He's mentioned you a few times! He must have fond memories from when you hung out as kids."

"Yeah, mom. I'm sure he does," I reply flatly, trying to hide the anger in my voice. "I'm really sorry. I don't think I can bring it with me. I have some really important things coming up and I really can't make it up there. Please pass along my best wishes to Aunt Meg?"

"Oh, of course, sweetie. Try not to work too hard. Maybe you can come up for Christmas? Or I can come down there, too!"

"Yeah, sure. Sounds like a great idea. I really need to get back to work. I'll talk to you later, okay?"

"Alright, honey. Don't work too hard or you'll work yourself into an early grave! I love you,

Cassie."

"Love you too, mom."

I hang up and resist the urge to toss the phone into the fire. The sound of his name makes my skin crawl, and the memories I managed to smother for the last half of my life are threatening to overtake me. Sure, I tried therapy when I was 18 and old enough to go without parental consent, but it never worked. They wanted to talk about everything else, or suggest I speak with a doctor, or shove pills down my throat, or go into special victim counseling. Me? A victim? I can't even stomach the thought of it, now. I just don't want to think about it. I don't want to remember him, or any of them. I felt abandoned when I needed my family the most, and I've found that I don't need them as much as I thought. I can do it alone. I've always done it alone. I've always managed to survive, and I'll survive now. I can't let this unravel me. I'm stronger than that.

Draining the rest of the wine from my glass, I place the half empty bottle in the fridge. I don't want to be home tonight. I don't want to sit around in silence and let my thoughts bombard me with fragmented pieces of the past which, just for fun, mixes with pieces from the present into a bleeding mirror ball that tells the story of my life. I want to be numb. I don't want to feel.

I walk up to my room, throw on something partially acceptable, and make the decision to head to the bar. If I'm going to go numb, at least I'll do it around people so I'll feel a little less pathetic. Maybe this will be good for me. Some fresh air may be a nice distraction. I may actually find someone who could use their brain for more than "Hey baby, what's your number?"

Grabbing my keys, I shove my phone in my coat pocket and start my walk to a local bar.

Chapter 17

The bar isn't much to look at. It's a squat, brown building the owners tried to spruce up with fake palm trees and Christmas tree lights year round, but since it's in a decent part of town there aren't many bar fights or rowdy crowds.

I walk up to the worn wooden bar and find a stool on the corner between a man in a black fedora and matching overcoat, and a blonde woman who looks as if she has had too much fun with Botox injections. In an attempt to turn her late 40 year old face into that of a 20 year old, she succeeded instead, on looking like a melting wax model held together with scotch tape.

The man in the fedora looks as if he's stepped out of an old black and white 1950's gangster movie. The overcoat hides a small beer gut brought on by an over indulgence in the frothy amber barrel, no doubt.

The woman is flirting and flipping her hair as she talks to a young 20-something with a Mercedes key ring and a thick wallet. I assume he's the one buying her drinks. What he sees in her is anyone's guess. She's laughing playfully as she inconspicuously works a diamond band off of her ring finger and tucks it into the purse sitting on the bar stool behind her. Slip it in a hiding place where no one ever goes, Mrs. Robinson. I won't tell a soul.

As I settle in, I'm greeted by the bartender. He's a man around his late 30's with an impressive beard and fitted black t-shirt. He's not bad looking at all, and the hint of toned abs presses beneath the cotton cloth of his shirt. He leans over the bar and flashes me a grin.

"What'll ya have, darlin'?"

His bulging biceps and broad chest ripple as he leans against the bar. He's hot in a very lumberjack sort of way, but his southern accent sets my teeth on edge. After living here for the last few years, I still haven't gotten used to it. It's more defined in some than others, but those who hold that strong accent make my skin prick with their words. I've found the majority of those down here are incredibly sweet and nice; it's not something you'd find up north...but that accent. I can't stand it.

Maybe I'll get used to it someday, but that day isn't today.

I share my sweetest smile with him in an attempt to hide my pained facial expression brought on by his southern drawl.

"I'd love a whiskey sour, please."

"Sure thing."

It's only been a couple of days since my evening with Delacroix, and I'm already aching to the point of frustration. I hate it. I don't want to feel that desire, especially not after that call.

Scolding myself, I dig my nails into the palm of my hand and grit my teeth. I might need a few drinks tonight…

The bartender brings my drink and I busy myself stirring with the cherry as I mentally go over my article again. Does it have the right feel to it? Will Angela like it? I really could use the money right now…

The gentleman to my left shifts and orders a drink, though his words are mumbled through a deep, harsh Irish accent. As I catch the drink being placed before him through the corner of my eye, he pushes it with the back of his hand till it rests glass to glass against my own drink. I cock an eyebrow and look over at him. He smiles, tips his hat and mutters…

"You look like you need it."

Who am I to argue with an Irishman about a drink? I shoot back the first drink, then tease the second with its' cherry as I pull out my phone and try to look occupied. As grateful as I may be for a free drink, I'm in no mood to really try and attempt conversation. Sadly, feigned occupation isn't exactly the biggest hint to some people.

"Come here a lot, do you?"

"Not usually." I mutter; my eyes still focused on the illuminated screen in my hand. Fuck, I'd make the trip to New Orleans at this hour just for another touch…

"Aye. Me neither. Actually my first time here, but they don't hold a candle to the pubs I'm used to. What brings you here tonight, if you don't mind?"

"I think I just needed a bit of fresh air. Time to clear out my head, you know?"

"Yeah? I know the feeling. We all need a bit of time to air out once in a while."

He seems to lose himself in the thoughts

swirling about in his glass and I'm grateful for the silence. I have absolutely no desire to make conversation this evening. The thoughts crashing through my head are all consuming, and I struggle to bring myself to the present. At the moment, I'm being rude.

I clear my throat as I struggle to grasp at some semblance of conversation but fail. He looks forlorn, and it tugs at my humanity and the deeply hidden instinctual feelings to try and make him feel better. I get the odd image of me grabbing him and hugging him tight just to squeeze the sadness from him, but know I wouldn't act on it. It would be quite odd to walk up to some stranger and give them a giant hug, and he could have me arrested for battery! Isn't that a sad thing, not wanting to hug someone for fear that they'll have you thrown in cuffs and booked? Kindness doesn't get you anywhere anymore.

Taking a breath, I clear the thought from my head.

"I'm sorry. I'm not very good with idle conversation. I never really have been. Thanks for the drink, though. It was nice to meet you."

They're empty pleasantries, but he accepts them graciously as he hides his eyes beneath the shadows cast by the brim of his hat.

I choose to walk the few blocks to the house instead of calling for a cab. It's a nice night, and I'm hoping the air will help untangle my thoughts.

The streets are ever-darkening as the lights span further and further between one another. The humidity adds an eerie shimmer to their yellowed glow. As I step through the door, I strain my ear for some sign or sound of Riley, but receive none. Hopefully, she's still out.

My body is on fire from the alcohol, and the internal battle between anger and shame is slowly drowned out. The lust always wins when the sun goes down.

Pulling out my phone, I browse the diminishing list of lovers. Maybe Riley won't come home tonight, but bringing someone to the house is far too risky. As I swipe through the contacts, settle on a particularly passionate lover. He's a sexy, beast of a man named Adrian. I send out the text and give him my home address to pick me up. We've known each other, and fed one another's lustful yearnings on more than one occasion since I moved here. I guess you can say we have developed an almost trusting relationship. Well, as trusting of a relationship as you can have with someone you fool yourself into believing doesn't exist unless you're tugging against your own leash, and slavering like a starved dog staring down at a fresh piece of meat.

Twenty minutes later, he pulls up outside the door. I slip into the passenger's side of his car and we make the drive back to his place. My body is writhing in anticipation as the alcohol courses through my blood. I reach over and rest my hand on his thigh, feeling the toned muscles tense beneath my fingertips. He casts a sidelong glance in my direction, the edge of his lip curling into a devilish grin as he returns the gesture, inching his fingers slowly up the inside of my thigh. Leaning over, I press my lips to the side of his neck as he drives, my fingers sliding further along the inside of his thigh. His breathing accelerates in time with the car as his blood throbs beneath my lips.

As we turn into his driveway, I can barely contain myself. He pulls his neck from my lips and hands as he turns off the car and walks around to open my door. I stand and close the door, gripping his shirt and slamming him against the car in a primal rage. My body running purely on instinct. On desire. Every nerve is tingling and burning, begging for the sweet release of his body against mine.

He gives in to my will, wrapping his arms around my hips as he presses his lips passionately against my neck. The thoughts of the day drain from my mind as our bodies meld with the shadows of the night. There's no Emmanuel, no mom, no Delacroix, no Ethan, no Riley. I'm nothing more than a starved animal. I need this like an addict needs their drug, and nothing will stop me from getting my fix.

My hands tremble as I tug at his clothes, threatening to tear the fabric, and his skin, to shreds if I have my way. Right now, I want him. Just…him, don't I?

His hands slip up my abdomen and lightly brush my breasts through my thin bra, causing my nipples to perk and harden instantly at his touch. I moan, my eyes fluttering as my teeth clamp down on my bottom lip. Groaning, he grabs my hips, turning my back to the car and lifting me onto the hood as I rip his shirt open and trace my lips down his neck and chest. His hands move from my breasts to my sides, tickling his fingertips along my hips as they slip to the small of my back. His dark, tanned skin shimmers with sweat in the faint light cast by the street lights.

I've lost track of time, but thankfully there aren't many houses on this street, and even less traffic at this hour. Not that I'd care at this point. I need it. I need *something*. It's been days now since I've had it, and before that, a month. I'm starving, and I haven't been properly satiated.

I need this.

My mind is reeling from the mixed scent of sex and the musk of his sweat, and my body drinks it in like a drug. Tugging my pants from my hips, his hands run up my back as he presses against me. I can feel his desire for me growing as he moves his lips to my neck. His kiss electrifies my already starved body, and causes me to shudder against him, gasping...moaning. His hands move further up my back, his nails lightly scratching against my skin. I rest my chin against his shoulder as he grinds his hardening erection against me. Whimpering in his ear, he continues to assault my neck with impassioned kisses and hungry licks. Higher and higher his hands travel, and my eyes flutter to a close. I want him. Hell, I want anyone right now.

His lips part and I feel his teeth grate against my neck, biting down hard as his hand reaches the back of my neck. His fingers tangle themselves in my hair as he rips his mouth from my neck and tugging my hair firmly.

My body tenses and, behind closed eyes, I can smell the smoke of Delacroix's cigarettes mingling with the scent drifting from Adrian's skin. My hands move to his back, digging my nails into his flesh and scratching deep, which only spurs him on. With one hand still in my hair, he moves his other down the front of my pants and between my thighs. His fingers easily worm their way beneath my panties and tease my sensitive clit, running his fingers back and forth before sliding one inside.

I gasp and moan as he slides his finger in and out... and Delacroix is there, sliding his fingers between my thighs, tugging my hair as he presses me against the wall and kisses me passionately with fire and desire on his lips. He's there, with his heated poison seeping between my lips to run rampant through my blood.

I drop one hand to my side, digging my own nails into my palm.

Stop it. Stop thinking about him.

Adrian picks up his pace, sliding them in and out faster and faster, and my head is swimming with a mix of desires. My mind teases out hallucinations of Alex's body against mine as he overtakes my senses, blocking out the feel of Adrian's rippling muscles beneath my fingers. My mind struggles to remain grounded; to remain in the moment, but my body refuses and begins to shut down. The tension and desires drip from my flesh, sailing away on the heat emanating from my body until I'm left as a hollow shell.

What the hell am I doing here?

I can still feel his hands groping my body, but the ache is gone. The daunting desires which drowned my damned soul have dissipated, devolving into the delicate disease of rationality. My body grows numb. The image of Adrian, the feel of the wind against my flesh, the heat rolling off his body. All of it slips away as my desire falters, seizes then shuts down.

He picks me up and carries me into the house, laying me on the bed as he hovers over me, and I'm disconnected; stuck watching the scene play out before my eyes. Watching him slide into me, watching my body writhe on the bed beneath him, hearing the convincing and very well-rehearsed moans slip from my lips. I can see and hear it all, but I'm not a part of it. It's akin to watching porn on my home computer. It's not happening to me, it's happening to someone else and I'm doomed to linger here…watching.

Once he's spent and panting, he cleans us both up, and offers to drive me home. I smile, agree and climb in the car, but I'm hollow. I'm lost. Completely void of all emotion and feeling from the moment I began to smell Alex's cigarettes, and feel his eyes, unwavering, on my trembling body.

Easing the door shut, I place my keys beside

Riley's in the dish we keep near the door. Removing my shoes, I walk slowly up the stairs in an effort to keep them from creaking beneath my feet. In my room, I close the door, strip down, take a quick shower and crawl into bed. As I close my eyes, he's waiting for me again; his jaw set and stars in his eyes as he runs his fingers playfully over coiled rope. His words drip into my ears,

"Why didn't you tell me you were so excited?"

My exhausted mind slips into an uneasy sleep; dreams permeate with flashing images of his eyes, the feel of his hot breath against my skin, the cold snap of cuffs around my wrists. He stands before me, and with a snarl, presses his hands against my chest, pushing me backward. My body balances on the edge of a precipice, and as I reach out to him with bound hands, he grins and stands stalwart with his arms at his sides. My heart bounds from my body and clings to the edge as my body slips away, disappearing over the lip of a large depression and falling…falling…plunging into darkness so complete that I cannot see my own hands in front of my face. And I become a memory. Nothing more than a disembodied voice on a ghost wind.

Chapter 18

Riley is sitting on the edge of my bed, gently shaking my shoulder as I groan. Is it so much to ask for a few more hours of sleep?

"Cass…" she whispers.

I roll my eyes and look over at her. She's dressed in a white, flowing skirt and black top. I glance out the window; it's still pitch black and she doesn't look like she's slept yet.

"Cass! Oh, thank god!" she squeals, and wraps her arms around me best she can, in a huge bear hug. She pauses, then inhales deeply with her arms still wrapped around me.

"Cass…" she hesitates as she pulls away, staring at me with scorned eyes "you smell weird. Musky, like a man…where have you been?"

"I went to a bar. I guess the shower didn't completely get rid of the stench of desperate, sweaty, gross men. Remind me never to go there again. And what do you mean 'Thank god'? I'm not dead."

"I came home last night and you weren't here, then I saw that you still weren't home by the time I finally went to bed. I called a few times and didn't get an answer. I was worried!"

"I'm fine. It's still dark…what time is it? Why are you waking me up? What are you dressed for?" I grumble. This is not exactly how I'd prefer to start my morning.

"You need to get up. Ethan will be here any minute."

"Ethan? For what?"

"How much did you drink last night, Cass?" she asks, raising an eyebrow. "You're supposed to take Ethan to the airport."

"What? No, that's tomorrow. What time is it?"

"It's 4 a.m."

"But he's not leaving till Wednesday."

"Cass, it *is* Wednesday."

Fuck.

I jump from the bed and rush to the bathroom, pulling on whatever I can find and dunking my head in the sink. As I run down the steps with the comb still picking through my curls, I open the door and am greeted by Ethan; his hand poised where the door had been just moments before in a pre-knock gesture.

"Ethan! I'm ready. Let's go."

Before he has time to say a word, I grab his hand and lead him to the car, hopping in and revving the engine.

"I'm so sorry," I explain frantically. "I must've lost track of the time…or days. I've been really busy lately…"

"It's fine Cass. We'll still make it on time." He reaches over and squeezes my hand gently as I shift the car into gear. My stomach lurches at his gesture; I feel like I'm going to throw up. Maybe I shouldn't have had those drinks.

The drive to the airport is quiet, though I suspect that's due more to the hour and how tired I'm sure we both are. I'm struggling to keep my eyes open in the darkness, the images of the last several days languidly sliding through my mind like drifting dreams etched out on the passing asphalt. How could I have gone through the last few days and completely forgotten what I've done? They're all one in the same, the hours and days. It's a monotonous droll of existence, and so, my mind seems to have seen fit to just merge it all into one. I really should get out more. Maybe the daylight will help to segment the days.

I peek quickly over at my passenger as we hit the spillway. His head is lolled off to the side, resting between the headrest and the window. His eyes are closed and his hair ruffles faintly in the current kicked up by the air conditioner, tickling the collar of his shirt.

We pull into a parking spot in the predictably empty airport, and I rouse him. Once we're inside, we navigate our way down stairwells and between over packed suitcases to the counter. As he picks up his tickets from the counter, he turns and wraps his arms around me. The smell of him clings to my body as I wrap my arms around him in turn, and hug tightly. For a brief second, his arms squeeze the stress and worries from my body. I inhale deeply, letting the turmoil fade from my head, and I feel happy. Happy, and at peace, and it does nothing but fuel a tiny spark of anger. I don't deserve this; I don't deserve any gesture so kind.

Not after who I am and what I've done. What…have I done?

I drop my arms to pull away but he doesn't release me. His face buries itself in my hair.

"I wish you could come with me." He murmurs softly, his voice muffled by my thick curls.

"I'm sorry?"

He finally releases me and holds my gaze; those ever shifting eyes of his are mesmerizing. Reaching up, he gently twirls one of my curls around his finger.

"I'll be up there for a few weeks. You should come with me. We could tour the city, and I know you miss your family there."

"Ethan, this isn't exactly something you can spring on me. I have work…I have prior obligations and appointments, and now is not the best for me to go back up there, anyhow."

"But don't you miss being with them? Where's that spontaneous spirit!"

"I really…I don't think I could see my family right now. I'm sure they're busy too."

My phone vibrates wildly in my back pocket and I reach for it, Ethan's eyes still holding mine as if he's daring me to answer it. I glance at the screen and my heart decides it's a fine time to travel into my throat. I silence the phone and slip it back.

I'd really rather not get into the reasons why I don't want to see my family, or why I can't just hop a plane and travel 1,300 miles away. Perhaps I could just defuse the situation.

I reach over and grab his hand, beaming sweetly at him.

"I'll still be here when you get back, and we can hang out more. Until then, you could always give me a call, you know. Besides, it'd be a bit awkward taking a trip when I have no luggage with me. I'm not spontaneous enough to hop a flight for several weeks without a single change of panties."

He smiles and leans down, kissing my cheek.

"Then I guess I shall say goodbye. I was hoping, on a whim, you'd join me in the air. Where is your sense of adventure!" he laughs, and brings my hand to his lips, kissing gently. "I look forward to seeing you upon my return."

"As do I." I smile forcefully, hoping that it

comes off as genuine. The chances of me allowing myself to warm up to him are slim, but he does have this very renaissance worthy nature. He possesses this sweet, hopeless romantic personality, and it sings to my secret pinning for a story book ending.

He releases my hand, straightens his dress coat with both hands, and takes off for the gate. As I wave him off, my phone begins vibrating again in my back pocket. I remove it and glare at the screen. It's him again. Of course it is. Days of unanswered replies to my scattered messages, and he expects me to jump whenever he calls upon me? Ridiculous.

Torn, mostly from guilt of ignoring a call regardless of the caller, I answer the phone.

"Hi…"

"What are your plans today?" he asks, stifling a yawn. Frankly, I'm surprised he's awake. It's just past six and I haven't known him to wake much before eight. Not that I know him well enough to predict his sleeping habits.

"I'm uh…" dare I tell him I'm even in the area? He hangs on the other end of the phone in silence, awaiting my answer, and I know lying to him wouldn't work. Lying to others isn't easy. Lying to myself, however, is a cake walk. Anyone can be convincing if they've first convinced themselves.

"My day is free, for the most part. I have to finish working on a piece that I'd like to have turned in by Friday."

"Ah. You should bring it over and let me take a look. Is it the one about me? Where are you?"

My heart is racing now from the sound of his voice playing their lovely lyrical notes through my ears.

"I'm at the airport. I was dropping off a friend..." Maybe he won't ask.

"Which airport?"

Damn.

"New Orleans."

"Oh wonderful. You're close, then. There's no excuse. Do you have your article with you?"

I thumb the flash drive on my keychain. It goes with me everywhere, and I have everything I've ever written backed up on it. This flash drive has traveled with me throughout my high school and college years, and has still held up strong. It still has every paper and poem I've written. I could never bring myself to delete anything, and often find myself reading back over things I've written in the past on whims of nostalgia.

"I have a copy," I answer softly "but it's on a flash drive. It's not a hard copy, or anything."

"That will do. You're about fifteen to twenty minutes away, yes? I expect you soon."

"Where should I…"

"The Quarter. I'm sure you remember how to get here." He interjects.

With that, he hangs up and I'm left listening to dead air. The busyness and general clamor of the airport builds around me to a deafening crescendo, as I catch up to my surroundings. I'd been whisked away from the moment I heard him, to a place where only the sound of his voice existed, and now find myself disoriented by the lights and sounds that are assaulting my senses.

Not wanting to disappoint, I head to my car and try to remember how to get to his home. As I weave through the small, confining one way streets of New Orleans, my heart rate begins to pick up with anticipation as I do a piss poor job of parallel parking just a block down the road from his house. Thankfully there's enough room for a bit of error between the two cars, and I manage to squeeze between them without causing any damage. I grip the wheel, take a deep breath, and convince myself to leave the car.

I walk through the courtyard, up the few steps to his front door and am surprised to find the door already cracked open. Walking through the expansive foyer to the back of the house, I find him sitting on the couch, his left ankle resting on his right knee to create a desk for his laptop. He looks up and smiles as the first hints of morning slip through the courtyard, shimmering down the foyer and brushing their fingertips on the edge of the living room.

"Come in! Please." He pulls the arm chair parallel to the couch, facing where he's seated. "Why don't you have a seat" he smirks.

Oh…I remember that chair.

I blush as I cover the few feet between us, and sit in front of him, my body shifting in the seat as memories of it shoulder their way to the front of my mind.

"So, Miss Roman, why don't we take a look at that article?"

My fingers wrap around my flash drive possessively. I've never let anyone touch it before.

It's my baby. My heart is in these files.

"I uhm… would you mind if I pulled it up for you?"

"Not at all."

He passes his laptop to me, and I run my fingers lightly over the keys, feeling the warmth from his hands still emanating from them. I plug the drive into the port, pulling up the article for him to peruse, then bite lightly on the inside of my cheek. It feels awkward having someone read my work while I'm there with them. I don't mind when dozens or hundreds of people read my article in the magazine, but I'm never physically there while someone pours over it and critiques it.

Pulling the laptop from my lap, his fingers brush lightly over my thigh, sending a warm tingle from my toes to my heart. He rests the computer back on the desk fashioned by his legs; eyes shifting as he scrolls through the document. It's impossible to read his expression. I'd hate to play poker with someone like him. What does he think? Does he approve? Does he think it's a complete utter piece of shit? It's not even finished yet. It's just…fragments. Ideas. Everything is scattered, and I'm frankly embarrassed that he's looking at it in this state.

After several minutes of silence and a few taps of his fingers to the keys, he saves the file and hands my flash drive back.

"It's not bad. I've made some minor grammatical corrections for you to review when you get home. All in all, color me a tad impressed, Miss Roman. Especially considering it isn't finished, and I didn't give you all that much to work with. Now, what about your other homework? I do hope that, after all this time, you've found the time to complete it."

His lips curl into a devious smirk, his eyes glinting just over the top of his glasses as he stares into my eyes. Oh those eyes. How I've missed them. My fingers lose their dexterity as I fumble over reattaching my flash drive to my key chain.

"My other homework?" I ask, attempting to sound innocent, but failing to hide the tremble in my voice.

He places the laptop on the floor, sliding it under the couch, then leans forward on his knees and holds my eyes firm with his own.

"Oh yes, Miss Roman. Your other homework. I really do hope you have it for me, lest there be consequences."

I find it hard to break from his gaze. It's penetrating; diving through my thoughts and seeking to unlock and unearth every deep secret. I pull my phone from my pocket, dropping my eyes to the screen and running my fingers hesitantly over it.

"Would you mind reminding me of the assignment…just to be sure, of course, that I have got it correct."

"I hope you aren't asking me to repeat my instructions, Cassandra."

He sits back, his hands resting relaxed on his thighs. He pats the side of the couch.

"Come sit down and show me your homework, quickly now. That's it. Now face me and read it to me."

As I settle in and face him, my hands begin to tremble with the phone in my hand. I'm not good at being put on the spot like this, even if it is just us. This man has seen every inch of my body, and now I'm speechless in front of him. I feel pathetic. I take a breath and bolster my courage.

"Okay well, you asked for a list, and so I typed one out with the intent of sending it as a message…"

"That's fine. Just read item by item. No need to spruce it up for me."

I clear my throat and bite my lip as my heart threatens to shatter my ribcage.

"Two thin twelve foot ropes, one pair of metal handcuffs, one pair of rope handcuffs, one vibrator and one pair of...uhm...beads."

"Beads hm? What kind of beads?"

It's embarrassing, and he's pushing for me to admit what they are. I'm sure he knows full well what kind of beads they are.

"A... uh. Well, they're anal beads..." I can feel the blood burst into my cheeks, threatening to set my face on fire from sheer embarrassment.

"Ah. Very good. What about the rest of your homework?"

I nod, and bring up the folder in my phone I've made solely to hide those pictures, then hand it over reluctantly. There are far more things in that phone than those pictures. Texts, calls, my entire illicit contact list...

He swipes through the photos with an uninterested look on his face, which only heightens my anxiety, then hands the phone back to me.

"Ropes and handcuffs? You're not such a novice after all, are you Miss Roman." He says casually.

"Very much a novice, I'm afraid. Just because I have those things doesn't mean I've actually had someone use them on me. It's been mostly for my own experimentation. My own interest in it…"

"Experimentation? On yourself?"

"Well yes, the best I can at least." I muster a small laugh. "It's made for a few panicked moments when I've gotten myself tangled and was too embarrassed to call for help."

He laughs, and squeezes my thigh, causing me to squirm under his hands. He takes notice, and that steeled gaze turns to a budding flame.

"Please stand for me, Miss Roman."

I oblige, convinced my beating heart can be seen pulsating through my skin and clothes. My fingertips press against my palm; nails bite into soft flesh in an attempt to calm my own nerves, and perhaps, to convince myself that I'm actually here with him again. It feels as if years have passed since I've felt his touch.

"It's quite hot, now that the sun is out, don't

you agree?"

I nod. The sun is streaming through the windows, turning the living area, with its large windows, into a giant green house. He stands from his seat and draws close to me. I can feel the heat of his skin against mine as he looks down at me, our foreheads an inch apart. He's so close and I want nothing more than to strip him down and run my hands over his heated skin. I want to feel that desire, that passion, seeping from him. I want to drink in his scent and feel his fingers drawing me to a much needed release, and yet, I daren't move a muscle. The ache grows as we stand in silence; the tension in every fiber of my body intensifying by the second. The minutes drag by and he says nothing, his eyes staring deep into mine until he unravels me. I tilt my head, my lips aching for a taste of his.

It's been so long…so long…hasn't it? How long has it been?

I feel like the night before never happened. It didn't, did it? Adrian doesn't exist, but Alex… I can't push him out. I don't want to push him out. I want him to envelope me and never let me go.

He smirks, pulling just out of reach of my lips. That's it. That's the look. That look in his eyes when he knows he has me.

"If you would be so kind, please remove your clothes, fold them, and place them on the table."

I smile, slyly, and begin to slowly pull my clothes off before him. I make no mention of the still open door that I neglected to close upon entering, or the unshaded windows. My eyes are on him, and I will damn well make sure that his are on me. The last few days didn't happen, and now I'm here with him again. I'm his again.

I lift my arms, pulling the hem of my shirt up with them. Then the pants, slowly, achingly tugging them from my wiggling hips. If he's going to be demanding, then I will take some of this for my own pleasure. I want him to ache for me; for him to want me the way I want him.

Obediently folding my top and pants, I place them on the table as requested, then bend over in front of him to remove my socks and shoes, being sure to offer him a full view of my body from behind. I can hear the floor creak as he shifts his weight. Smiling, I run my hands up my smooth legs then stand and face him, reaching behind to unsnap my bra and toss it on the neatly folded pile of clothes. I move to the couch and sit, spreading my thighs for him. I've wanted him every waking moment since the day we met, and it's about time

I've shown him just how much. Grinning at him, his eyes fixate on my body as I slip my hand from my breasts between my legs, lightly teasing myself through my panties. My eyes flutter, and my mouth gapes as I sigh and moan.

"Miss Roman, I don't believe I asked you to sit."

"Alex…" I moan as I slip a single finger under my panties and lightly tease my dampening slit.

"Stand up. Now."

I smirk, my defiance finally peeking through and putting its foot down. I've been lost in lust for this man, and I've finally got him here in front of me. I will let him know what it feels like to ache.

The power in his voice is hard to hold against, but I hold my ground, and pull my panties to the side, offering a glance at what the thought of him does to me. I gaze into his eyes and watch as those budding flames transition to a growing hunger.

Carnal and blood thirsty, he takes a deep, shuddering breath and sits in the arm chair across from me. Leaning forward, he places his elbows on his knees.

"Cassandra, we need to talk about the rules."

"I thought we had this discussion? Or did we not finish it. That night was a bit of a blur for me, honestly."

"We started. You gave one rule for the night, but threw yourself at me shortly after, and I dare say, we didn't quite get around to finishing our discussion." His head drops, his hand slipping along the back of his neck, and rubbing thoughtfully as he stares at the floor between his feet. "Cassandra, I don't normally do things like that. There's always structure. There are rules. Everything is hashed out beforehand so we know what to expect from one another. ...Do you know what this is?"

I sigh, the burning need in my body being smothered by his abrupt change of subject.

"Do I know what this is? To be quite honest, I don't. I don't know who you are, or what you want with me. What *is* this, Alex? Do you just like it a little rough now and then? Does spanking get you off? I'm all for spanking." I smirk, leaning forward and resting my elbows on my thighs. I peek at him as he raises his head, staring at me with an amused look in his eyes. "How deep does the rabbit hole go, Alex..."

"I need to know hard limits, soft limits, and

your desires. I need to know what *you* want, Cassandra. I need to know what excites you; what makes your blood burn with desire. And most importantly, I need to earn your trust."

I cock an eyebrow and rifle through my thoughts. Do I have any hard limits? I'm familiar with limits, but I've never sat down and had a talk with someone about desires and what I would and wouldn't do. Usually the conversations are about them. Their wants and desires...I don't often bring my own needs into play with my lovers. In the end, I wind up getting what I need, anyhow. What else matters?

"My trust?"

"Yes."

"I barely know you."

"Well, we'll have to fix that at some point, then, won't we?" He leans back in his chair, his fingers lightly dancing along the arm rest. "I need to know what I can, and cannot do with you."

"I'm uh. Honestly, I've never had this kind of conversation with someone before. I don't know if I have any hard limits, though I guess if I had to name anything...the thought of human excrement's and blood isn't exactly my thing. In addition to being incredibly unsanitary, it's a bit dangerous, isn't it? Speaking of which, we should probably…I'm assuming condoms will be a consistent thing?"

"Of course, unless you have another option. In the off chance that you do…" he leans back, grabbing a few papers from the coffee table and handing them over to me. I glance over them, thumbing through the three pages.

"These are…"

"Lab reports. Yes. To remove any doubt, of course. I'm not running around with any hidden diseases, and I have not engaged in any other sexual activities since you and I met. I'd assume something similar from you, as well, if you prefer to forego the usual latex jacket." He steeples his fingers under his chin and eyes me, a smile in his eyes.

"So this is something monogamous then?"

"I told you before that I tend to get a bit wrapped up in work, and can't really dedicate myself to a more long term or traditional relationship, but it doesn't mean we can't have a bit of fun, if you're willing."

I'm trying desperately to grasp his words, but they're sliding through me like water. Seeing him so close, being able to smell his scent and feel the heat from his body. His words no longer hold the same meaning. They're lustful promises whispered to a parched body, washing over me and coaxing me closer with the songs of promised pleasures. The more he talks, the more I want him and the less control I have over the movements of my own body. I'm sitting before him, near nude, trying to keep the conversation going and failing poorly. I want more from him. More than he can offer me, but I would kick myself for walking away from him. I've never been so…enchanted.

"Cassandra?"

I stare blankly at him. I hear him, but my mind isn't able fully comprehend what he is saying. My blood is pounding in my ears, an electric current washing over me from head to toe and back again, poising me on the edge of pleasure.

"I want you." I stutter.

"Please try and keep yourself focused."

"Alex, I don't care what you do to me; within reason of course. I'm willing to try anything once, and I haven't exactly had many experiences with a ton of different fetishes. The ones I have had experience with have been a bit less extreme, and on the more mundane side. Some blindfolds, some scratching. Nothing extreme, and so, I think it'll be fun to find out something new. If there's anything I don't like, I'll let you know and we'll go from there. Is that acceptable?"

He stares at me with a mixture of confusion and disbelief. I guess he wasn't expecting that kind of response.

"I suppose. It will need some revision as we go along…"

"I want to see how far I'll go. I want to see how much I can take, and experience all the things I've only ever fantasized about in my most fevered dreams. I want us to push each other's limits, and maybe, finally, find some contentment at the end of the night. That's what I want right now…out of…whatever this is."

"Pushing limits? Do you know what you're asking, Miss Roman?"

"Oh, I hope so." I smirk.

He stands, pulling me up into his arms in one swift motion, and presses his lips against mine. My body crashes against his like a wave on the cliffs as I liquefy, dripping through his gripping fingers. I inhale deeply, drinking in the scent of his body as his arms wrap around me tighter. His touch, fueled by animalistic desire, surges through my skin. I moan against his lips, relishing in the feel of our bodies pressed perfectly against one another. My fingers slide up the side of his face, teasing over the rough, unshaven beard, and tangle themselves in his hair. I love the feel of his curls in my hands, and can't help but caress each lovely twirl. His fingers grip my back, slipping down to my panties. He shows no remorse as he pulls them, their thin fabric straining against his fingers till they finally gave way and tear. The feel of cloth ripping leaves me stunned and aching as my body erupts in a deadly mix of pent up desires for him alone; fabricated by my addicted, delusional mind during lonely nights. The cage lifts in that moment, and my slavering beast consumes my body.

My skin prickles, each muscle tense as if assaulted by a raging typhoon as he wraps his arms around me and lifts, my legs wrapping around his waist. His hands grip under my thighs, holding me firmly in his grip, then kneels, leaning me back to rest on the couch. His hand slips along the floor under the couch, and he pulls out a thin, coiled rope.

"Do you trust me? Right here and now…do you trust me not to hurt you?"

I nod, breathless as my heart pounds out a rhythm that sings of heat and passion against my ribs.

"Stay still." He orders, though it seems near impossible.

My body is pulsating with each beat of my racing heart. It's no longer my own, and the overpowering strength of this raging monster is almost too much for me to handle.

A few deep breaths, and I manage to still my trembling body, if only for a few seconds. He straddles my thighs, pressing his forehead against mine. The heat of his breath washes over my skin as I struggle to keep myself from tilting my hips up against his body. Grabbing my wrists, he joins them above my head, then weaves the rope around and between them, securing them together from wrist to elbow in a delicate series of complicated knots with deft, expert fingers. His heated breath drips onto my skin, his lips following, gently kissing down my temples and over my cheeks as he secures the rope to the frame of the couch. My arms are bound tightly above my head, and I can't resist testing the knots. I tug hesitantly, and find I can barely move them. Damn. He's good.

He slides down my body, his tongue twisting over my body in an agonizing dance. I writhe beneath him, his tongue sparking a dozen stars to erupt along the surface of my skin. My eyes flutter, the worry and anxiety over feeling so exposed has become buried beneath a heady mix of lustful desires. He slips his tongue between my breasts and down my stomach, and as he approaches my hips, he smiles and pulls away. Placing his hands on the arms of the chair, he draws himself up and settles across from me.

My chest rises and falls too quick to count; my heart throbbing along with the rest of my body. I'm panting, struggling to control myself. Pulling away from me was agonizing, as if he'd severed a limb with a rusted machete. The pain was immediate, tearing through my body and leaving me to fall deeper, that hungry beast tearing pieces of my flesh and devouring me from the inside out. I tug against my binds, whimpering and begging.

"Please touch me."

His eyes flicker with a combination of hunger and amusement as he watches me thrash about on his couch like a fish on a hook.

"We will finish our discussion."

I whimper, tugging against the harsh ropes until they bite into my skin, threatening to rip the skin from my wrists, but something about the pain is almost soothing. It gives me something to concentrate on, and I draw in a shuddering breath and nod.

"How are you supposed to respond? Come now. We've gone over this once, and I hate repeating myself."

"Yes, Sir."

He smiles, leaning forward and running his finger lightly along the inside of my knee.

"You look delicious like that, and once we're done talking, we can get back to it."

How can he exhibit such control over himself? The heat coursing through me is enough to bring me to the brink of orgasm, alone.

"Since you seem unable to focus long enough to tell me what you want and don't; or rather, too inexperienced in this type of relationship to do so, I will tell you what I expect of you."

I guess my earlier spout wasn't good enough for him. His gaze holds mine once firmly and I'm hypnotized by them.

"I expect you to make yourself available whenever I call upon you. I'm not an unreasonable man, and so, if you have prior engagements, we can work around them. Though we haven't spent too much time together, after our first meeting, I realized that you have quite an insatiable hunger. With that said, I do expect you to exhibit control over yourself. This is, more or less, a monogamous relationship, with few exceptions that may be discussed at a later date. I need to trust you, and you'll need to trust me in turn."

Exceptions?

"Therefore, I fully expect you not to engage in any unapproved sexual relations with other men, or women for that matter. Understood?"

"Yes, Sir."

"Mm, you can be such a good little girl. You're doing so well controlling yourself. I haven't seen you thrash against those bonds for several moments, now."

He moves his finger from my knee and trails the tip further and further up, tracing circles along my inner thighs. I bite down on my bottom lip. I want to please him. I want to show him that I can control myself.

"Very good." He comments "When we stay the night together, I expect to wake up the next morning with a show of what a hungry little slut you are."

Slut? Is that what he thinks of me?

Somehow the sound of it doesn't sound degrading to my ears. It's almost like a compliment. I can see the desire grow in his eyes as his finger slips between my thighs, teasing along already damp lips.

"And my little slut is exactly what you'll be, isn't it?"

I'm doing everything I can to hold myself from moving, but hearing his words causes me to whimper.

What has he done to me?

"Y…yes, Sir. I will be your little slut."

Oh god, it feels good to say that. Why does it feel so damn good?

"Very good. Do you have any comments? Any additions? Suggestions?"

I shake my head, not daring to speak, as I'm sure the words that may fall from my lips at this point, would be a jumbled mass of incoherent sounds.

"Cassandra…" and I can see the disappointment on his lips. I guess I have a lot to learn about what he wants.

"No, Sir, I have nothing to add at this time." I blurt out; my body on the edge of falling to miniscule pieces.

He moves next to me on the couch, his finger sliding smoothly inside of me and tracing slow circles inside of me. His lips are at my neck, breathing in my scent and littering my skin with lingering kisses. I shudder against him.

"You're quite wet, aren't you?" he purrs. His voice causes my eyes to flutter. Oh how I love hearing him speak.

And this time, a nod is sufficient for him as he plunges his finger deeper into me. His tongue lightly, lazily licks along my earlobe as my phone begins to vibrate from the table. He glances over, and stands, leaving my body to steam. Walking over to it, he glances at the screen, then brings it back to me. Smiling, he swipes the screen to answer it, and places it to my ear.

"You have a call, Miss Roman." he grins.

My eyes open wide, my mouth falling open as I stare at him in disbelief. He's teased me for what feels like several lifetimes in the span of the time it takes someone to eat a quick breakfast and down some coffee, and now he expects me to speak to whoever is waiting on the other line?

"Speak." he mouths.

"H...hello?"

"Cass, where are you? It's nearly 8 and you still aren't home yet. Are you on your way?"

Fucking Riley. Of course it is. Who else would it be?

"Oh, uh, no. Something came up. I'll be home later, okay?"

There's silence on the other end. It's impossible to hide anything from her, but what would I tell her? 'Sorry, Riley. I can't come home right now. I'm too busy hopefully getting screwed so hard I won't be able to sit down for a week without feeling pain.'? Yeah. I'm sure she'll take that well.

"Cass, what is wrong with you. What's going on? Are you like, addicted to drugs? Are you off at a bar this early? I don't even know where you run off to anymore."

She's hysterical, and Alex is taking this time to move his lips to my sensitive breast. His tongue wraps around my nipple, letting his tongue dance along my skin as he suckles and nibbles on the hardening nub. I'm trembling from pure exaltation, and it's a struggle to keep my breathing normal. His hand is still holding the phone to my ear and he's gazing up at me with a wicked grin curling the corners of his mouth.

"Riley, this really isn't the time…"

"It's never the time! You never have the time, anymore! What's happened to you?! To us?! And who is that fucking guy that seems to have twisted you into a knot?! I'll kick his fucking ass!"

I'm blushing as he stares at me. I'm sure he can hear her from the phone, she's certainly loud enough. He tilts my head so I'm holding the phone between my ear and shoulder then smirks as he kisses down my stomach, and I squirm in shame. I hate my stomach, and it makes no sense for me to suddenly become self-conscious, but something about him touching it and kissing it makes me uneasy. His eyes flash against mine, holding me firmly.

"Shhh…stop hiding from me…" he coos.

His fingers pry my thighs apart, grip behind my knees then they lift them till my feet rest on the edge of the couch. I feel like a puppet; his hands molding me into the perfect position for his plans. He then grips my hips firmly, and tilts them forward.

Please don't…not now.

"Riley, I really need to go."

There's no way I can hold it together with her on the phone for long. Not with him…

"No. You're going to explain everything to me. Right now. I deserve to know what the hell is going on and where the hell you are! I *worry* about you, idiot! You've never hidden things from me, before! "

His tongue traces the outer edge of my pussy, moving ever closer to the center as he holds my thighs apart. I'm struggling to clamp them together, to hint somehow…to beg him not to…but he's surprisingly strong for his lean stature. He's holding my thighs spread without much effort and gazing up at me as if waiting for me to continue the conversation.

"I'll tell you when I'm on my way home." I snap.

"That's not good enough!"

She's screaming, on the verge of bursting into hysterical tears, and I'm caught somewhere between ecstasy and grief.

"I know it's not. Just please don't worry

about me. Please just…"

My sentence is cut off with a sharp gasp as he buries his mouth between my thighs, his tongue lightly flicking over my clit before plunging deep into me. It slithers around, drawing circles and coaxing waves of pleasure from my body. My thoughts grow hazy, my hips tilting higher to meet his mouth. I bite back a groan of pleasure, my eyes fluttering as the room grows hazy and clouded.

"Riley, trust me, please." I manage to stutter. "I'll call you when I'm on my way."

He pulls the phone down from my shoulder, never missing a beat with his lips and tongue, and hits the 'End Call' button before Riley can reply. He tosses the phone to the side where it begins vibrating wildly against the wood floor, but I'm too far gone to care.

Moving up, he kisses me passionately, slipping his soaked tongue between my lips. In my ravenous hunger, I return his kiss deeply, sucking his tongue and lapping the taste of my body from his lips. Reaching up, he unfastens my hands from the couch, then leads me down the hall and up the winding stairs to the bedroom, by the rope. He places me on the bed face down, slipping pillows under my hips to prop me up then ties the rope to the head of the bed and moves behind me. Leaning down, he kisses along my spine from my lower back to my neck, causing my back to arch in response and my lips to gasp. Words seem to fail me, as I'm washed away by his presence.

He crawls onto the bed behind me and places a hand on my lower back, letting his thumb dip down and gently rub against my ass, as he positions the tip of his cock against my dripping lips.

"Mm yes, you will be perfect..." he moans as he slides into me in one, smooth thrust.

Slowly, he rocks his agile body back and forth, sliding every inch of his impressive cock into me, burying it deep then drawing it out for a second and repeating. The ravenous beast within me roars in triumph, finally being given what it's wanted and craved. It spreads its arms, stares into the sky and roars in exaltation, sending my skin prickling and my hair to stand on end as its voice pulses through my body.

He picks up speed, the tip of his thumb tentatively slipping into my tight hole as slams inside of me. Faster, faster, and I feel every inch of my body throbbing in pleasure. More...more. I need more.

The nails of his free hand dig into my hip as

he guides me back onto him. His panting, grunts and moans dance in the air, mingling and mixing with my own. Louder and louder; my moans drift effortlessly though my lips and my vision grows fuzzy and dim, my eyes choosing, instead, to roll back and enjoy as he takes every inch of me, and makes me his. As our bodies slip into a common rhythm; his thrusts become more intense and my body presses back against him to drive him deep. The movements become a blur, an unconscious need that doesn't require my brain to give the go-ahead. It's an instinctual coupling, and I can think of nothing. Nothing except the feeling of his body against mine.

"Please…please don't stop" I beg through gritted teeth.

My muscles tense, my wrists tug against my bonds, fingernails biting into my palm. My heart forces blood through my veins in time with his thrusts. Just as I teeter on the edge of the precipice, his hand slips down my back and knots itself in my hair, tugging back.

"Come for me. *Scream* for me!"

My voice rings out for the entire Quarter to hear, and I can't stop it. The screams flow unchecked, mixed with the mutilated fractions of words somehow stringing themselves together into incomprehensible begging. A desperate plea for him.

Finding renewed strength, he thrusts harder, threatening to rip my body into pieces. My orgasm crashes against my body with the strength of fifteen Mack trucks, and leaves me blind. My vision shifts from pure blackness to blinding red speckled with dancing lights. Every sound...every material thing in the room slips and melts, falling away from us and leaving our bodies exposed. The world around us falls away as we find ourselves caught in this beautiful, sweat-splattered dance, and I love every second of it. I breathe it in and taste it on my lips. I feel it in every cell...in every spark that gives me life, and know I'm hopelessly addicted to a drug like no other.

My heart slows its racing rhythm; my muscles too exhausted to tremble. The weight of his body collapses upon my back, where he stays for a few seconds, and his thumbs use this time to run lightly over my shoulder blades. He rolls to the side, still struggling to catch his breath, and releases the ropes from the headboard. His fingers delicately loosen the binds around my wrists, the indentation of which can still be seen against my skin, and the rope falls lifelessly to the floor. As he turns me on my side, he holds me close, pulling my head to his chest. Neither of us can speak as we lay there; sweat glistening from our skin from the morning's workout. His heart is pounding, beating out an intense rhythm in my ears as he reaches over and strokes my hair gently, and after several moments, it seems he's found his voice.

"You are an incredibly alluring woman. Your moans…your screams. I love listening to you. A man can become addicted to sounds like those." He breathes.

I blush, and bury my face against his chest, kissing the glistening skin and tasting the salt from his sweat on my lips. He kisses my forehead as my eyes flutter and close, my body completely drained of every ounce of energy. I can't muster enough to speak, and I let myself succumb to darkness and my dreams.

Chapter 19

I'm alone in his bed. The sun is high in the sky, and the heat caused from its intrusion through the windows this morning has waned, if only slightly. I pad into the living room, where he's typing away on his laptop in the same position he always seems to be in. I'm still naked, and quickly move over to the table to grab my clothes while attempting to cover myself with my hands. He peeks up at me as I scurry by, and chuckles.

"Please, my dear. I've seen it all, now. There's no need to feel embarrassed."

"I know…" I reply, suddenly very aware of my nakedness "but if it's all the same, I'd like to get dressed."

He waves his hand as if giving me permission, and I scoop up my clothes and pull them on sans panties, as they're still lying, shredded, on the floor at his feet. I find my phone on the table next to my clothes; he must've picked it up for me.

"I took the liberty of talking to your friend."

I cock an eyebrow at him, but he doesn't break his eyes from his work.

"You were asleep, and she must've called a dozen times. I didn't want to be responsible for sending your friend to the hospital with a panic attack, and so, I spoke with her to ease her mind."

He did what?

He glances up for a moment to assess the look on my face then turns back to his work.

"I explained to her that I was a friend of yours, and that you were tired from making the trip so early in the morning. I reassured her that you were safe, that I would let no harm come to you, and that you stopped here at my request. I told her I had you eat, then you were so tired you could barely stand, and so I let you sleep a bit before your trip back home. She sounded quite grateful. She's a pleasant girl, that friend of yours. She cares and worries deeply for you. So as not to make me out to be a liar, I have some eggs and toast on the counter if you're hungry."

I take a deep breath to ease my anger. I don't like anyone touching my phone, and him taking the liberty of speaking with Riley was entirely inappropriate, even if it was under the best intentions.

"I'm not all that hungry. Thank you, though."

"Suit yourself."

I'm speechless. I would be incredibly surprised if she really believed anything he said. I'm sure she's at least a bit suspicious; however, he is quite gifted with his words, so maybe it isn't as farfetched as I may think…

"I do owe you a trip around town, sometime. Sadly, it won't be today. I have a lot of work to catch up on and it's already past noon. You'll forgive me, I hope?"

His passion and warmth have disappeared from his voice, and his demeanor makes me question my own memories of the hours before. He voice, though tinged with that hint of concern that so often accompanies his words, sounds a bit more business-like than I was hoping for. It sounds like we're just discussing work, and nothing more.

"That's fine. I probably should head home soon anyway."

"Mhm." he mumbles, his fingers dancing along the keys of his computer.

I grab my keys and belongings, and move towards the door. He gets so engrossed in his work, and I can relate. I understand…don't I?

As I open the door, I feel his hand on my shoulder. The silence of his movements is a bit unsettling, and I jump at his touch. He turns me to face him, wraps me in his arms and presses his lips passionately against mine. As he pulls away, he tucks one of my curls behind my ear then kisses my forehead. The touch of his lips to my head sends relief washing through my body mixed with …something I can't quite put my finger on. What is that feeling?

"I had fun." He smiles, running the tip of his finger over my nose. I can still smell myself on his skin, and it's so sexy.

"Me too."

Heat rushes to my cheeks. I haven't felt this infatuated since high school, and silently scold myself for acting so childish. Blushing on a dime is embarrassing. I should have a better hold on myself.

"The next time we meet, I expect you to bring all of those lovely little toys you've shown me."

The blush deepens and he smiles, leaning down to press another gentle kiss to my lips before moving back to the couch to continue his work. I walk out the door and slip into my car, my mind still struggling to believe everything that has happened despite my body showing all the evidence. I slip in my headset and call Riley, praying to whatever divine being exists that she won't shiv me when I walk through the door.

"Hey, Cass!" she answers excitedly.

Wow, she sounds chipper.

"Riley, I'm sorry about earlier, I must've..."

"Oh, Cass, I had no idea you were so exhausted! Why didn't you just say that? You poor thing. Are you on your way home? I can make dinner. What about a steak? It's a nice day so far, and I bet it'd be a great evening to break out the grill. I'm still mad, why didn't you tell me you'd been working so hard! Here, I thought something awful was going on, like you were hooked on cocaine or something." She chirps. It doesn't sound like she took a single breath, and I'm surprised when she stops talking so abruptly.

"Riley, when have you ever known me to take drugs?"

"Well! I don't know. Never, I suppose. That doesn't mean you wouldn't start!"

I laugh and tell her to pick whatever she wants for dinner, then hang up to continue the drive. That girl has one of the most active imaginations I've ever seen. Cocaine. Really? Silly girl; alcohol and sex are the only drugs I need.

Chapter 20

The sun streams through the windshield and plays along my hands as images of the hours before meld with the open road. His scent permeates my car, drifting from my clothes to mingle with the interior. It's saturated in every cotton thread of my clothing and I'm hopelessly addicted. My attempt to take even the slightest bit of control of the situation, and of myself, only ended in my complete and utter obliteration. I caved, and I silently chastise myself up over it. When will I be able to gain control over my own actions and desires? I'm a slave to that ever present fuming fire. The smallest spark and I'm consumed, doomed to burst and scatter as ash on the winds.

I sigh and roll down the windows to take a breath of fresh air, no matter how hot and stifling it may be. Slipping on the radio, I silently pray that

I'll find something a bit more upbeat, but have no such luck.

Another deep breath. In through the nose, out through the mouth. Nice and slow. I have other things I should be thinking about. My work. My friends. Well, friend, at least.

I'm struggling and grasping for some ground over my heart and the lust-filled beast. The thought of going home and pining over this man who seems to have taken control of me disgusts me. Why? Why should I wait on him if he's too busy to keep in regular contact with me?

My hands grip the steering wheel and I push the memories aside. Oh, but how wonderful they are. But what is this pain that keeps gnawing at me…

Ugh.

I dig my nails into my palm.

Wake the fuck up. I groan. *Every thought should not scream for him. This is no way to live.*

I pull into the driveway of the house, a constant war within my head raging the entire drive home. I'm assaulted at the door by Riley, who practically throws herself at me and wraps her arms around me in a giant hug. It seems that, whatever

Delacroix said, has made her feel guilty about giving me such a hard time. I feel bad letting her think my demeanor was anything other than selfish, but I am too emotionally exhausted to try and set the record straight.

I smile, and hug her back. Satisfied with my gesture, she dashes into the kitchen. I follow her, but only to grab a bottle of wine and a glass, then walk out the back door and settle into an outdoor couch. I start a spark in the fire pit and curl up, my arm propped under my head as I lay on my side. The temperature is brutal outdoors, but I don't care. I want to focus on something other than him, and the dancing flames coupled with the wine may help. I hope.

As the flames begin to pick up, Riley comes out with a tray of sliced watermelon and sets it on the small table between my couch, and the matching armchair she settles into. She picks at the watermelon as she stares into the flames.

"Cass, how long have I known you?"

I bite back my response. I hope this isn't one of her talks about trust and openness and communication. Sometimes I feel like she's my wife instead of my friend. I wonder if it's like that with everyone; where your best friend becomes so close that they're more like your relationship partner than just your friend, or perhaps we're a special case.

"Eight or nine years, now, I think? We met our second year in high school."

"It feels like so much longer."

She draws her feet up on the chair and rests her chin on her knees; her arms wrapped around her legs. The flickering flames dance in our eyes.

"It's been awhile since we've come out here together."

"Yeah…"

"Do you love him?"

My eyes never break from the flames, but I feel that same feeling from earlier tug on my heart. The ache hurts more and more the longer I try to ignore it. It couldn't be that, could it?

I can't bring myself to speak, because my throat feels as if it's closed up on itself. There's no point in asking who she's talking about, because I know. She knows. Hiding things from her has never been an easy feat, and with the way I'm feeling, it's no wonder she can see it all, painted on my face, etched out in the fresh scars of heartache and confusion.

"How could I love him? I don't really know him that well. I barely know anything about him. Like, what's his favorite color, or does he have any siblings, or where did he grow up. I don't know what he likes to eat, or if he likes to do anything other than work." I whisper, but my voice betrays me. It cracks and pitches at the end as I choke back my emotions. How can I love someone I don't know? I want him, sure, but love him? That's insane.

"You can love someone you don't know. You can feel it." She says, as she stares into the flames "Right there in your heart. You feel the ache and realize that, even if they never touched you, you'd still love them because it goes deeper. You love their heart, and their mind. You love listening to them talk, and love being around them. You can't explain it. It is pain and joy, and all encompassing. It's mean, and loving, and agonizing. It hurts, but it's also complete and total bliss. You don't have to know someone's favorite color or their hobbies, sometimes. Sometimes, it's just something that happens. It doesn't make sense. It's not something you can label or dissect or approach analytically. Your heart calls out for theirs, and their heart answers. You can love someone in an instant, Cass…even if you don't know them as well as you'd like to. It's still love."

I'm stronger than this.

I repeat it over and over until the words feel wooden and void of life. Just a lie I've repeated to myself so many times that it's formed this armor around my body; an impenetrable wall around me that's allowed me to engage in promiscuous acts and forget them the next morning. Why? So I wouldn't feel like this, so I wouldn't feel this kind of emotion. Sex was simple. It was natural, primal and…simple. Love and emotions are different. They're complex, living, breathing things that grow deep in your heart and sprout. No matter how many times you take an axe to it, no matter how many times you throw a match and watch its branches go up in flames, it comes back, sprouting and reaching its fingers into every inch of your body.

Yearning and aching, this feeling refuses to be snuffed out, and makes me both happy and completely miserable. Both glowing in the morning light, and a desecrated corpse rotting beneath the earth. There seems to be no winning when it comes to this, and emotions were the last thing I ever wanted to feel. How did this sneak up on me? How could I let myself become so careless? And with him, of all people out there. The unobtainable and yet, so enticing, Delacroix.

This isn't how it was supposed to be.

"Cass…" she whispered, as she moved from her seat to curl next to me. She rests her hand on my shoulder, gently stroking her fingers over my arm. "It's okay."

And I cried. Unabated and unrestrained, the tears seared my eyes and burned trails down my skin. Riley slid to her knees on the ground in front of me, holding me in her arms, and I cried. It was a pent up release of every emotion I've felt since meeting him. Why was I crying? Was it frustration, loneliness, or longing? Perhaps it was confusion or desire. Maybe it was even this…love…Riley spoke about. Just thinking of the word makes me want to rip my tongue from my mouth, and throw it into the ashes. Love…

Whatever the reason, the tears refused to end. All my strength…all those walls I put up to hide the memories, had shattered in an instant, and the tide I'd held back for so long, threatened to claim my life here and now. How many things have I done? How many questionable, unethical things have I succumbed to in the desire to satisfy my perceived needs? How many people have I hurt, used, and led on for my own selfish whims?

The memories flashed through my mind like a collage. Fractions of thoughts buried so deep as to have been forgotten by my conscious mind, were now bubbling at the surface and overwhelming me. They found release in my tears, in my incoherent babbling into Riley's shoulder as she held me tight to keep me from shattering into a million, glittering pieces.

I told her everything. It had been so long since I let anyone in, and I couldn't hold it back anymore. I had hid so much from myself and everyone around me, and I just wasn't strong enough anymore.

I spoke of the lovers, of my nights in the company of all of those I had buried away and attempted to purge from every thought. I cried over my inner turmoil and exposed my demons to her, and she held me even tighter. She cried with me before the dancing flames of the fire pit and the amber glow of the setting sun. She sat by me, pulled me into her lap and cradled me as I continued to sob against her chest. Wet stains from my tears splattered over her pale blue skirt as she rubbed my back and whispered soothing words, the only ones of which I understood where her asking "More wine?"

"Hell yes." I stutter between sobs.

As I drain the glass, I take a deep breath and look to the sky to gain some composure, willing my tears to stop flowing.

Deep breaths. I'm okay. Everyone needs a little emotional release once in a while.

With my eyes still focused on the sky as the blues blend to oranges and purples, I reach over and place my hand on Riley's, squeezing it tight as I steady my breathing.

In and out.

She grips my hand just as tightly and we sit in silence as the sun dips beneath the horizon, giving way to the brilliant, star-littered blanket of night sky. The fire burns low, allowing the light from the stars glimmer blindingly from their place in the heavens.

She's the first to break the silence, which had sat between us like a welcomed stranger for what must've been hours, and yet, I enjoyed it. The feel of a faint breeze caressing my skin, the popping and sizzling from the burning wood, and the silence, was a pleasing respite. Even my mind was silent, and I almost broke down and cried again at the relief of it. There were no racing thoughts, no anxiety over 'what ifs' and it had finally become so calm and clear. I feel as if the combined weight of the last half of my life had somehow been lifted and tossed into the dying coals of the fire. None of it mattered anymore. For the first time in months, I smiled from happiness so genuine, I was near giddy.

So long had I been living with so much dragging me down that I hadn't noticed the toll it had taken.

Riley stood up, smiling down at me with her hand still holding mine.

"Come on, it's late. Why don't we head inside, and you can get some rest."

I nod, smiling in return as I let her lead me to my room. She gives me another hug, squeezing the remnants of a shattered, broken body back into place. The smile never leaves my lips as we both crawl into bed, her arms wrapping around me and holding me close. I bury my face against her chest, and breathe in deep as her hands gently rub my back. Her chin rests on the top of my head as she whispers soothingly to me, coaxing my eyes to close with the promise of a much deserved.

My dreams, however, are less than kind. They are a dark and turbulent nightmare.

I am standing in a darkened room, staring at myself. Not merely a reflection, but a flesh and blood copy. She stands there with a smirk on her face, flocked by a dozen different lovers both past and present. They surrounded her, a surging mass of human bodies, and she relishes in it. She drinks in their attention, finds rapture in their touch. She was pure sex in human form and she's loving every second.

From the darkness beyond the scene, walks a tall man, well over 6 feet with tanned skin, dark hair, and a familiar boyish face. He parts the crowd and she cowers from him, growing younger before my eyes. He moves toward her, wrapping his arm possessively around her, and she averts her eyes, her body shifting uncomfortably as he trails a finger over her collar bone. I wanted to scream, to beg, to somehow convince myself to wake up, but I was forced to watch, my body frozen as I stared helplessly. His finger moves from her collar bone to the center of her chest as he presses his lips close to her ear.

"You won't tell anyone, will you, baby."

Shimmering tears fall from her eyes and pool on the floor beneath her, slowly filling the room until it's a swirling, salty maelstrom. I can't move; I can't keep myself from drowning. And through the water, I hear her distorted sobs, carried on the turbulent waves.

Chapter 21

The sun bursts through the window, assaulting my face. A tear-stained pillow is clutched to my chest, and the smell of bacon is in the air.

Mmm, bacon.

I crawl out of bed, wash up, and slip downstairs; the nightmare already filing itself away neatly in a box without much effort. I've done it so many times before, that it's become habit; as natural as taking a breath of air.

Downstairs, Riley is a whirlwind in the kitchen, whipping up scrambled eggs with bacon and toast. She spots me as I step off the stairs, and runs to greet me with a big hug.

"Good morning! I've made breakfast, but then I have a few deliveries to make."

Over the last few weeks, she found a way to make money off of her talents. About a week ago, she ventured into creating a webpage, and went crazy taking pictures of various desserts that she's managed to whip up in our kitchen. To my surprise, her website really took off, and within that small window, she managed to pull in half a dozen orders. Not bad considering the small time frame, and frankly, it's about time she started helping with the rent.

She ushers me to the table, sits me down then brings out our plates along with freshly squeezed orange juice.

"How are you feeling?" she asks cautiously, eying me from across the table.

Ah, so this is what it's all about. This is a stop-feeling-like-shit breakfast. I should've known.

"Better." I smile as I take a slice of fatty, greasy goodness and chomp down. Oh man, bacon. It's better than sex, at least, for the moment.

We eat and clean up over the some light conversation. She talks a bit about Tom, and his newest building project. He's an architectural consult for the city, and has been fairly busy over the last week with work. He always finds time for her though, and it makes me smile with a bit of hopeless longing. I'm happy for her. I love her, and if she's happy than I'm happy.

They've somehow managed to keep their spark alive, and have kept the butterflies fluttering between them for almost two years now. They've had their fair share of fights, but I think they've both learned a little give and take. Especially Riley, who can be very demanding of attention at times, and not just from Tom, but from me as well.

This thing she's began building up for herself is the start of her personal independence, and it's nice to see her doing something that she's so passionate about. She had been swimming in a sea of lost ideas. Things she wanted to do with her life but didn't act on, which led to a general hopelessness at times, followed by a shopping spree with money she didn't have.

We help each other out, and I hate the thought that maybe, one day, Tom will whisk her away and she'll be too busy carrying around a baby on her hip and reading Good Housekeeping, to have time for me. She'll be happy, and I'll be ecstatic for her, but the thought of being alone, hurts.

My writing has always been an escape for me, but it only holds for so long, because once the pencil falls, the silence presses in around me, bringing with it whispered thoughts from the past.

It's suffocating; an agonizing pain with which I've struggled to deal with my entire life. My coping mechanisms aren't always the best either, I'm afraid, but everyone has their vices. Everyone has their own little unique way to deal with the harshness of the world. Everyone finds a little addiction deep inside that drives away the pain of the day to day, even if it's for a second. How else would you get through the day? I know I'm rationalizing. I know the unhealthy ways to cope, and I've touched on every single one of them at one point or another. I like to think we all do. It's what helps me feel like I'm not such an abnormality.

After checking on me yet again to make sure I'm okay, Riley busies herself in the kitchen to double check her paperwork, then she begins to gather her deliveries. I joke that if she winds up being some famous chef, she's buying my next house, and she laughs.

I head upstairs and sit at my desk, which overlooks the front yard, and scowl at the desk calendar which hadn't had its' pages torn off for several weeks now. I cheat a peek at my phone to verify the date. It's Thursday. Fuck. I missed another class day. Of course I did. I've been so shot for the last several days that it's a miracle I remembered to brush my teeth this morning.

I turn on my monitor and pull up my inbox, sending out one mass email to my students basically saying 'Hey, things came up, do this for the next time we meet' then run my fingers absently over my flash drive.

Slipping it into the USB slot, I pull up my brainstorming ideas, then remember that Delacroix had edited my article on him. I don't really mind that he had some suggestions for my article, but having someone I barely know reading something I wrote, one on one, is almost like peeling back my skin and baring my soul to their scrutiny. It's unnerving.

What if he read it and found it horrendous? The biggest fear being; what if he finds that I'm not as intelligent and well-spoken as he may have previously suspected? There are other fish in the sea though, right? I'm sure if I wait around long enough, I'll eventually find some hunky, well-spoken man who's just as eloquent, and he'll sweep me off my feet and whisk me off into the sunset.

I stifle a giggle at the thought. Hah…yeah, a regular knight in shining armor. They don't exist. It's just not practical. There is no perfect man, and with that said, there's also no perfect women. Besides, I'm not one much for the typical specimen of hyper-masculinity.

We're all a little fucked up. There is no fairytale ending. I am by no means saying you should settle. I've tried that. I settled for this man who I thought was great, at first. He was a wonderful guy for the most part, but not entirely affectionate. We sat on separate couches when watching movies, and apart from the kiss we'd share when we first saw each other for the day, there were no other real intimate encounters.

He was completely and utterly devoid of desire. That's all well and good if sex wasn't all that important to me, but I guess I'm a bit of an asshole in that way. Sex is incredibly important, and not only is it important, but it has to mean something. I need to be able to feel my partner's passion and emotions during it, or it does nothing for me. I need to know they want it, and want me. It was something that lacked from every brief sexual encounter we had together, and it got to a point where I threw my hands up in exasperation and tried to find other ways in which to cope.

Finding other reasons to stick around proved to be a lot harder than I thought it'd be. What did we really have in common? The conversations began to dull until evenings out were nothing more than sharing a meal across from one another with no actual conversation, and my attempts to spark one, always fell flat. Without any real input from him, the conversation would die after one word answers, and yet I held on. He was cute, and he was incredibly sweet. A hold-the-door-open kind of man, a flowers-for-your-birthday kind of guy, but that intimacy was lacking and the longer I held out, the more it pushed me into a deep depression.

I'm sure it's my own short comings that cause things like that to happen. It could've been low self-esteem, maybe a bit of anxiety or a touch of depression. He was so stable in his life and I wanted to be a part of that, but after that experience, I'm convinced that living that white, picket fence life, just isn't in the cards for me. Maybe I don't want it to be.

Delacroix doesn't seem much like a white, picket fence kind of guy, either.

So, what is there to work with when you don't even know what you two are? Are labels even necessary? Maybe a lack of them would make all of this a little easier to deal with; a little less stressful, but I need to be able to define what him and I are. I *need* to know how to label him.

I gaze over his corrections and find that they're minor; a missed comma here and a needed semicolon there. Nothing overly serious, and there is no change in my wording. At the end of the document is a note from him.

I formally request your presence for a show at the Mahalia Jackson Theater for the Performing Arts. It's still a week away, but I'd like to ask now, lest I forget. Please respond via text as soon as you're able.

Sincerely yours,

A.R. Delacroix

Excitedly, I pull out my phone and reply; all previous musings over titles and relationship status', and stress over him are wisps in the wind.

I'd love to go with you. Thank you for the invitation. I wouldn't miss it.

*Wonderful. I'm assuming you'll be driving here alone. We'll make arrangements on where to meet up when the date draws closer. How are you feeling? Where you able to catch up on sleep? *

When the date draws closer? It is one week away. Does he plan to spring our meeting place on me, the day of? I shake my head dismissively. He's not one for ironing out all the details well in advance, it seems.

*Yes, I did. I'm feeling much better, thanks. How's your work coming along? *

Busy, as always. What are you wearing?

His text comes as a bit of a surprise, but it's enough to start fanning those flames. I smirk, proud in the fact that I've left him wanting enough to ask a question such as that. And so what else is there to do, other than lie. I'm not exactly sitting in the most flattering attire, and it's much better to let him fuel that fantasy in his head than kill it with a comment about my butterfly pajama bottoms and tank top.

His voice is in my ear again, and the glint in his eye, as we spoke over the rules and his expectations.

"I need to be able to trust you."

I sigh. Butterfly pajamas, it is.

Nothing all that flattering. I'm wearing a pair of pajama pants with blue butterflies on them, and a black tank top. .

What about your bra and panties?

*What bra and panties ;) *

Are you alone?

Yes...

Take off your shirt, fold it, and place it at the end of your bed, then take a picture to show me you've done as you're told.

I obey his instructions without another question, being sure to slip over to my door and lock it. Trying to explain what I'm doing undressing and taking pictures to Riley, is something I really don't want to do.

I send the pictures as requested, and a few seconds later, I receive a reply. This is a record for him. Consecutive texts with no more than a minute or so between them? It's unheard of!

Slip out of your pants, lay face down on the bed and place a pillow just at the lower end of your abdomen, so your hips are tilted up

Yes, Sir. I reply.

The act of calling him Sir still sends a little tingle down my spine.

Slip a finger between your legs and rub your clit in slow circles. Do you like being fucked in this position?

Very much so. I manage to type, with one finger tapping out the keys.

How do you feel now?

My body is tingling as I read over his words, the sound of his voice in my ear with each message.

Hungry for more. I want more.

Good girl. Slide a single finger inside of you. Nice and slow. How wet are you?

I'm soaked, Alex, and aching. I wish you were here with me...

I want you to close your eyes while you slide your finger in. Slow at first then gradually pick up speed. Imagine me there with you, my hands running over your sexy ass and gripping your hips. Think of how it feels when I slide into you, when I kiss your back, and when I tug your hair. Open your eyes and text me when you get close. You must ask permission before you come.

Yes, Sir. I reply.

I close my eyes as requested, and plunge my finger into me as deep as it'll go. It feels amazing thinking of him sitting on his couch, picturing me here, on my bed, touching myself for him.

I slowly pick up speed, the muscles in my legs tensing as I feel myself draw closer and closer. My breathing grows labored, and I stifle my moans into my pillow as I draw closer. My body trembled, and I hold myself on that edge as I bring up his message.

Please Sir, may I come? I ask.

My body is begging, over and over, for blessed release. A minute passes then two, and I move my finger barely just to keep myself hanging on the edge.

Please...please Sir. I need to come.

This would be a terrible time for him to get caught up in work. Finally, a reply comes.

No. You may not. You may, however, go over to that little bag of toys you have, and slip in those balls. I expect you to keep them in whenever possible. I'll be in your area tomorrow. See you then.

I gape at the response, my legs still trembling in the anticipation of release. One little touch… just a bit harder, and I'd scream; my body wrapped in an orgasm. He'd never know, and I could still put the balls in and walk around.

Oh, but that wouldn't be nearly as exciting, would it?

I love the torture. I love the tease, and so I pull my finger reluctantly away, and slip the Ben Wa balls inside of me. For good measure, I snap a picture of them inside of me and send it to him. Let's see how well he does with my little visual tease.

He doesn't respond, but I entertain the thought of him squirming with a hard to hide hard-on pressing against his jeans, and smile.

I walk into the bathroom with the balls inside of me, the metal bells wrapped in a silicone covering clanking together and sending pulses of pleasure to every part of my body with each sway of my hips.

I wash up, and pull on a night gown. It's the only nightgown I have in my closet, as I'm more prone to sleeping nude or in panties and a tank top, and is a deep red with lace trimming around the edges, and a plunging neckline. The straps are nothing more than thin strings, and the way the silk rests on my breasts and hips heightens my feelings of excitement.

I feel sexy, even if it's just me in my room. There's no chance of me going out anywhere today, anyhow and it's getting quite late, so why should I bother putting on everyday clothes?

I get a bit more work done at my computer and decide to call it an early night, sticking to my instructions on keeping them inside of me.

I receive a text from him around 11 p.m., which wakes me from an uneasy slumber.

How are you feeling?

Teased and tired.

*Did I wake you? You can take them out for the

night if you still have them in. It may keep you from getting adequate sleep. Do you work tomorrow?*

*Yes, just for a few hours. 12-3. *

*I want you to wear the balls again for those 3 hours. Where do you work? *

Linden College.

And the silence I've began expecting from him follows. No reply and no explanation. Instead of worrying and obsessing, I laugh, silence my phone and curl up for bed. It's felt like a long, dragging day that consisted of me doing essentially nothing, and I'm all too anxious to try my hand at getting a decent nights rest.

Chapter 22

After I dress for my mid-morning class, I insert my 'homework', and head for the door. Tom's shoes are resting innocently just inside the front door, and seeing as how Riley isn't dancing around the kitchen over eggs while blasting music, I assume she's still curled up in bed with her long-time love-muffin.

As I step into the classroom, I am greeted by 10 smiling faces. Incredible. It's a new record! Halfway through the semester and these fuckers finally decide to show up. They'll be sorely disappointed when their final grades come in.

The clock crawls, as I work on suppressing the waves of pleasure originating from the Ben Wa balls buried inside of me. I manage to drag through the first half of the lesson, flip on a movie, and try my best to pay attention. Once the short clips ends, and I've collected the various half-assed papers from my students, I grace them with an early release, then spend some time in the empty room. The silence allows my thoughts to shuffle; pieces of Delacroix's face…his lips, his eyes, his curls, piece together into a perfect picture of a man, dancing its' way between the desks as the sunlight shimmers through his phantom form.

Closing my eyes to banish the ghost from the room, I pull out the first paper that had been turned in and begin reading. Surprisingly, it isn't half bad, and I'm grateful to know that at least one student has bothered to listen to the lectures and read over what I post. Soon, I'm losing myself in the students essay; a tale of death and heartache. It's a sad story spun by a girl far too young to experience these tortures of the world, but then again, I was like that once.

Wrapping up my first paper, I pull out the second and Delacroix tugs at my thoughts as the balls shift inside of me. His texts and his voice pick at the surface and I rest my head in my hand, closing my eyes tight in an attempt to push those feelings down just for a bit longer. I'm too old to be fussing over labels and 'boyfriend/girlfriend' shit. The constant battle of what we are is idiotic, and I really need to get over it. I'm too old to be thinking about silly things like this, and obsessing over someone so completely is unbecoming. Stress is causing me to gray before my time. They're there every morning, staring me in the face like the petrified coils of medusa's snakes.

I close up my books, pack my bag and head for the door. Something about the silence of an empty room can be so peaceful and calming, and it's always a bit heart wrenching to leave, knowing I'll be bombarded by the stomping footsteps and overwhelming chatter of countless students swarming the halls.

As I step over the threshold into the hallway, I catch someone leaning against the wall just outside the door, with a hat pulled low over their eyes. My eyes catch the glint of a pair of familiar glasses, just visible beneath the lid, and auburn curls carefully tucked beneath a well-worn Saint's hat.

"Miss Roman."

My heart plummets into the pit of my stomach.

"I hope your classes went well. Have you done your homework?"

I nod, my eyes darting around the hall in paranoia. My lips part to speak but nothing comes out. He smiles, and takes my hand, leading me down the hallway and into a stairwell. I can hear the commotion of the surging mass of students traveling along the hallways and stairs, but this stairway is a bit further out of the way, and is usually empty around this time. He pins me between his body and the wall, pushing his lips hungrily against mine. His tongue slips past my lips to invade my mouth, and I can do nothing against him. My legs tremble beneath me as he presses himself against me, his hands reaching up and tugging my hair as I moan against his lips. The kiss lasts a mere few seconds, but leaves me flushed and trembling as he pulls away.

I feel like I'm doing something terrible...something forbidden, like a high school student sneaking a make-out session with a member of the football team. The excitement is there, but there's a level of professionalism expected of me. Doing something here...no. What if we were caught? I could lose my job! No, if he wants more, we need to move somewhere else.

His eyes lock with mine and his face is a mix of hunger and hesitation.

"It's a bit risky for you to come here, isn't it?"

"Yes. I had to meet with my agent nearby, and figured I'd stop in. I couldn't leave without seeing you..."

"Did you...want to find somewhere a bit more private?"

Pulling away, he grins, then runs his fingers through his hair.

"Actually, I wanted to ask you to a coffee. I'm not often in this area, is there anything you suggest?"

"There's a coffee shop not too far, maybe 10 or 15 minutes away."

"That sounds fine. We can take my car if you wish?"

I nod, and let him lead me out of the building. He doesn't hold my hand, and I'm grateful. Displays of affection, especially around my workplace, are something I don't condone when there are watchful eyes. The last thing I need are rumors of me and some guy holding hands and walking around campus like a couple of teenagers. I already feel like the higher-ups are out to get me, though I don't help my situation with all the classes I miss.

He leads me through the parking garage and to a midnight blue Lexus, which sparkles beneath the harsh, florescent lights of the parking garage.

It's a beautiful car; the type I'd often bring up on my computer, and fantasize about owning one day but know I'd never make enough money to afford something so extravagant.

He walks to the passenger side and holds the door open as I crawl in; the black leather seat conforming to the shape of my body and cradling me in its arms. I look over at him and smile as he crawls in the drivers' seat, then my eyes drop to the shift. Yes! A manual transmission! Oh how I love a man who can drive a stick.

He shifts the car into gear as I guide him through the streets toward my favorite coffee shop. It doesn't look like much from the outside; a brown building shoved in the corner between a tanning salon and a subway, and I could see the doubt on his face. We slip in the front doors and are assaulted by all the wonderful aromas I've come to associate with a good coffee spot; the scent of coffee and the smell of freshly baked goods. Muffins and pastries decorate the glass cases that make up the front counter, and most of the tables are already occupied. We place our order with a short, blonde girl with a round face, cherry red cheeks and a squeaky voice. She's all too eager to take our requests, and moments later, we're making our way to a lone table in the back corner, with hot coffee in our hands.

I choose the seat against the wall as he settles in next to me, and immediately brings the scalding liquid to his lips. He stares across the table at me; his eyes drawing me in, tugging me down, and threatening to drown me within them. They're filled with years of sorrow, of love, of heartache, of desire, and of his steeled drive and confidence. They flash his dominant nature, mixed with a soft, caring hand, and I'm enraptured. He smiles softly, reaching across the table to take my hand. His thumb gently caresses the top of my hand.

"How was work?" he asks gently.

"It was the same as it always is, I suppose. Tiring, and frustrating. I never thought I'd be teaching students like this, I guess. I was expecting something entirely different. What about you? How are things?"

"They're going," he chuckles. "I'm afraid it's just that. It's a lot of back and forth, but I will have it squared away eventually. I was pleased with your article, and must thank you for such a finely crafted piece. I can't wait to see it finished and in print."

Blood rushes to my cheeks, and a smirk paints across his face. He reaches under the table, his hand still warm from holding the coffee, and lets his fingers dance along my knee. I squirm in my seat uncomfortably as the barista from the front counter comes to ask if we need anything further, then leaves promptly as he waves her off.

"How are those balls feeling, my dear?" he asks, innocently, the moment the barista leaves.

"They're agonizing" I groan, careful to keep my voice low. "It makes it a bit difficult to concentrate."

"But you will find that control, won't you?"

"Yes, Sir…" I murmur, glancing around nervously for fear that someone may hear our conversation.

"You're such a good girl." he breathes, leaning over the table. His fingers lightly brush along the underside of my forearm, and it sends a shocking pulse through my body. I never knew a gesture like that would bring so much…pleasure. At that moment, I find that my lip has become oddly appetizing, and begin nibbling mercilessly on the corner of it.

When we're done our drinks, he helps me stand, and leads me to his car. Once we're housed within the tinted windows, lush leather interior and metal frame, he leans over and presses his lips to my neck. I inhale sharply and writhe in the seat, feeling myself dampen immediately in excitement.

"Alex…" I whisper.

He pulls away, letting one hand linger on my thigh for a few seconds before he starts the car.

"I have a meeting at 5 for drinks with my agent, and he's always very punctual so I must be sure to be on time. I always love seeing you, though, and wanted the chance to feel you while I'm here."

Feel me? I want you to feel more of me…

"So, I won't see you again till our theater date?" As soon as the words are out of my mouth, I immediately regret saying the word 'date'. It feels so informal…so juvenile, but he doesn't seem to take notice, or he doesn't care. I'm sure I'm making that silly statement out to be far worse than it really is.

"Correct. I need to get back to my room and get a few things together before the meeting. I'll be gone first thing in the morning, and I don't imagine I'll be available later this evening."

"Oh…"

I try to mask my disappointment, after all, I have a life of my own too. It just involves sitting on the couch with a bottle of wine and watching reruns of my favorite British sci-fi show. I don't want him to feel guilty, but for the first time, he's actually in my area. To know I've only had time for a quick touch, and for him to tease me to a near breaking point without having the chance to bring him home, is torture. I want to have his scent permeating my bed sheets. Leaning towards me, his lips press faintly against my cheek, then shifts the car into gear and drives me back to the school.

As we say our goodbyes, he wraps me in his arms and kisses my forehead amidst the students surging through the parking garage, then takes off.

My heart is aching, as well as that delicious, soaking spot between my thighs, but the heart ache is overwhelming. It overshadows the lustful beast, reaching its sobbing tendrils into every crevice of my body. It's as if he drove off with my still beating heart, secured in his back pocket, and there's not a thing I can do about it. Shaking my head, I climb in my car and head home.

Just block it out.

If I can convince myself that it didn't happen, maybe it won't hurt so much.

Chapter 23

Riley has, once again, outdone herself as she slaps a perfect medium rare steak on my plate, and a matching one onto Tom's. He's become a fairly regular guest at our table, and has taken to entertaining us with stories from his childhood and from work. He has this way of spinning a story that always makes us laugh, and it's managed to lighten a bit of the ache which has settled deep in my body.

I can't help but feel like a third wheel in their happiness, sometimes. They find ways to keep me included, but I can't always push away the sting of loneliness when I see the loving glances and secret smiles they share.

Riley comes to the table with the last addition to the table; a lovely, precious bottle of red wine. Alcohol has always been a necessary sustenance, and though I'm trying so hard not to drink as much, it's often my go-to for numbness in the absence of me grabbing a random person off the street to fuck senseless.

As she fills our glasses and settles in next to Tom, my phone buzzes from my back pocket. Riley and I have developed this very strict 'no phones at the table' policy. We both have agreed that it distracts from the conversation and social aspect of a meal, and that phones are better left turned off and thrown in a corner somewhere. However, she's been lenient with me, and allows me to leave mine on vibrate for the purposes of anything work related that may come up.

As Riley and Tom wrap themselves in their own private joke, I sneak a peek at the phone. Surprisingly, it's Ethan. He's sent me a text to remind me that he's thinking of me, and wishing I were closer. A picture accompanies it, of him wrapped in a wool coat with a scarf around his neck. It's nearing the end of October, now, and it's already gotten cold up north. The same, however, cannot be said for the bipolar weather of Louisiana. It's in the 40's one day, and mid 80's the next. I have a hard time keeping up with the constant wardrobe changes.

I smile at the picture and managed to get it tucked back into my pocket when there's a knock at the door. Frustrated at the sight of my poor steak sitting untouched on my plate and getting colder by the second, I grudgingly go to the door. Riley and Tom can't be bothered, as they're stuck in their own little world, and probably haven't noticed the knock, much less, me leaving the table.

I reach for the door, wrench it open, and am greeted by none other than Alexander Delacroix standing before me in a pair of black slacks and a pale blue collared shirt. I'm shocked, and attempted to hide my emotions from striking themselves across my face. I thought his night was booked? I thought he didn't have time for me this evening, and more importantly, how the hell did he know where I live?

He smiles, the gold flecks in his brown eyes glinting, as he stands patiently at the threshold.

"May I come in?"

"Uh, yeah, I guess. How did you get my address?"

"I spoke with Angela. She was more than happy to give out your information. You may want to speak with her about that." He chuckles.

I step aside and let him walk in. Riley has just gotten up to make her way to the door when she stops dead in her tracks. Her eyes move from him, to me, then back again. I can see the question already bubbling in her eyes, but Riley, being the perfect hostess, must introduce herself properly. She walks up to Delacroix and holds out her hand, the sweetest smile slipping across her lips.

"Oh! I didn't realize we were expecting more company. I'm Riley Moreau, and who might you be?"

He takes her hand, lifts it to his lips, and gently kisses the top of her hand. Her cheeks blush in immediate response, and she pulls her hand away quickly, thoughtfully rubbing the spot where his lips had been just seconds before.

"I apologize if I'm intruding. I'm the man you spoke with the other day; the one who had been with Cass after her trip to the airport. I don't think I ever told you my name. I'm Alexander Delacroix. It's a pleasure."

"It's a pleasure, Mister Delacroix." She says in response, then steps to the side and sweeps her arm towards the dining room. "Please, come in."

Tom has risen from the table to see what all the commotion was, and at his approach, his eyes widen to a near comical size.

"Sweetie," Riley says lovingly, "this is…"

"Alexander Delacroix! It's an absolute pleasure, Sir." He rushes forward, grabbing one of Alex's hands in both of his own, and shakes enthusiastically. "I'm Thomas Locke. It's wonderful to meet you!"

Riley rolls her eyes at Tom's enthusiasm, then turns her attention back to Alex. "Have you eaten, yet? I have an extra plate, and would be honored if you joined us for dinner."

"Thank you, Miss Moreau. I'd hate to intrude…"

"Oh, not at all! Please, come in and have a seat! I'll grab a plate."

Of course there's extra food. Riley is more apt to cook for a dozen people than a party of three, and often has leftovers stored in the fridge that I use for my lunch during the week.

Before he can fully digest her words, she's grabbed his hand and set him in the seat next to my own. She's a tempest as she moves through the kitchen, dragging me along with her as she prepares a plate for him. As she slips a steak onto his plate and spoons mashed potatoes and green beans, her voice takes on an urgent whisper.

"Is that him?"

"Yes…"

"He's kind of cute! Why didn't you tell me he was cute? You should've warned me!"

"I guess it never came up."

"Well good for you! Now put that man in his place."

I stifle a laugh, and peek over at the table where Tom has engaged Alex in conversation. It's a low murmur that I can barely make out, then I see Tom reach over and grasp Alex's hand, shaking it enthusiastically once more. The look on Alex's face is a mask, carefully placed as to not offend the overly excited Thomas Locke.

Riley and I make our way back to the table with her gingerly placing a plate before Alex, and outfitting his place with silverware and a wine glass, which she fills halfway.

"Riley! This is Alexander Delacroix!" Tom says enthusiastically.

"Yes, sweetie, he told me that when he came in, and you repeated it yet again at the door. And again…just now. I think I've gotten the point."

"Do you know who that is?"

"Someone Cass knows, obviously."

"Riley, I love you, but I think I need to expand your reading collection."

Riley shoots a heated look at Tom, clearly not impressed with his lack of manners when he's wound up. Tom chokes back his next words and clears his throat, his eyes taking on an apologetic look.

"What I meant to say is, he's the author of one of my favorite books. I guess I'm just a bit excited. Do we have tea? I could really use a cup of tea. Can I get you cup of tea, Mister Delacroix?"

"No, I'm quite fine with the wine, thank you."

Tom jumps from his seat, rushes to the kitchen, and comes back minutes later with a piping hot cup.

Alex shifts uncomfortably under Tom's attentions, and tries his best to keep his eyes focused on his plate as Tom rattles off about the book and everything he knows about the illustrious Alexander Delacroix to Riley.

Once Alex has checked to make sure Riley

is completely engrossed in Tom's ramblings, he busies himself by finding a distraction of his own from the conversation.

His hand slips under the table and rests on my thigh, squeezing affectionately. I nearly choke on the piece of steak I've slipped between my lips, and I shift in my seat. His lips curl into an impish smile as he casts a side glance in my direction. I still have those balls buried deep inside of me, at his request, and I desperately ache to feel him rip them out of me and replace them with him.

His fingers slide over my inner thigh, slowly working their way up higher...higher. My heart picks up its' pace, moving from a slow dance to a pounding drumbeat in my ears. I bite my lip and absently stare at my food as my mind soaks in his touch. Glancing up, I notice Riley's eyes locked on mine, tuning out Tom's voice. She grins that knowing grin, and clears her throat.

"So, Alexander, I hear you're treating Cass to a show this upcoming weekend?"

His hand wrenches away from my leg and leaves me yearning. I don't want him to stop. I don't care who is watching. I want him to throw me on this table and fuck me till I scream.

"Ah, yes. I have. It's one that I'm quite fond

of, and I know she has yet to see it. I was hoping she'd find as much enjoyment in it as I do."

Oh I'm sure I'll find plenty of enjoyment if his hands are roaming over my body during it.

"She's always talking about how she wants to see something at the theater, but she never takes the time to go act on those impulses! I'm glad you two are going. You will keep her safe in the city, I hope? I'm always hearing about a murder or rape, or some other heinous crime in that city. I need someone to pay the bills, so losing her would be a huge inconvenience."

He smiles, the same smile that roped me into trusting him within minutes.

"I'll keep her safe, I promise."

We finish our meal, and Alex leaves shortly after. Tom is still gushing over being able to get his autograph, and pummeling me with questions about how I met him, and the nature of our relationship while he busies himself with making yet another cup of tea. I explain how I did an article on him, and how we've become friends, but nothing further. This isn't high school; I don't kiss and tell.

Riley has decided to take care of the clean up on her own, so I grab a glass of wine and head back up to my room. The toy inside of me is driving me wild, and having the chance to catch the scent of him this evening as left the ache of wanting on my lips. I wanted to kiss him…to push him against that wall and rip his clothes from his body. I wanted to see that fire in his eyes again, and yet, it was just out of reach.

Chapter 24

I received a text from him later that night with instructions to slip the balls into me whenever I left my house. He also firmly pressed that I wasn't allowed to orgasm at all until I saw him that weekend for the show, and at that time, he may give permission.

Fantasies of the various possibilities of our upcoming meeting danced through my head every night as I went to sleep. The thought of him pinning me to a corner seat in a dark theater, teasing his fingertips along my body until I was soaked and aching, stifling moans so I wouldn't be overheard by the guests, drove me wild.

I count down the days, the hours, the minutes until I can see him again. My heart races when I dream of what he will do to me that evening, and the thought of needing his permission to come is…enticing. I wonder how long I've craved that kind of control; for someone to try and tame the animal that I've let run rampant through my body for so long.

Texts from Ethan have come on a fairly regular basis; one or two a day with pictures of the various sites around New York City, and updates on how the convention is going. He's acting like such a tourist, and it's almost adorable.

I entertain his texts with brief spurts of information about how Riley and Tom are doing, and how it's nice to hear from him, but my sentiments feel hollow to my own fingers as I type them. The longer he's gone, the less I can remember what he looks like or the sound of his voice, and Alexander has pushed his way to the forefront of my mind. It's hard to fathom that he ever left that spot in the first place.

The day of the show quickly approaches, which I've finally found out is the opera Carmen, and Alex didn't bother to send meet up directions until four hours before the drive into New Orleans. I had put off getting ready, afraid that he'd cancel our plans, so at the last moment I'm stuck throwing on a long black dress, and pinning my hair up in a makeshift clip. I don't look *too* terrible, and once I pat on some makeup and a simple diamond pendant around my neck, I leave the house and head to the theater.

We decided to meet just outside of the theater. He's standing on a charming, wooden walking bridge over a man-made lake with sparkling fountains spouting up around him. The water reflects and refracts the lights from the theater, casting glittering starlight on him as he stands there, waiting. He smiles as I approach the apex of the bridge and holds out his arm for me to take.

"You are stunning, Miss Roman. As always." He whispers against my skin as he presses his lips to my cheek.

Blushing, I slip my arm in his and let him lead me into the theater. I can't tear my eyes off of him. He's dashing, dressed in a perfectly fitted three piece suit which mimics the ocean on a starless night, and a pale blue shirt accented with a black tie decorated with a silver fleur de Lis pin. His curls fall carelessly from his head, lightly dusting over his collar. I had often imagined how he would look in something other than a pair of jeans, but my dreams didn't prepare me for how he looks tonight.

We take our seats near the front, and talk quietly over the dull roar of the audience behind us. The butterflies in my stomach are in full swing as we await the performance. I never thought I would actually witness an opera; it seems like one of those things that only the super-refined attend, and though I've always wanted to come, I never thought I was good enough. I often keep myself from attending things like this, based on that notion; the thought that I'm not good enough to be seen in a certain place. I feel like I'd stick out among the crowd, and wind up not enjoying the experience because I was too busy worrying about how everyone else saw me.

Sitting here beside Alex, chased those thoughts away. I belong here with him, and no scoff or rude glance from anyone could convince me otherwise.

The theater is a cavernous room dressed in cream colored ceilings and walls, with the stage carefully concealed in a blood red curtain. As patrons filed in and took their seats, the lights dimmed, and the opera commenced. There were no stolen glances from him, or any sneaking touches. We sat still in our seats, entranced by the brilliant performance before us, and as it came to an end, I wished they would find a reason to keep going. I dreaded the curtain's fall; this moment is so perfect, and I don't want it to end.

He stands as the lights fill the capacious

theater, and offers his hand, which I graciously accept. Wordlessly, he leads me out into the night, winding us through brilliantly lit streets, back to his home. The silence between us is anything but uncomfortable. It's more of a peaceful contentment, in which words would only serve to clutter and tangle the delicate strands of threaded between us.

My desire for him had grown steadily over the last few months, and tonight, it has warped into something more than a steaming primal lust. I want more; something more than the hunger in his eyes, and the twist of pleasure as our bodies bind together. I wish to hold him, run my fingers through his hair, and fall asleep in his arms. For once, the beast was absent. It wasn't clawing through my skin and bones for a chance to taste his heat on my lips, and I just want to feel…loved, and perhaps, less lonely, if even for a single night. I ache for the gentle touch of a soft hand, and the whispered acceptance and reciprocation of those feelings from him.

"Thank you for joining me." He says, hesitantly, breaking the silence between us as we make the last turn towards his home.

"Thank you for inviting me." I offer, my fingers lacing with his and squeezing affectionately.

Smiling, he slows his stride to a leisurely

pace, and slips his fingers out of my grasp. His hand slides up the side of my arm, and drapes around my shoulders as we walk the few feet through the courtyard, and up the steps to his door. Guiding me through the foyer, he kicks off his shoes and pulls me into the couch. I curl close, leaning against him. His arm wraps around me, his fingers gently twisting my curls as I rest my head against his chest. He's so warm…so soft, and his gentle demeanor smothers me like a blanket fresh from the dryer on a frigid evening.

"This is nice…" I whisper

"It is. Can I get you anything? Are you hungry?"

"No…"

He leans down and kisses the top of my head as we sit in silence together. His phone begins vibrating from his pocket, and reaching in, he turns it off.

"Are you allowed to do that?" I laugh, teasingly.

"I am tonight."

"What makes tonight different?"

"I need a day off, and I've decided today is

going to be that day. So, for the rest of the night, no phone calls."

He tosses his phone onto the table among the rolling hills of books, then flips on music, which fills the house. It begins in soft, muted notes, building in intensity with each passing second. A beautiful, tenor voice rings out to join the notes; powerful and filled with passion. It sends chills through my body.

"Ah, I'm quite fond of this one." He sighs as he closes his eyes. His head leans back on the couch as he lets melody wash over his body, content in letting the music fill him till he drowns.

Looking up at him, the corners of my mouth lift. My fingers delicately slip up the side of his neck, and I tentatively stroke his cheek. He's wonderful. The embodiment of everything I ever wanted, but never felt I deserved. Perhaps I still don't.

He leans his head towards mine, as the voice flooding the house reaches a compelling crescendo. His fingers slide fluidly under my chin, tilt it up and he presses his lips against mine, his heat surging against my lips.

The sweet, soft touch of his lips threatens to replace my monsters' lustful feelings with an ache in the core of my heart. The scent of his skin mingles with that delicious, old book smell wafting from the written tomes that fill every corner, and I feel myself drowning in him once again. Taking my hand, he stands and draws me up.

"Will you join me on the terrace? It's a clear, beautiful night. We should enjoy the air."

Without waiting for an answer, he grabs a bottle of wine from the kitchen, two crystalline glasses, and leads me out the back door onto the terrace. The moonlight shines against the flagstones, causing them to glow with its pure light as we step outside. The terrace is filled to the brim with palm trees, and vibrantly colored tropical plants. There's a three tiered fountain in the center, and several small tables and chairs scattered amongst the foliage. He leads me to a chair furthest from the fountain, and pours a glass of wine. The music from the house streams into the night air from speakers planted outside of the house, and I feel as if I've been led, in secret, into his personal oasis.

We share our drink in silence, with the bubbling water and music as our background, but I can't seem to keep my mouth shut for long. There's so much I want to know. So much I need to know.

"Do you live here by yourself…?"

"Yes."

"It's an awfully big place."

"I enjoy my space, and my solitude. Usually."

Silence follows, and I'm hesitant to try and spark more of a conversation, but our entire relationship has been shrouded. I know nothing personal about him, and I'm aching to know more.

With his eyes fixated on the sky, his lips part once more.

"It wasn't always so empty. There was a time where I enjoyed having people over. A time when the house, and terrace, were filled with the laughter and joy of friends and family. It was another time…a lifetime away from the here and now…"

"What…happened?"

He shakes his head, his eyes sliding to the fountain as he loses himself in the sparkling waters.

"I saw death. I saw agony, and fear, and saw people turn on one another with the savagery of untamed animals. Those closest to me…those I loved, were ripped away unfairly. Unjustly. It forced me to see the world as more than just joy and happiness. Now…now, I enjoy my solitude. It gives me time to think, and time to work."

He looks over at me as he speaks, locking me in an intense gaze, then noticing my sadness, his expression softens.

"Cassandra, please don't pity me. Death is everywhere. Whether we choose to believe it or not, it is an inescapable, irrefutable fact. I lost someone very near and dear to me, and it took me quite a long time to piece together some semblance of a life. Everyone goes through these things at some time or another. I just became something more than the carefree youth I was before. Life is filled with happiness, sadness, pain and pleasure. If it weren't, if it were only filled with happiness, we would cease to appreciate everything good in our lives. There is no happiness without sadness, and no pleasure without a sense of pain."

I gaze up through the trees. The center of the terrace is unobscured, offering a full view into the clear, sparkling night sky as I digest his words. I can't imagine living in this place on my own. Doesn't he get lonely? I'm at a loss as to what to say in response. What could I say that doesn't sound rude or patronizing?

"What's the name of this piece?" I ask, straining. It's lovely, and I'm sure I'm making myself sound a bit less refined in not knowing what it is.

"Nessun dorma."

"It's beautiful."

He turns to me, his eyes sparkle in the night as he smiles lovingly. Reaching over, he takes my hand in his, absently stroking his thumb along the back of my hand.

"It's from an opera named Turandot. This song is sung by a prince, who falls in love with a beautiful princess with a heart of ice." His eyes return to the sky, my hand still held in his. "We should go see it sometime…"

My heart can't decide whether it wants to beat faster or ache in longing. The emotions run, conflicted and clashing, through my body as I struggle to piece him together.

The song shifts, and violins now sing out into the still air. He eases onto his feet, my hand still in his, and draws me up to him.

"Dance with me…" he whispers, his eyes gazing into mine.

His words sweep over me in a gentle, relaxing wave as he wraps one arm around my waist and holds me close, his other hand clasping mine. An arresting look in his eyes holds me against him as he leads me in soft, swaying movements to the exquisite notes of Pachelbel's Canon. Each movement is premeditated, as if we're playing out our parts in a scene, on a stage all our own. This is something that is only ever dreamed of; some flight of fancy that never happens in the real world. This is…he is…

The music swells as we glide across the terrace, tracing the fountain and its splatter of crystal droplets. Our eyes are fixed on one another, never wavering, never moving. The music steals us away as the background shimmers into a muddled mix of greens and browns, and flashes of pinks and oranges, as we circle one another in an endless dance. I am breathless, caught in the beauty of him. His hands effortlessly move my body with his own, synchronizing each step, each sway, and each breath.

"Will you stay the night?" he asks softly.

"Of course I will."

His hand cups my cheek, his thumb lightly stroking my bottom lip. Oh, it feels wonderful, like the whispered breath of an angel against my skin.

His lips follow his thumb, pressing against

mine; soft, gentle and tender. Taking my hand, he leads me upstairs to his bed. Our bodies shift as he pulls me firmly against him; absently moving with the beat of the slow, passionate tunes streaming from the sound system.

Thin, lithe fingers slowly unzip my dress, pulling it from my shoulders and letting it rest peacefully on the wooden floor. My fingers stumble against his suit as I help him undress, and I internally plead, please don't make this sexual. This is too nice…too wonderful. I don't want it to turn into something…primal and lustful and painful. My heart couldn't handle it. Not now…

His hands slide up, through my hair, gently guiding my eyes into his own. He hovers over me, one hand petting my hair and the other, stroking my cheek. Those eyes…the world swirls in their depths. The room, the sky, the earth, and so much more. And I'm reflected in them. My fear and pain. My ghosts, my demons, my insecurities, are swallowed by them. Snuffed out of existence. Inconsequential.

I don't deserve this…

My head dips against his chest, tears threatening to pool at the corners of my eyes, and he wraps his arms protectively around me, kissing the top of my head.

"Say you'll be mine..." he whispers against my hair, and my heart twists in its' cage, wrung out of all its life sustaining blood. It hurts...it's agonizing. Why does it hurt so much? I should be blissfully happy.

Pulling back, I breathe and regain my composure, shooting him a wry look, then curl a smile on my lips.

"Yours? But Mister Delacroix, I thought you didn't *do* those types of relationships? I thought you didn't have the time."

"I want to make the time," he groans against my lips. His fingers slip through my hair lovingly, then lightly brush over my cheek. Turning my lips into his hand, I softly kiss his palm.

I find myself unable to speak, and afraid to. What would I say? No? Yes? Is there an answer? His lips press against mine, kissing me with such a deep urgency that fills me with a feeling of such blinding love, that it'd rival the suns' light.

Breaking the kiss reluctantly, he scoops me effortlessly into his arms, carrying me to the bed, and laying me gingerly upon the sheets. Walking to the foot of the bed, he slithers up my body like a vine on a tree, leaving nectar kisses in his wake. The moon streaming in through the large windows, reflects off his shimmering skin; each strong, lean muscle defined in its purifying light.

He is gorgeous. Beauty the likes of which I've never seen. We are programmed to think only the epitome of manliness; some hyper-masculine being with bulging muscles and broad shoulders, is the height of sexuality. But no, no. This is… this lithe, beautiful, intelligent male has drugged me with his words, with his gentle demeanor, and I'm a puppet on his string. I ache for him, heart, body and soul.

As he slides beside me, he pulls the covers over both of us, pressing flush against my body and wraps me in his arms, resting his chin on the top of my head. His chest rises and falls with each, deep, deliberate breath and for once, I feel calm and content. My thoughts are silent. The rushing, doubtful inquiries about what-ifs are gone. The insecurities and uncertainties have disappeared, as if they had never existed to begin with. This is where I'm meant to be.

I take a deep breath, soothed by the scent of his skin, and feel his arms tighten around my slowly chilling body. His heated hands run absently over me, moving to my hair and stroking gently through the strands until my eyes grow heavy.

Chapter 25

I'm cast into darkness again, my body taking on that of a small child, and I'm pined against a wall.

He's come home drunk again, and I was unfortunate enough to wander into the kitchen for a glass of milk at the very moment he stumbled through the door. The smell of beer on his breath was stomach-churning, and I found myself choking down vomit from the words spilling out of his lips.

His arm shot out against the wall in a sorry attempt to hold him steady him, barring my escape from his clutches, as a sinister smile curled on his lips. He was too close…too close.

The heat from his body mixes with the poison from his lips, and my brain starts panicking.

I need to get away…I want to get away. This is wrong and I don't want this. What is he going to do to me?

My eyes dart back and forth, trying to find some gap in his defenses as he sways in front of me.

Too close…too close.

He leans down toward me, and my panicked brain finally breaks. I push my much-too-small hands against his chest, trying with all my strength to move him, and finally manage to push him off balance. I quickly duck under his arm and race to my room, slamming my door shut and locking it, then checking and double checking the handle just to make sure it was, indeed, locked.

Shuffling quietly to the opposite corner of the room, I curl up on the cold, concrete floor and pull my legs against my chest. I stifle my cries as I stare at the door for hours, afraid that he'd break it down.

A small knock, and my whispered name from his lips, then everything goes quiet except for the sounds of the bugs screaming in the night. I stare at the door until the sun begins to peek up over the horizon, afraid that in some rush of frustration, he would break the door down and come after me, but he doesn't. I'm safe…at least, for now.

Chapter 26

"Cassandra. Cassandra..."

Alex is hovering over me, propped up on his elbow and lightly stroking my hair. His eyes are dark, hooded, worried. Did something happen?

His fingers slip over the edges of my eyes, wiping away tears which glimmer on his fingertips as he holds them up to his face.

Oh, I was crying.

The dried tracks made by tears running down the side of my eyes, pull at my skin as I blink a few stray drops from my eyelashes.

"Are you okay?"

"I'm fine..." I murmur, as I pull away from him and sit up in the bed as I struggle to recall my tormented nightmare, but it's already quickly slipping beneath the surface, filed away in some dark, dilapidated box. All I could pull from it were fragments that refused to join together into a cohesive painting.

"Are you sure?"

"Yeah. I'm sorry, I'm not really sure why that happened, but I'm okay. Really, I am." I smile, and the corner of his lips tug downward as he regards me with a skeptical look.

"If you insist. I made some eggs, if you're hungry. You're welcome to stay as long as you'd like…"

"Thanks, but I haven't really brought anything with me, and would feel awkward sitting about your house in a dress. I should head home…"

"Are you sure? I have a shirt and some pants you can slip on if you'd like to be more comfortable."

"I'm sure," I smile "thank you, though."

His eyes are pleading for my company, and I want to stay more than anything, but the fractured remnants of my dream have left an unpleasant taste in my mouth. I feel sick; on the verge of vomiting.

I make my way to his shower where I wash up and try to make myself a bit more presentable. I haven't brought anything with me, and so, am stuck in the same gown I wore the night before. I feel a bit out of place in it, but thank him for the night, offer a hug, and slip from his home.

The desire to stay is overwhelming, but the way he was acting last night has left my thoughts in a constant tug of war over what it all meant. He took on the features of the man that my white-picket-fence side has always wanted, and those two parts of me don't seem to mesh together all that well. There was no man who could cater to all of me; I have become comfortable with that realization, and his actions are making me question everything.

As I pull onto the interstate, the sun reaches its highest point in the sky, filling my car with an unbearably stifling heat, but I can't bring myself to close the windows. I love the smell of the air, and so, I suffer through the uncomfortable feeling of my clothes sticking against my skin, and the frizzing of my curls to near treasure-troll proportions.

The roads are, thankfully, empty, and the near barren asphalt offers my mind a certain kind of tranquility to accompany my drive home. I begin to draw myself into thinking of golden beaches and crystal blue waters, and think of just how much I really need a vacation to get away from everything and everyone when my phone rings. I flip on the Bluetooth and hear Angela's frantic voice on the other end.

"Cass, there's an event I need you to cover in two weeks. Are you busy? Can you handle it?"

"Ah, Angela. Great timing, as always…" I grumble under my breath, trying to hide the sarcasm from my voice.

"You know, I could always find someone else if you don't want the work. If you're going to bitch about it…"

"No! Sorry, it's been a long week. You should probably start by telling me what event, where it is, and what exactly you need me to do."

"I was getting there! But it'd be pointless to waste my breath if you didn't have the time free."

"I'm free, I'm fairly certain. So, tell me about it?"

"It's a festival for everything! Literature, performing arts, music, everything you can think of. It's this huge thing that happens every year, but I've never had someone willing to stick around for the whole thing and write up anything more than a small article. I'd like for you to stay at least a full week and cover it for me, though the event itself can sometimes span several weeks. We'll pick up the tab for your hotel stay, of course, but you'll have to cover your own food and drinks. We already have a room booked for two weeks just in case you decide you're up for staying longer. Are you in?"

"Sounds fun, I guess. Yeah, sure. I'll hang out for a week. Bit late notice, though, especially for you." I roll my eyes. Late notice? At least I have two weeks. The last job she sent me on — with Delacroix — I had barely 24 hours' notice. This is an improvement, at least.

"Yeah, well, I had someone else all set up for it and he flaked out on me, so now I'm scrambling for a replacement."

"Awe, Angela, I wasn't your first choice? I'm genuinely hurt." I chide.

"Oh shut up. You'll have fun, I promise. Just get me something good to work with, okay?"

"Yeah. Sure."

"Good. I'll email you all the details of the event, and the name of where you'll be staying."

"Sounds good.

"Thanks, Cass. I really appreciate this."

"Yeah, no problem."

With an audible click, she hangs up, and I'm left alone once again with my struggled thoughts of a beautiful quiet beach.

I guess I won't be taking that vacation any time soon…

Chapter 27

It was the day of the festival, and I was more excited than I thought I'd be. To use the age old cliché, I felt like a kid on Christmas. I picked out my outfit last week in anticipation. A simple knee length black skirt hugged my hips, paired with a crisp light blue button up shirt and a pair of black ankle boots, and now I find myself in front of the open closet, staring at it, mentally mixing and matching various accessories that may go along with it. I'm usually more comfortable slipping into a pair of black slacks and a blouse at best, but this is different. This little work assignment has turned out to be a very special occasion, indeed.

It's been a couple of weeks since Delacroix and I have had another chance to spend time together, though we still did manage to swap a few texts once every 3-7 days depending more on his schedule than my own.

Two weeks ago, I received a call from Angela to hang out at this big festival happening in New Orleans. It was due to be a several week event and the L*Addict* had already booked my hotel, as well as given me a list of all the events planned for that span of time.

By a very happy coincidence, it seems that my very own Alexander Delacroix was due to be a part of this fest, and my mind immediately began weaving a slew of fantasies ranging from being taken in a wild public display of passion, to a more subtle 'Prince Charming' encounter. And so, I picked out this outfit as a sort of introduction for my first day at the fest. I know it's completely impractical to walk around for several blocks and stand for hours on end in heels, so I have decided to pack along a few pairs of fashionable flats as well.

I went all out. I actually paid a visit to the salon, and I'm happier with the results than I would've thought. No hair products needed for this girl! Just soft, shiny loose curls, and as I check myself out in the mirror, I realize for the first time that I'm pretty damn hot. Usually I only feel that way when I'm high on hormones once the lights go out, and the raw musk of sex is in the air. I've always felt my most confident in the bedroom, but now? Well, being embarrassed in my own skin is the furthest thing from my mind.

I run my hands over my curves, and adjust myself in my bra, leaving a button carelessly unfastened to show a tasteful hint of cleavage. I flash a smile at my reflection. Damn. I'd do me.

Laughing at the thought, I grab my bags and head downstairs. Riley is furiously writing down several numbers on a piece of paper and shoving it at me as I reach the first floor.

"Cass, you're going to be gone forever! You have my number, but here's the number to my parents, and to Tom, and to Ryan if you need him! And you have Ethan's, right? Well, what help would he be. He's not here…anyway! You could still call him if you can't get a hold of myself or Tom. I also wrote down the numbers to our neighbors just in case you can't get a hold of us or anything, but I'll have my phone on the whole time you're gone!"

"Riley, I'm staying in a nice place, and I'm not a child. Really, I can take care of myself. I'll be just fine!"

"But it's a two whole weeks! What am I going to do for two weeks?! And it's New Orleans!

It's a big city! It's big and scary and crowded and who knows what could happen!"

Amidst her mini panic attack, she stops suddenly and stares at me while I stand before her, bags in hand with the paper of numbers she so hastily stuck in my mouth, since I had no other way to grab it.

"Cass…" she whispers as she draws closer, eyeing me up and down. She pulls me to the center of the room and paces a full circle around me

"How the *hell* are you going to walk around in those shoes? Are you INSANE?"

She bolts to the closet by the door and starts rummaging through her shoes, dragging out various boots, flats, sneakers, and flip flops.

"Riley, I already packed a few pairs of comfortable shoes."

"Oh…" she sighs "well okay…"

"You can call me, you know. While I'm away…"

"I know, but you're going to be busy. I don't want to bother you."

"I'll try to call you every night. Maybe

every other night, okay? I'll at least text every day with a few pictures!"

"I guess that's okay. I wish I could go with you, but I promised Tom I'd go with him to his parents this weekend. It's his mom's birthday or something. I still have to bake the cake…"

I set my bags down and wrap her in a big hug.

"I'm going to miss you too, Riley."

She hugs back tightly and lingers for several moments before I manage to wiggle from her hold. I smile, and she places a kiss on my cheek then sets on my way.

After checking in at the hotel, I entertain the thought of letting him know I'm in the area, but think better of it. After all, it may be a nice little surprise, wouldn't it?

I settle in, grab my camera, pull out my pen and notepad from my duffle bag and transfer them to my purse. I'm not much of a photographer, but I'm sure I can produce semi decent things to go along with the article and at worst, they will remind me of the festival and contribute to the descriptions I'll use when putting together my piece for Angela. If she decides not to use them, it's not like I'm losing anything.

The festival takes place a mere three blocks from my hotel, so I decide to walk there in order to get a feel of this area of New Orleans. I've shoved an emergency pair of shoes in my purse and pray I can hold out for a few hours before the blisters start to form.

It's a surprisingly crisp day for this time of year, and by crisp, I mean it's hovering somewhere around the low 70's. That's chilly, considering our normal weather, but it's beautiful nonetheless. The humidity isn't stifling for once, and there's a gentle breeze meandering its way through the catacomb of buildings.

The music of the festival is audible from the moment I leave the hotel doors, and I'm lured towards it as if it were a siren's song. The sounds of joy and laughter intermingle with the rhythmic notes streaming from the festival band, and as I approach it, I feel the spirit of the festival grip me.

The event is massive, and though I find the energy of the music and the colorful people exhilarating, I begin to worry that I won't find Alex in this overwhelming crowd of people.

Closing my eyes for just a second, I push the thought from my mind. After all, he's not the reason

I'm here. I'm here to work, give a detailed account of the events to Angela and let her worry about piecing together the mass of information I'll be sending in. If I have to spend two weeks in a hotel without a good, home-cooked meal, than she's going to spend a few days shifting through everything I'm sending back to her!

Navigating through the festival, I dance between bodies clad in every imaginable shade and color. Some are dressed like me, models of the semi-professional, and others are a bit more outlandish.

Black business suits and ties mingle with vivid feathered hats. Smart, gray pinstripe skirts dance with radiant corsets with thigh-high buckled boots. And the alcohol overflows from every corner, freely consumed in the streets that burst with the heightened energy of jubilant laughter and excited whispers.

Shifting and sliding through the crowd, I attempt to blend with the local population, swallowing my anxiety from being engulfed by the crowd in such an unfamiliar place. A few trips for less than a few hours to this vibrant city, does not a local, make.

I stop by a stand and grab a drink - a rum and coke - and continue making my way through the crowd, snapping pictures which people all too happily pose for. They express, in their eager words, how wonderful this festival is for the local artistic community.

Jotting down names and quotes, I gather as much information as I can before the sun begins to set. I begin making my staggered way back to the hotel room. Delacroix was nowhere to be found, but the energy from the festival mixing with the alcohol, which danced through my blood stream, had a welcome effect on my body. I feel warm, calm, happy and comfortable in my own skin, which is something that, sadly, isn't all that common. I feel completely joyous, without a single care slipping through my mind. I'm simply happy to be here, and getting to really learn about the culture of this city, is exciting! I daresay, I almost want to stay, and find myself musing over the thought of buying a place here in the city to experience all the wonderful things it has to offer.

It's silly. I'm sure it's just the alcohol.

Slipping past the front desk, I barely catch the elevator, and make my way to my room. Some pizza and a night with my feet up while I listen to the music slip in through the hotel window, seems like the perfect end to a fun filled day.

I let my hair down and kick off my boots,

my feet numb from the walk. I'm sure I'll feel the blisters in the morning.

The festival still pumps through my veins as a knock comes to the door. Raking my fingers through my hair to shake out my curls and massage my scalp, I move to the door. My shirt is unbuttoned to my naval from the heat of the room, and the fire that so often accompanies alcohol, but I refuse to care even if I were walking down the hall completely naked. It wouldn't be all that much of an anomaly here anyhow, if what I've seen on the streets is any indication.

Wrenching the door open, I find the delivery guy, whose eyes are fixed on the crests of my breasts, and the fabric of my laced bra. With a wink and a smirk, I slip him a nice tip, and shut the door quickly, lest my body take over and act upon its heated impulses.

Fantasies flash through my mind of the oh-so-typical delivery guy sex scene, and I briefly entertain the thought of him naked and strapped to my bed.

Tossing the pizza unceremoniously on the table, I pull out my phone and am about to call Riley when another knock taps against the door. Oh how delicious it would be, if it were my little delivery guy.

I opened the door to gold-flecked brown eyes set behind gleaming silver rims, and auburn curls. His eyes quickly move from mine, slipping down my neck and breasts, then back to my eyes.

Shifting uncomfortably under his gaze; I could feel his eyes boring into me with disappointment. Biting my lip and down-casting my eyes, I wave meekly, muttering a soft greeting. This isn't exactly the state I had wanted him to see me in. I feel like I have some image I should uphold. Some sense of sophistication I wanted to prove to him. I wanted him to look at me and feel respect first, and desire second. To feel as if I were unobtainable and yet, oh-so-desirable. I wanted him to want me the way I want him. To feel that obsession crawl up his spine. That anticipation of waiting for a call or text from me. To feel helpless, the way I'd always felt when it came to him; and all of it was slipping away from me. And suddenly I'm angry that he's here when I couldn't find him anywhere at the festival to make our meeting on my terms. I'm upset that he hasn't contacted me at all, for days. Is this going to be a constant thing with him?

"Is this the way you normally answer the door, Miss Roman?" he sighs, his lips set in a disappointed line.

My lips and tongue refuses to form the

syllables required for any kind of coherent sentence, and all I can do is shake my head.

No, it's not.

I move my hands to my shirt, and begin to button it up, pulling my hair over one shoulder. I can do nothing but stare at the ground, ashamed of how I must look to him.

"Well? It's rude to leave me standing out here. Are you going to invite me in?"

Nodding, I move aside, waving my arm to welcome him into the room.

As he walks in, I pull a chair for him to sit, and sit in the chair directly across. I rest my elbows on the table between us and lace my fingers, then cradle my chin on them, still uncomfortable with the idea of looking him in the eye. He settles into the chair and props his ankle up on his opposite knee, his hands lacing themselves together in his lap.

"I didn't know you were staying here until I saw you walk in as I was sitting at the café."

He points to a small coffee shop opposite of the hotel room. I hadn't noticed it was there before.

"Why didn't you tell me you were going to

be in town? I feel like we've had this conversation, already, and I do hate repeating myself."

"I sent you a text days ago just to say hi, but you never replied. I didn't even know you were going to be here until just a few days before I left."

"You could have contacted me at that point and told me you were coming. You arrived today?"

"Yes."

"And yet, I've no text from you today, or even yesterday, stating your plans to be in the area."

"When you didn't respond to my other messages, I figured you'd gotten too busy and I didn't want to be a bother."

"When I don't reply, it doesn't mean I don't want to talk to you or don't want to see what you've written or sent to me. I just get wrapped up in other things. I'm disappointed. I expect it won't happen again."

"I'm sorry." I whisper meekly, my eyes tracing the small lines in the table as a way to keep tears from welling in my eyes. Am I that intoxicated that I can't keep my emotions in check? I feel like a child being chastised by her father for breaking the rules. "I just didn't want to interrupt anything. I know how busy you can be...and I thought that maybe you'd grown bored with me."

The chair shuffles, but I don't bother to look up. I can only assume he's become so disgusted by talking to me, that he's decided to leave, and I don't want my last image of him to be of him walking out the door.

My heart is hammering and I can feel the tears about to break. I close my eyes tight and take a deep breath, remembering how agonizing it could be at times to not receive the smallest response to a message from him. How long could it honestly take to send a simple response?

My thoughts waver, and I grow furious. How dare he make me feel like shit, always hanging on a limb waiting to hear from him, nervously glancing at my phone waiting for the lights to flash for a new message, and yet it never comes. I came here, steeling myself to be the one in control. I came here convincing myself that I'd turn the tables and perhaps, make him want me instead of me sitting around questioning myself, as I feel my confidence dwindle away because of a single man.

Then, the cool touch of his fingers press under my chin as he lifts my face, forcing my eyes into his. He's moved near me; his body, dangerously close. The electricity from his skin jumps the void between us, sparking against my skin as his pulls me into his arms, and his lips embrace mine. I breathe in deep, taking in his musky scent, as my heart pounds and aches against my rib cage.

He pulls away; his speckled, brown eyes melting my body as he strokes his thumb against my cheek.

"I'm the one who should be apologizing. I told you I'd try to be better with communicating, and I haven't been doing a very good job. So many different things demand my attention, but you shouldn't be suffering for it."

He apologized to me. A real, heartfelt apology. I can see his eyes begging me for forgiveness, and as much as I don't want to give in, I do.

Standing firm, I grip the front of his shirt and pull him close, kissing him with the full might of every emotion that's wracked my body since the day I met him. My body is on fire, and every memory of those unanswered texts float away on the waves of music flowing through the city. His arms wrap around me as his hands slip through my hair, tugging lightly; seductively.

Riley was right; I love with this man. Against all rhyme and reason, I am hopelessly in love. Completely, lustfully and overwhelmingly entangled in him. I can't fathom how this will work, as I feel the need for constant attention. Even if it's just a small phone call for five minutes, or a text to check up on me. In my twisted and broken mind, I need some kind of reaffirmation that he hasn't let someone else catch his eye, or that he hasn't simply grown bored with me. I need to feel like I'm good enough.

And yet when he's with me, I can't imagine how I was so foolish as to think something so absurd. He is so…there were no words. He's wonderful, incredible, eloquent, successful, intoxicating. A testosterone-infused cocktail of romance and seething dominance. Those words alone doesn't seem to do him justice. He is absolutely beautiful in every way. His eyes, his body, his mind and his words are sweet notes of a symphony that enraptured my heart. They wrapped me in a blanket and whispered promises, reaffirming that he is one of a kind. I'm obsessed; totally and completely. I'm drunk off of his presence and high from his scent; as if everything I built up to protect myself has come crashing to the ground, exposing raw unadulterated passion, desire, and aching, painful love whenever I am close to him.

Our kiss deepens, and my fingers run

through his hair; each soft curl giving way beneath my tender touch.

He sighs heatedly, near inaudibly, against my lips and pulls me closer. My hands move down, slowly unbuttoning his shirt. It sags off of his shoulders as he runs his fingers through my curls, and holds my head firm against the kiss. Ripping his shirt off, my hands press desperately against his warm chest and relish in the feel of his soft flesh beneath my fingertips. His hands move down my back then over my chest, unbuttoning my shirt and pulling it down over my shoulders, exposing my bra. His lips move to my neck, kissing the sensitive skin and pulling me firmly against him. His hard, thick erection presses against me, a wave of pleasure crashes through my body in anticipation.

Knowing I can excite him like this heightens my own pleasure all the more, and I'm aching for him. My entire body, now singing with the passion in my heart, as they cry out in unison for him.

Pulling away, a sly smile spreads over his lips as he moves to the window. He tugs the windows open, letting the music waft in on the evening air, and allowing the heat to fill the room. Beckoning me closer, he points out the window.

"Right there. Do you see it?" He whispers, his lips dangerously close to my ear.

My eyes flutter as his words slide through my ears, and I struggle to see what he's pointing at but I only see the throbbing crowd below.

"The group of people?"

"Mhm." He whispers as his hands wrap around me from behind, holding me tight as he sways our bodies to the music. "I don't want you to take your eyes off of them. Watch…knowing at any moment, they could look up and see my hands on your beautiful body."

His lips move to my neck once more, and kiss along it softly, moving from right below my ear to my shoulder then swapping to the side. His hands move over my breasts and tease over my collar bone. The muscles in my body tense as he does; flashes of pain from so long ago…

I close my eyes tight, strangling the memories, lighting them on fire and watching in pleasure as they burn to ash.

It didn't happen. Those memories…that life…doesn't exist and never has.

His hands stop, and he moves them to my hips.

"Is something wrong? Are you all right?"

"…yeah. Just, please don't touch me there… it makes me uncomfortable…"

"Then let me make up for it."

He turns me to face him and gazes into my eyes as he runs his fingers through my hair. I have to bite my tongue to keep from my lips from betraying me. Do I love him? I want nothing more than to tell him right here and now. My heart aches, my throat clenches, but I hold it back. His eyes, and his touch, banish the darkness of old, painful memories.

"When all of the festivities are over, and my obligations complete, I'd like you to come stay with me for a few days. If you can. Perhaps a weekend? I would love to spend some more time with you. Uninterrupted, of course."

"Uninterrupted? That's hard to pass up."

I run my fingers along his prominent jaw line, then tilt my face up to meet his, lightly tracing my lips along his. They're soft and supple, like running my lips over the ripe flesh of freshly opened rose petals. Everything about this man makes me crave more. He's my drug, my freedom. I want nothing more than to be locked in this moment for eternity.

Smiling, he kisses along my cheek and down my neck as he hooks his thumbs into the waist of my skirt and tugs it down to splash at my feet. He lightly traces his fingertips over the front of my laced panties, then slides his lips down further, lightly licking between my breasts as he leans down and wraps his arms around my waist, lifting me and placing my butt on the windowsill, my body pressing against the transparent glass.

If anyone were to look up, they probably wouldn't be phased by seeing a naked woman against a window, not like I'd care what they thought at this moment, anyhow. They didn't exist. It's just him and I in my world, and at this moment, that's all I ever want it to be.

Thoughts of Riley, Ethan, Angela; they weren't there. My home, my car, my money, my past; it didn't exist. It's him and I, and I want nothing more than to feel my body meld with him, be a part of him, and float on his ocean until I drown.

He slips his fingers in the band of my panties, wiggling me out of them, and as he pulls them from my feet, he kneels down in front of me and presses his lips against my ankle. He slithers his tongue against my skin, sending shocks through my body strong enough to draw moans from my lips.

I've never felt something so incredible, nor had I ever thought that my ankles were as sensitive as they were proving to be.

What kind of sex did I have before him? It all seems terribly mundane and boring in comparison, as if I'd never fully experienced it. As if nothing, at all, could ever compare.

Moving to the other ankle, his lips go back to work. My fingers dig into the windowsill as my head tilts back, my eyes fluttering as my moans grow with each touch.

I don't want him to stop, and as his lips work against my ankles, my muscles clench. My body and mind are wrapped in a fit of ecstasy within seconds, without warning, and as my back arches, I feel that all-too-familiar sensation welling up deep in my body.

"Please, Alex…"

"Come for me, my lovely girl."

My body rebels against my will, trembling and writhing against the window as my lips moan his name.

He stands, wrapping me up in his arms, and carries me to the bed.

"You're so erotic, my dear. And so sensitive…"

"Please," I gasp, burying my face against his shoulder, "I need more. Please."

He strips the rest of his clothes, his body glistening in the evening sunlight like a golden statue.

Crawling on me, he gathers my wrists in one hand, and pins my arms above my head. My breasts tremble with each labored breath, my sensitive nipples pressing against his chest as I bend my knees and press my thighs against his hips. He kisses my lips, his tongue hungrily wrapping around my own as he strokes his free hand down my side and grips the small of my back.

Slowly, agonizingly, he slides himself inside of me, and my body screams in delight. Still sensitive from my orgasm mere moments before, my body shudders as wave after wave of pleasure wracks through me.

He begins slow, sliding in and out with calculated movements. Running my hands over his back, I grip tight; my nails bite into his skin, raking against his flesh. He lets out a guttural growl and dives into me, driving hard and deep. My back arches against him as my head presses back into the bed. He's so deep, shoving every inch into me, and it's almost too much. It hurts, but oh…it feels so damn good.

"Take me!" I scream as my body trembles, my lips unable to bite back the words any longer.

And he obliges, slamming mercilessly into me, moaning against my neck. His lips vibrate with his primal, carnal groans of pleasure, and the sound of pure sex assaults my ears.

Swiftly, he props himself on his knees, pulling my legs over his shoulders while still buried deep inside of me. Gripping my hips, he pulls out, agonizingly, then thrusts into me in one sift motion, as his lips find my ankles and kiss them lovingly. Every inch pushes and stretches my sensitive sex around him.

He looks down at my body, his eyes hungry, flaming with desire as he presses his hips against me, steadily quickening in response to my lust-filled scream. Gripping the bed, fisting the sheets as he takes me, my nails threatening to rip them to shreds as my body tenses and aches.

"Please…don't stop…" I beg.

My body writhes, contorting into an image of pure pleasure, as I grip his arms. He increases his pace, sliding effortlessly into me until I'm left trembling beneath his body. My back arches, my eyes fluttering as I scream. Each delectable contraction squeezes him, as I throw myself from the edge of another, earth shattering orgasm.

My legs slip from his shoulders, weakened, as my body twitches and trembles, but he doesn't stop. He grips my thighs firmly, thrusting into me harder and faster as his eyes roll back and his eyes flutter to a close.

"Oh, God, Cass…you feel incredible" he groans.

He's panting, sweat glistening on his body as his rock hard cock fills me to a near breaking point.

Spearing into me with an animalistic ferocity, his eyes take on a wild look, his damp curls clinging to his face and neck as his perfectly trimmed nails bite into my thighs. Wincing in delectable pain, the small jolt spreading like a wildfire from his fingertips, throughout my body into a mix of fire and lightning, churning in the middle of a maelstrom. I'm melting into him, each limb and bit of skin indistinguishable as our bodies press perfectly into one another, each movement a carefully calculated note of exquisite harmony.

His eyes blaze, head tilting back as I feel him grow inside of me. His breathing comes ragged, struggled from his lips as every muscle tenses against me. He groans, moans, then grows silent as his breath catches in his chest, and he comes. Bliss and ecstasy flashes in his eyes for the briefest of moments before he collapses on top of me, tilting my face to meet his.

"You're wonderful." he whispers breathlessly, kissing my lips.

Rolling off of me, he wraps me in his arms, and I feel safe and carefree. It's the only place I can ever imagine being, the only place I ever want to be.

His chin rests on the top of my head as I wrap my arm and leg around him, taking in his scent mixed with the lusty smell of our lovemaking, and I feel lucky to have him. Never had I thought I'd be lying in a bed with this man, who enraptures all with his written and spoken words, and yet here I am. And I know I'm his. There are other men who may capture my eye, and yet none have captured my soul as much as this man, with nothing more than a few words and a look from his eye.

Tracing my nails lightly over his chest, I listen to his heart pound against my ear. He reaches down and softly pets my hair, leaning down for a moment to kiss the top of my head, and I can't help but smile. If only every night were like this…

"What does your schedule look like for tomorrow?" I ask cautiously, willing him to tell me he's not busy so I could selfishly steal him away for the entire day.

"I have a meeting tomorrow morning, then back to managing my part of the festivities." He responds nonchalantly.

"Oh…"

"I may have some time tomorrow night…maybe we can have dinner?"

"I'd like that." I smile.

"How long are you here for?"

"For the duration of the festival."

"The entire two weeks?"

"If I choose to be, yes."

"Good. I rather like the thought of you being so close, for once."

Gathering me in his arms, his fingers lightly stroke my curls. "Rest, now, my dear."

Chapter 28

It's just past 3 A.M as I roll over, glaring at the icy blue numbers of the nightstand clock. Surprisingly, he's still here, and is curled up against my back cuddling close against me. I lightly run my fingers over the hand he has draped over my hip, then slip out from beneath his arm and make my way to the bathroom. My makeup is a mess, and my hair is even worse. I scowl at the clock sitting on the counter; I never do sleep all that well when I drink.

Looking back at the mirror, I try in vain to remove the black smudged eyeliner from under my eyes, but to no avail. I run the shower, hoping it's not loud enough to wake him. Sneaking a quick peek out of the bathroom door to the bed, I find him still lying there, fast asleep.

The hot water soaks my aching body,

washing the sweat and fluids from my skin and coaxing them down the drain. Once finished, I wrap myself in a towel and move over to the window in the main room, gazing out at the people still wandering the streets. Even at this late hour, there are still hordes of them walking around; drinking, laughing, and dancing to the music that's still being drummed out and amplified.

The sky breaks, and a light splattering of rain trickles down gray clouds that must have moved in overnight. The people below are unfazed, letting the sweet sounds of music seduce them into a world without a single wet drop.

I let my finger trace a miniscule tear as it dances down the window pane, memories and thoughts swirling within the reflective orb. I'm aching, both in desire and in loss. He's here with me, and yet I know it won't be forever. Tomorrow, he'll be gone again. The sun will come and he'll be gone, just like the gray clouds when they're pushed off into the horizon. Just how long can I fool myself into thinking I'll ever be satisfied with the arrangement we've managed to piece together from broken shards of our desires. What is it he wants from this? What is it that I want?

Collapsing at the table, water tickles my skin as it slides down my back from my soaked hair. The rain drops accumulate on the window pane, growing larger and larger till they're softly drumming out the song of my heart, as they dance in torrents with one another, and I'm transfixed by them. I watch the world below, in their distorted image, trying to find a place to fit this…well, whatever this is. Running my fingers over my chest, the ache increases; my heart threatening to bleed and push its' way through the hole it will inevitably create in my chest. My thoughts fixed, I glance at the bed from the corner of my eye and he's gone. The blanket tossed aside, pillows askew, and he's nowhere to be found.

I press my hands against my temples, closing my eyes tight as I hang my head and let the sound of the rain fill my ears. It aches; my body and heart are so pained that I feel as if I'll simply break apart, shattering into jagged shards of carelessly strewn glass.

Taking a deep, shuddering breath and willing back the tears that I can feel welling up, his hands rest softly on my shoulders, thumbs gently rubbing themselves over my skin. He leans down behind me, kissing the top of my head.

"My dear Cassandra, why are you always so sad?" he asks softly, and my body betrays me as I attempt to stifle my sobs. It's almost a cry of joy, as I'm surprised he's still here. Question my own sanity, I question if he's really just some elaborate figment of my imagination.

"I don't know." I sob.

"You don't know? Or you don't wish to share."

He pulls me up in his arms and holds me close as I sob against his shoulder. Why am I so sad? Why do I feel so empty and hollow at the thought of being alone, without him?

His hands are in my hair, softly petting the back of my head as his other hand strokes my back, his lips murmuring soft reassurances in an attempt to calm me, and the tears finally ease.

My demons have been chased away, but I know it's only temporary. They're still there, nipping at my heels and threatening to consume me. I just want them to go away...to stay away, but for him to have even accomplished this temporary feat is unheard of. Usually such respites come at the end of an impassioned night, and only due to exhaustion and copious amounts of alcohol.

I've grown to, dare I say it, love him and hate him, and I can't grasp the idea of living without everything he's awakened inside of me. He's filled parts of my life that I didn't realize were missing, and as much as I may despise the thought of it, I can't seem to stop it. I can't wrestle him from my thoughts and reassert my dominance. I feel so weak against him, and my body relents to the comfort of being held and protected by him.

I feel desperate and pathetic, and it makes me sick, but my heart wins this war, and wills my arms to wrap around him in return. I don't want him to shut me out again. I don't want him to abandon me…

"I want to be a part of your life." I plead. Oh how desperate I must sound; like a child clinging to her first crush in response to an absent father.

"My life is hectic." he responds matter-of-factly. "It involves cameras and interviews, and I'm always working."

"I don't care."

"You're not exactly close, distance wise."

"I don't care."

Shut up, Cass. You sound desperate!

He chuckles, leaning down and kissing me gently on the lips, then pulling away till our foreheads and noses still touch.

"Well, perhaps you can come stay with me for a weekend once everything settles down. We'll see how things go, and take them slow. I don't expect you to leave the life you have to come away with me."

I think back on Riley and give pause; after all, she'll probably move in with Tom soon, won't she? I couldn't leave her before then, though. How would she pay rent without me?!

"Perhaps…to be closer…"

"And your job? Are you so willing to drop everything?"

"Do I really have to drop everything to be with you?"

He smiles, and it was such a genuine gesture, that I found my heart sighing in pure pleasure.

"I wouldn't be happy if you did. No one should have to change their entire lives for someone else. It wouldn't be fair for you to give up everything so I could give up nothing."

He tilts my head up and smiles, his thumb running along my cheek. My eyes flutter, and I press my cheek into the palm of his hand, enjoying the warmth and softness of his touch.

"I want you to live your life, and in return, I need to live mine."

Wrapping my arms tightly around him, I breathe in his delicious, musk and basil infused scent. It goes straight to my head, causing every nerve to tingle.

"Now, why don't we go back to bed?"

Taking my hand, he leads me to the bed, and with a single gesture, pulls off my towel and tosses it over one of the chairs. Crawling in to the bed, I'm pulled in after him. With my head on his chest and strong, lean arms wrapped around me, I fall peacefully into him, my body smothered in his warmth.

"Thank you..." I whisper, then let exhaustion take hold.

Chapter 29

Filtering lazily through half-drawn blinds, the suns' light streaks across the wall, casting long shadows throughout the room like phantom fingers come to steal away the night. Breathing in the warm sunshine, I glance around the room, and he's gone. The bed is empty and the room is completely silent. There's no evidence that he's been here, not even a wrinkle in the sheets beside me.

My body takes on a zombie-like state as I walk to the shower. What did I really expect from him? To wake up next to him; waste away the day cuddled in his arms while we ordered room service and watched bad 80's movies? Ah…that would've been a perfect date night. Maybe we could…

Look at me. Still clinging to the hope that I

mean something to him. Hanging on to the whispered promises of a late night. Does he really want me to stay with him? Why would he say such a thing, and leave me without a second thought. Even a note, for Christ's sake.

Rolling my eyes, I let out an exasperated sigh as I let the near-scalding water cascade over my aching body. Once again, he has me questioning my own sanity, as I struggle to convince my mind that he was just a dream. He always has been. It's so much easier to believe that last night was nothing more than some feverish fantasy…there's less pain that way. I'll simply cut him off. I won't try to send a message, or let my finger hover over his name in the contacts list, and after a while, he'll fade just like everyone else.

Cutting off the water, I wrap myself in the complimentary plush white bathrobe, and am assaulted by the smells of bacon, eggs and fresh baked bread. The smell is intense, and wonderful, and immediately draws an embarrassing growl from my stomach. I guess I'm hungrier than I thought I was.

Padding lightly across the bathroom, I dismiss the smell. I must've left a window open. I should definitely find out which place is cooking up that delectable aroma, though. I'm starving!

Running my fingers through my drenched curls, I cross the bathroom threshold, musing over what I'm getting for breakfast, when I catch his silhouette in the window, framed in shadows and gold.

Turning to face me with a steaming cup of coffee in each hand, a warmth floods his eyes as his lips curl into a smile filled with such genuine happiness, that it draws the sun itself into my hotel room to chase away the shadows from every corner of the room, and my thoughts.

How could I have thought, for one second, that he would get up and leave me? He wasn't just another lover to be cast aside when I was done. There was no agreement between us for him to leave the way he came, and my rules for the lovers simply weren't mentioned to him. He was something so much more, something I couldn't purge from my body and I hope he feels the same.

Of course he does. You can't lie through your eyes, or perhaps, I'm only seeing what I want to see.

No. No more damaging thoughts. I deserve to be happy, no matter how fleeting it may be.

On the table, are two paper plates, each holding a beautifully crafted breakfast sandwich from the Gods themselves! Fresh French bread wraps lovingly around fluffy eggs, bacon and diced tomatoes. Walking over, he places the coffee in my hands and twists a sopping curl between his fingers. Placing his lips against my forehead, his kiss floods my body with an overwhelming peace and tranquility.

As the mornings rays set his hair aflame, and causes his body to glow from within with light and joy, there is no doubt in my mind. He has become my angel in a world filled with pain, and sorrow, darkness and regret.

"Good morning, my dear." He says, while rubbing the tip of his nose against mine. "I hope you don't mind. I figured you'd be hungry, since the pizza you ordered last night was barely touched. Join me?"

Well played, Mister Delacroix. Let's add mind reader to your list of perfections, and the fact that you remembered how I take my coffee is a lovely touch.

Words have failed me, and I'm still reeling over him being here. I was so convinced he'd leave. What else have I been wrong of? What else have I so, whole-heartedly convinced myself was real, that turned out to be false?

He ushers me into a chair at the table, then joins me. His auburn waves are hanging, damp, from his scalp, no doubt from the humidity brought on by last nights' rain and the festering sun.

"Cassandra, might I ask you something? It may be a bit personal…"

Personal? What…he wants to know what I use to shave my legs? Or when my monthly 'friend' comes to visit? I don't know how comfortable I'd feel disclosing that kind of information

"Sure…" I mumble between bites of food. My God, this tastes amazing.

"This is difficult to ask…" he states shyly, his eyes averting to some corner of the floor as his fingers rake through his hair. "I'd just…like to know…why do you cry in your sleep?"

I cry in my sleep? How embarrassing. I swallow hard and stare into the coffee cup, as if it could offer some answer for him. I didn't realize I had. I wonder why I do...

"It was probably just a nightmare." I state, as I wave a hand dismissively. Nightmares happen to everyone. Surely I'm not the only person who has a bad one now and then, and cries because of it. I wish I could remember what it was, though. Maybe then I could offer more of an explanation.

"I realize we haven't spent much time together, but every night we have, you've cried and whimpered in your sleep. I've tried to soothe you, but it does no good. I feel so helpless…maybe if I knew why you did it, I could help. Do you have a lot of nightmares?"

"I don't know. I guess? It's not something I think about. I don't remember my dreams too often."

A blatant lie. I remember every single one of them. Every painful, minute detail of every single nightmare, and often, they'll jumble themselves together at night just to drive me closer to the edge of insanity. Sure, I can drown them out, but every night they will remind me that they're still there. Memories of nightmares, perversions of a painful past bubbling just beneath the surface, waiting to take hold.

I glance out the window, suddenly losing my appetite at the turn the conversation has taken. Sliding across the glass are phantom images of a little girl, an older man…and pain. Immense, unbearable pain. Moving my eyes to the sky, I feel a warm tear slip from my eyes. Why…

"Cassandra…I think you do remember

them." He reaches across the table, wiping away my tear with a delicate touch of his finger. "What are they about?"

"I don't remember."

"Cassandra, I thought we went over this. I don't want you to feel like you have to hide from me. I'm not here to judge you, if that's what you're afraid of. I'm the last person who should be judging anyone."

Hide? I'm not hiding anything. Why the sudden interest in my life, anyhow.

"Why does this matter?!" I snap, unexpectedly. The tone surprises me. I had expected to say it an entirely different way, but my voice took on a mind of its' own. Why are we talking about me? All of these questions are pushing the limits of my patience. Can't we talk about more pleasurable things? Like sex, or the festival, or the goddamn weather. Or why talk at all? I'd rather just strip down. Then I don't have to think. Then…my mind is quiet.

"Because it may help you…" he murmurs. His voice is soothing, filled with worry and concern. How easy it would be to melt into him again, but at the moment, the gentle voice sparks a deep-seated anger.

Standing abruptly, my chair clatters to the floor as I walk to the other side of the room, busying myself by straightening up. I don't want to look at him. I don't even want to hear him speak.

"Please, Cassandra."

"Cass. It's Cass. Stop calling me Cassandra. I hate it. And how the fuck do you know what will help me? Who gave you the authority to say there's anything *wrong* with me!? I'm perfectly fine. I don't need your help, or anyone else's. I've always, *always* gotten by on my own, without anyone…without you or Riley or my family. I don't need *you*, Alex, to *help* me. I'm not some charity case. You can't throw those sad eyes at me, and sweep me off my feet and expect to squeeze every fucking shattered piece back together into a portrait to hang on your wall. I don't need yours, or anyone's, sympathy. No, don't look at me like that, like I'm some child with a skinned knee that you have to protect. Fuck you."

My face is burning. Tears are gushing down my cheeks, soaking my neck, and I'm trying in vain to hide them. I don't cry in front of anyone, and now Riley *and* Alex, have seen it, and I'm thoroughly disgusted with myself for it. It's a weakness that I can't afford to show. I'm stronger than that. I'm stronger…

He stands and moves behind me, wrapping his arms around me and pulling me against his chest, where my tears soak through his shirt. My body is trembling, and the memories threaten to break through. They chip away at the wall, exposing pinholes large enough for the smallest pieces of my past to sneak through, and even those, are overwhelming. I can't...I can't hold out much longer. I can't fall apart. Not in front of him.

Pressing my hands against his chest, I push him back more forcefully than I wanted to, and he staggers.

"Just get away...please."

The memories are painful, and my fingers press against my temples, gripping my hair tightly in hopes that physical pain will drive back emotional pain. It's always easier to deal with something physical than the daggers that are slicing away at my chest.

"Don't push me out, Cassandra. Please don't."

The monsters are there, nipping at my heels, ripping their teeth into flesh and sinew, and I can feel every small piece ripped violently from my body. My heart aches, on the verge of melting between their gnashing jaws. The memories...no.

No, they didn't happen...they didn't happen. Nothing happened.

"There's nothing wrong with me." I whimper, stifling sobs, my eyes tightly shut, blocking him out as my body curls on the bed. "I was a good girl...an innocent girl. I did nothing wrong. I was raised by a loving family...they loved me, and it was perfect. My childhood was perfect. My life was bliss. We were happy...we were always happy." But the words are hollow against my lips, dried and cracking like blood baked in the sun. It hurts, oh god, it hurts. "Nothing happened...nothing happened."

He sits on the bed beside me, his hand gently rubbing my shoulder, but he feels so far away. So distant, as if it were another time, another world, another life.

"Tell me what happened..."

I set my jaw, sucking back the tears and taking a deep breath. Deep breaths...I will not break.

"Please get out." The words are almost too much to squeeze out. I don't want him to see me like this. I don't need his pity.

"Burying things isn't the way to cope."

"Get…the hell…out!"

Several seconds of silence stretch on for eternity with us sitting in silence before I hear the door shut, and I'm alone. Completely, and utterly alone. But this is what I wanted, isn't it?

Running to the bathroom to splash cold water in my face, I begin going through the notions to piece together my shattering reality. He wasn't here. He didn't try to drag up my past. It didn't happen.

After another shower, I dress and rip open the shades, looking over the crowds of people that have already begun forming for the festivities. Straining an ear, the lively notes of the band caress against my skin. The sun rays beat against my eyelids, flowing through me from head to toe, and I breathe it in. Soft, slow, deliberate, the heat of the morning and the smell of the city seep into my soul.

Today is all about getting my work done, and enjoying my time in the city. Nothing else matters.

Checking the mirror, I pull on my mask — a perfect, near genuine smile — and head out into the world.

Chapter 30

The week went by smoothly, and I had successfully been able to keep my thoughts focused on work. At least, during the day. Once night fell — and I lacked a true distraction brought on by the festivities — I found it hard to keep my mind off of him, and reached eagerly for my bottled poison. I sat at the table and, regardless of my attempts to bury the memories, I couldn't keep the scenes from replaying over in my head. Was I too harsh to send him away? Did I really want him gone? I desperately want to see him again...maybe I just need to get away from this city.

Despite my desire to completely cut him off, my fingers slipped over his name and sent him a message, but I received no response. I even wandered around the festival, trying to catch a glimpse of him. Maybe...maybe I could try to explain it to him; try to apologize, but I didn't have the good fortune of running in to him again. He disappeared like smoke in the wind.

The end of the two weeks had finally arrived, and I'm more than happy to get away from the city, and away from him. I wanted to apologize and try to work things out, but he, apparently — from his lack of response— wasn't interested. This is why I hate getting tangled up in someone. It's nothing but a festering mix of pain, confusion, frustration and heartache. My previous arrangements were always so clear cut. Simple. No drama, no attachments, no expectations.

I make the drive home, pushing the speedometer well past the speed limit just for the rush it gives me, and its help in blocking out my thoughts. Riley isn't home by the time I get there, and I'm glad for it. I'm not sure how I'm feeling now, and the last thing I want is to snap at her.

Climbing the steps to my room, I rest a bottle of vodka on the desk that my fingers reached for before I could even think about it.

Work. Work will distract me, and I know what else Angela wants; the article on the ever-elusive Delacroix. It'd been such a catch for Angela to get him to agree to an interview, and now after I've met him and had, whatever this is with him, I want nothing more than to slander his name across the pages and show his colors. But what has he really done to me? Stroked that dark side of me; coaxed out those wild feelings and have me finally become comfortable in my own skin in front of someone for the first time in my life. Is that such a bad thing?

But it made me needy and desperate. It made me addicted to him and to that feeling. I wanted to be comfortable, I wanted to accept myself for once, and he gave me the excuse I was looking for.

Then he ruined it. He asked too many questions; questions I can't answer. But this feeling…it's excruciating, and I don't know how to bury it away. I've willed myself to forget him; begged myself. I've tried to slip him inside the deepest hole of my mind and yet he seems to peek his way through. I see him in the eyes of the cashier, in the scent of a passing stranger on the streets and in the voice of our neighbor. He's everywhere and all I want to do is escape the thought of him and these acidic feelings.

I grip the shot glass on my desk, already filled to the brim, and toss my head back. Sliding into the chair, I bring up the article on him as my body is smothered in warmth. It's littered with these wonderful accomplishments of his, most of which can be found with any quick Google search. His face lights up the heading with a sparkle in his eye that every photographer who's ever taken his picture, has captured. His eyes bore through me from the picture; shuffling through each hidden box that I've buried deep, and prying each one open. He coaxes those memories out of their hiding places and lightly stroking over their head as if to reassure them and welcome them into the light.

"You don't have to hide from me."

His words echo like nectar in my ashen heart, singing through my body. He gave me a reason to pull down the mask I show the world, but would he accept all of me? My broken past and the twisted present have borne some deviant incarnation of childhood traumas that manifests itself into a salivating nightmare clawing its way through my body, seeking some release from the world. That release has always been a bottle mixed with the heady scents of sex, but now I can't enjoy sex, or even the mere thought of it, with anyone but him.

I close my eyes, take a deep breath, and down another shot. And as my head begins to swim and my ears to buzz, I place my fingers over the keys and begin editing the biggest piece of bullshit I've ever written in my life. An article flourished with Alexander Roderick Delacroix's accomplishments, a list of his most prominent works, and his philanthropic activities for the local New Orleans community as well as his involvement in the current Fest.

I weave it all into a written work that melds him with the heart of New Orleans, and the festival I spent the last week of my life walking through. Another shot or two, and three hours later, I sit back to admire my work. It's beautiful; unlike anything I've ever written before, and it's the only thing I've written that I'm actually a little proud of. I have taken my feelings for him, and the pulse of the music from the fest, and melded it between every word.

I'm finally done, and I hope I never have to see his name again.

Chapter 31

Something about my article appealed to Angela, because several days after I slammed it onto her desk, I found a box of chocolate raspberry truffles on a new desk at the office, with my name scribbled on a plaque and set on its wooden surface. I suppose this is her way of officially inviting me to be a part of her family, though I'm not quite sure how I didn't get my ass kicked out the door for taking so long to bring it in.

The week after, my story was featured in the magazine and it was on that day that I decided to spend time at the office with my feet resting on the surface of my new desk, picking at the truffles she left me the week prior. It's a miracle they survived this long, honestly.

No one has bothered me, but it's no surprise. I look like shit. I wouldn't even want to talk to myself, if I had the option, but I welcome the solitude. I want to be alone, but not so pathetic that I wanted to be alone at home.

Am I still pissed off over what happened with Delacroix? Of course I am. I let myself drop my normal defenses for an asshole with a grasp of the English language greater than that of your everyday idiot. He wasn't special, and I let myself get so caught up that I almost lost everything I built up. I almost lost my grasp on my personal reality, and that's something I never want to be close to losing again.

As I shift through the half-finished articles I've shoved into the various drawers of my desk, my phone buzzes on the polished wood. There's a text flashing on the screen from Riley informing me that her and Tom had just picked up Ethan from the airport and are on their way to pick me up. I wasn't expecting him back in the area so soon, but then again, my sense of time has been skewed lately. Honestly, for a while, I almost forgot he existed.

I sigh as I make my way to the ladies room to make myself seem a bit presentable then make it down just in time for Riley and Tom to pull up. The second the car stops, Ethan hops out and rushes to my side, wrapping me up in his arms. He smells of cologne…oh I've forgotten the name of it, but it makes my eyes flutter at the scent. Musk and…basil. Like the scent of a perfect summers day.

"I've missed you." He murmurs against my hair, breathing in deep to take in the scent of my shampoo. His voice seeps into my skin and melts me from the inside out. I didn't realize just how much I missed the sound of it until this very moment.

"I've missed you too." I smile through a fake mask of happiness. Hugs are good for that; for hiding your emotions, and my voice is convincing enough for him to not question me. He pulls away and the moment his face comes into view, I plaster on the most genuine smile I can muster. He returns it, and runs his finger along my jaw line.

"You're still just as lovely as ever, Miss Roman." He sighs. This ongoing joke of his to pay compliments to me when I clearly look like shit is getting really old.

He opens the door for me to slide in, and we take off to a restaurant where Tom and Riley had their first date. It's their anniversary, and so, they decided to take us all out since Ethan was due to arrive today as well. It was a quaint little place reminiscent of an old log cabin. It looked a bit shabby from the outside, but the food was something often praised on every site covering the food culture of Louisiana. And oh…the barbecued shrimp were something out of an exquisite dream.

Ethan rattles off about his trip and passes around pictures that I absently browse through. The majority of the conversation drowns itself out with the rest of the noise of the restaurant as I fall into a haze, and it flew by. Dinner, then home, then Tom and Ethan bidding us farewell and going home for the night. Riley murmured something, gave me a hug, commented about how great dinner was and I went up to my room and closed the door. The night had sped by. Some inconsequential outing that I felt I had to put up with, even when none of it held any meaning for me. I love Riley. I do, and I can feel a small bit of affection for Ethan, but what is he? He's a friend, and far too good for someone like me. I could live a thousand life times and never deserve someone like him. Day after day, he's been there letting me know he was thinking of me, or seeing something on his trip and saying how he wanted to share it with me some day. He was patiently waiting for me to come and open up to him, but I can't. He deserves a good, honest woman and I am so far from that. I am toxic, broken, and unworthy.

But as the weeks went by, I found his constant presence a needed comfort. He came over with Tom every visit, and would sit and keep me company into all hours of the night while Tom and Riley went off giggling to do whatever it was they did. We'd watch T.V, share a bottle of wine, and talk. Just talk. There were no stolen kisses or hand holding. There were no passionate embraces and rough romping in the bedroom or on the couch. It was nice and pleasant, and though I was hesitant to ever open up, I did find myself comfortable enough to walk around in pajamas with no make-up on a fairly regular basis.

It had been a month since I last heard from Delacroix; first one, then two, then three. I found myself finally easing the hammer of my heart in response to thoughts of him, and found comfort and security in Ethan. He became a constant source of solace in my life. He made himself available for me when I wanted to vent about work, or Angela, or even Riley. He came and held me while we binge watched shows on T.V when I was upset, or pissed and just needed something to occupy myself.

And somehow, that raging beast became subdued, lightly scratching just beneath the surface and begging for more just to be smothered down by me. I held that foul thing beneath a pillow until its' kicking stopped, and its body lie twitching with Alexander's voice whispered from its lips.

I fooled myself into thinking I could be

normal. I tricked myself into thinking I could be just as sane and regular as Riley and everyone else that went about their daily lives without the tortures I found in myself. I could be like them. I could be *just* like them, and live my perfect life with this wonderful, caring man. I could live, get married, pop out babies, and be absolutely happy in my quaint little house with the delicately manicured lawn and purposefully placed white fence. I could do it, right?

And one day I woke up to the birds singing, my phone buzzing on the nightstand, and the sun filtering through the window pane, casting its welcomed warmth on my skin. It'd been nearly five months, now, since I heard from Alexander Delacroix.

I felt like I owed it to Ethan. He had invested so much time and energy in me, and had nothing to show for it for so long. I owed him a chance, and perhaps, I owed myself a chance with someone like him.

Turning to my side, wiping the sleep from my eyes, I scowl at the little light flashing on my phone. It was early, just barely 8:30, and I was so comfortable sleeping in Ethan's arms. He kept me warm, safe and secure, and I loved the thought of spending forever in bed, soaking in a life that was too good to be my own, but I still felt so hollow. So alone, like I was living a life meant for someone else.

This is how it was supposed to be. A normal life with a man who was so good, in fact, that he didn't want to have sex before marriage. That beast would occasionally tug at my brain, screaming 'What if he sucks in bed!' and was quickly choked out. I can do this. I can be a perfect little girlfriend, and a perfect little wife who doesn't need sex for anything other than having babies, right? Yes, of course I can.

Propping myself up on my side, Ethan turns to nuzzle his face against my bare back. The feel of his lips against my skin brings a sad smile to my lips. This is how it's supposed to be, right?

"Who is it?" he mumbles against my skin, his words a slurred mix of deep, resonant tones that vibrate to my core.

"Probably just work." My fingers trace over the arm he has draped over my waist as I unlock the phone with my free hand, and I saw it…

The message reaches out from the screen and wraps around my throat, ripping it from my body and throwing the poor, shattered remnants into a blender on puree. It's Alexander Delacroix.

Come to me…